Deadly Mayhem

Deadly Mayhem

Dakota Destruction Book 2

Millie Copper

Written by Millie Copper

Edited by Ameryn Tucker

Proofread by MDC Proofreading and WMH Cheryl

Cover design by Dauntless Cover Design

Also by Millie Copper

The Havoc in Wyoming Series

When a series of coordinated attacks devastate the United States, the people of Bakerville, Wyoming, must come together to survive. Unfortunately, not everyone has the town's best interest at heart. Some are striving for personal gain during the apocalypse.

The Montana Mayhem Series

A group from Bakerville, Wyoming strikes out on their own while searching for the desires of their heart. Unfortunately, the road will not be easy, and sometimes the heart is hardened and deceitful. When things don't work out as they hoped, will they become stranded in the wilderness? Or will each be able to find their way home?

The Dakota Destruction Series

After a series of coordinated attacks devastate the United States, Katie and Leo sacrifice everything to help their country. But some things aren't as they seem. Is it time to go home and start fresh, or can something good come out of this terrible situation?

Nonfiction Books

Millie has penned seven nonfiction, traditional food focused books, sharing how, with a little creativity, anyone can transition to a real foods diet without overwhelming their food budget. Many of her books also include preparedness and food storage tips.

Find these titles at:
MillieCopper.com

Join My Reader's Club!

Receive a complimentary copy of *Looming Mayhem: A Dakota Destruction Prequel.* As part of my reader's club, you'll be the first to know about new releases and specials. I also share info on books I'm reading, preparedness tips, and more. Please sign up at:

MillieCopper.com/Join

Chapter 1

Merissa

"You'll take care of my mom? Courtney too?"

"I will. You know I will." I put my hand to Braedon's face. "Please, be safe. I need you." I reach for his hand and place his palm against my stomach. "*We* need you!"

He swallows hard. "I'll come for you when it's over. Walt will be with you." He brushes his finger across my chin. "I love you. Go! Hurry!"

"See you soon." I give Braedon a quick kiss before running to catch up with my sister-in-law, Courtney, and mother-in-law, Pearl.

I don't want to be sent with the evacuees. I want to stay and fight by my husband's side. When the guerrilla attacks on our community escalated, we knew the day—or night—for an all-out battle would happen. We've been training for it. We set the trap, and they took the bait.

Now our fighters, including Braedon and his brother, Tomas, will end this. We'll end the tactics being employed by our aggressors. Then we can go back to the important stuff.

Survival.

Survival in a world without electricity. Without the ease of dropping by a restaurant for a hot meal. Without even grocery stores, phones, computers, or any of the things we took for granted.

Courtney and Mother Pearl are at the back of the line that's scurrying out of the subdivision. When I reach them, I glance back to where I left my husband and his brother. I can't see them in the dark, but I know they're running toward the fight. They'll do what's needed to keep us safe.

The night wears on seemingly forever. The shooting and screams continue. When the dark sky is lit up, not by the rising sun but from a purposely ignited inferno, I know the battle is nearly over. This is the noose around their neck, the way we finish the assaults on our community and stop the aggressors. Even though I wasn't included in the final battle, this part was all me.

As a professional wildland firefighter, I used every bit of knowledge I had to fill a row of empty houses with soured gas and other accelerants. Someone was designated to ignite the homes, trapping the aggressors between our gated community and the town, and allowing our snipers to pick them off.

When the sun finally peeks over the horizon, the conflict is over. We won. We can now get back to our lives. I can't wait to see Braedon, to pull my husband tight and—

"Merissa? What are you doing in here?"

I slam the notebook shut and drop the pen. Letting out a slow breath, I lift my gaze to Mother Pearl. "Just, uh . . . you know."

"Journalling again?" Disapproval blankets her face as she leans heavily on her cane.

"Did you need something?"

"This house . . . " She waves her hand. "It's so tiny."

I blink a few times while I work to keep my face even. It's an average-sized house, larger than the condo Braedon and I owned in Livingston, Montana. They've made it comfortable for us, setting things up to operate without electricity and running water. In many ways, it's better than Pearl's McMansion, especially for riding out the apocalypse.

But the location is the best part—less than a block away from my new job at the Guard District Hospital off West Main Street in Rapid City, South Dakota.

We've come a long way from our Montana home.

"What are you writing about in that book, anyway?" Mother Pearl narrows her eyes. "Is it about me?"

I chuckle and shake my head. "Of course it is." I don't mention how she thinks everything's about her, even when it isn't.

Mother Pearl crosses her arms and lets out a huff. "I'm going out to Opal's ranch tomorrow. She's sending my nephew to pick me up. Maybe I should stay there."

"We've discussed this. If you think living at the ranch is the better choice for you, you should. I'm staying here. I'm going to work at the hospital and attend their new medical school. It's the right choice for me. I want to help with— "

She thumps her cane. "I know, I know. You want to help with the reconstruction efforts. You've told me. Not that I understand why you think it's so important. We could work on the ranch. Opal has plenty for us to do."

I force my hand to remain on the desk instead of traveling to my expanding stomach. Thanks to heavy sweatshirts and other cold weather garb, Pearl has yet to notice. I won't be able to keep it from her forever, but for now, it's best left unsaid.

While living and working at the ranch does have some appeal, being offered a medic position at the hospital while training for their doctor program is a huge honor.

Because the hospital needs people now and the medical school is starting in only a few days, everything happened quickly. A messenger arrived at Opal's ranch with a note from the hospital director, Dr. Williams, who prefers to be addressed as *captain* since he's part of the South Dakota National Guard. He wanted to meet with me.

At first, I thought it was because something showed up on the exam I had. Opal Maher, Pearl's younger sister, took both Pearl and me to the hospital the day before. She was concerned about our health after our long journey from Montana. When the note arrived, Opal immediately had her son Shawn hitch up the wagon and take me to the hospital.

I was nothing short of shocked when, after a short interview, Captain Williams offered me a position as a medic, starting immediately, and a spot in his fast-track doctor training program. Working at the hospital and attending school just might be the perfect choice for my current condition.

I do feel a little bad I didn't tell Captain Williams I'm expecting, though. A few of the other staff know since they examined me, but I don't think they told him. He didn't give me any weird looks or even suggest he knows I'm pregnant.

Opal, though . . . I think *she* suspects I'm pregnant. She's given me a few curious looks. Pearl, always wrapped up in her own world, is unlikely to notice. At least I have that on my side for keeping it quiet.

Not even considering what Pearl wanted, I accepted the medic job and the school position. I realize now it was selfish of me. But I think, in my mind, I figured she'd want to stay with Opal on the ranch.

The captain had a house available that he'd set up for another med student who ended up not needing it, and I was able to move in immediately.

Orientation begins tomorrow with a blood-borne pathogens class put on by a husband-and-wife team who also works at the hospital, followed by shadowing the medic on duty.

I'll admit, I'm nervous. But I'm mostly excited. Pearl, though . . . she's a special problem. I'll be gone so much, and I can't see how she'll manage here on her own. Living at the ranch with Opal may be better for her.

"Opal does have plenty to do. So does the hospital. Really, Mother Pearl, I'm fine here if you want to live at the ranch and stay out there with Walt . . . " I lift my eyebrows at her.

"That Walt Cox has nothing to do with this. I don't even know why he followed us here. Other than thinking he needed to get us here safely. Says he wanted a fresh start, but I know the truth about him. He felt he owed it to Braedon and Tomas. That's all."

I push down the lump forming in my throat and let out a long breath. "That's part of it. But not all. I think he cares for you."

She gives her cane a solid thump against the hardwood floor. "Pshaw. He's made himself right at home out at Opal's place. Settled in and everything." She narrows her eyes. "When are you going to ride the horses? Don't you need to keep training them?"

"Walt's taking care of that. He's working with them and is doing fine."

Pearl shakes her head. "You know that mounted archery stuff is beyond me, but Walt says it's important to keep up your skills. Especially with ammunition in short supply. He says he might even go out with a hunting group that's trying to bring in more meat before the snow gets too deep. You could go with them, take down a deer like you did back home up on Emigrant Peak. I still can't believe you shot him with your bow on the back of your horse."

She gives me a crooked smile. "Braedon was right proud of you." She turns from the doorway, and in a soft voice, she adds, "So was I."

Her words catch me by surprise. My mother-in-law is not an easy woman to love. For most of my marriage to Braedon, I simply tolerated her. While she didn't come right out and tell me how she truly felt about me—I wasn't nearly good enough for her youngest son—she'd narrow her eyes and let out dramatic sighs.

There were times she'd ask, in a disapproving tone, why I wasn't more like my sister-in-law. If anyone would've told me a year and a half ago, before the nuclear bombs changed everything, that I'd be the one living with Pearl instead of Courtney, I'd have called them crazy. I was definitely not the favorite daughter-in-law.

After the assault on our home in Livingston left us both widowed, Courtney decided to head west to find her family while I went east with Pearl. Walt Cox did feel an obligation to Braedon, to make sure we arrived in Rapid City safely. But whether Pearl wants to admit it or not, he also has a thing for my cantankerous mother-in-law. And even though she denies it, I know the feeling's mutual.

I open my notebook and return to my page. After Braedon was killed in the attack, I struggled with my grief. Part of me wanted to die alongside him. On the day of the memorial service for all of those killed in the attack, including my husband and brother-in-law, Pearl received a letter from her sister Opal. Though unreliable, mail service was being attempted.

Opal invited us to join her at her ranch. Staying in Livingston would've been difficult. Like many other homes in the subdivision, our place was caught in the crossfire. The damage was substantial, and all the ground-floor windows were shot out.

We made the impulsive decision to travel to Rapid City before winter so we could have a fresh start. Thankfully, some enterprising people set up transportation systems once the military cleared the interstate, using buses and other means to ferry people and even animals. Living on Interstate 90 in Montana, and Rapid City also being on Interstate 90 in South Dakota, was a huge help.

Pearl and I took the commercial transport while Walt, two teens who were orphaned in the attack, and another couple brought our horses and other essentials. Our first bus ride ended in Billings, only a few hours from Livingston, where we waited several days for Walt and the others to catch up.

It was there, staying in what Pearl referred to as a *seedy motel*, that I found a half-used, dog-eared notebook. That notebook became my first journal. I started pouring my heart out on the remaining pages, filling it up within a few days. Even though paper is a commodity in our fallen world, I was able to scrounge up another book when we arrived in Sheridan, Wyoming.

Sheridan, a former college town, had a good bartering area set up. When gathering supplies, I spied the partially used yellow legal pad and traded one of Pearl's small trinkets for it. I filled the legal pad by the time we got to Spearfish, South Dakota. This new notebook is a proper hard-sided journal given to me by Opal.

In some ways, I find it amusing that I'm writing. It's not something I ever did before. I was way too busy and spent as much time as I could outdoors—either working with the forest service as an engine captain on the wildland fire crew, riding our horses and practicing mounted archery with my husband, or doing physical training to keep in shape for all my obligations.

Now undernourished and weak from the trip and my pregnancy, writing seems to keep my brain occupied. It doesn't even bother me that I write the same words over and over, that I keep reliving the same events. How many times have I written about that night? Six? Eight? A dozen? I repeatedly replay it, trying to make sense of everything as the words fill the paper. It'll never help.

I let out a sigh and shut the journal, then scoot my chair back and extinguish the oil lamp. Writing about it isn't going to bring my husband back. Maybe, if I could change the ending, things would be different.

Not possible. He's dead. And I'm here in Rapid City with Pearl.

At least I have my baby—someone to remember Braedon by. I place my hand on my stomach. "I'm going to love you enough for both of us."

Chapter 2

Katie

"Now squeeze my hands with both of your hands. Good. A little more." His words are toneless, and the look on his face is completely passive. His calm, laid-back demeanor is almost annoying.

We were told Dr. Bollinger at Monument District Hospital is the most qualified orthopedist to assess Leo's injuries. Both his arms are still in casts after falling off a horse almost two months ago, and we've done everything possible for his healing, so Captain Williams suggested we see Bollinger.

Leo's left wrist has been in a hard cast since shortly after the fall, and his right humerus has been splinted between the elbow and shoulder. Both arms seemed to be improving as expected. At least, we thought everything was going okay . . . until Leo tripped a few weeks ago and fell flat on his face.

Luckily, his teeth and nose seem to have healed okay, with the swelling completely gone. I do notice a slight bulge on his nose, but in today's world, a mildly misshapen nose isn't much to worry about. It almost looks good on him.

A broken wrist and humerus are a big deal, though. The bones in Leo's wrist shifted so much that he should've had surgery. That didn't happen.

Surgery—cutting someone open—is done only as a last resort. Not only do we not have electricity, but we also don't have the medical supplies needed. The terrorist attacks and electromagnetic pulse made sure of that, sending us back to what some refer to as the 1800s. Others say it's the Middle Ages because of the violence some areas are experiencing.

"Well, Leo." Dr. Bollinger leans back on his wheeled stool. "Let's discuss the right arm first. The humerus fracture was simple. It's healed nicely. There's no indication of nerve damage, which is sometimes a concern with this type of break, or any residual issues. The abscess on your shoulder still needs to be monitored, though. You got lucky. A wound like that could've killed you in today's world." He snorts. "Even in the old world."

My cheeks redden at the mention of the ulceration. I still feel bad about it. Thankfully, the infection didn't become systemic, but it's been a battle to get the lesion to heal. It's only recently improved, thanks to herbalist Stella Swenson and one of her medicinal salves.

"And the wrist?" Leo leans forward slightly.

Bollinger clicks his tongue. His handsome, well-tanned face contorts. "The news isn't as good."

My stomach turns hollow. As soon as the cast came off and I saw exactly how it looked, I knew the report on Leo's wrist wouldn't be great. Even from my seat several feet away, I can see it has an awkward bulge to it.

Leo looks down at his wrist and gives a solemn nod. "How bad?"

"The bones weren't aligned properly. The displaced ends have filled in with new bones. We call it a malunion. It happens sometimes with wrist fractures. Even before—*before the apocalypse*—we'd see it on occasion. In those cases, we'd do surgery to rebreak the bone and start the process again."

"And now?"

Dr. Bollinger tilts his head, his thick silver hair picking up the late afternoon light that's filtering through the western-facing window. "Now . . . " He shakes his head.

Leo gently flexes the fingers of his shriveled left arm. "Will I be able to use my arm?"

"You may return to a partial degree of mobility."

I clear my throat. "May?"

Bollinger glances at me with his piercing blue eyes. "We'll give your husband some exercises to do. Gentle stretching exercises at first before progressing to strength training. The big question is, why didn't the bones heal properly? You were cast at the hospital in the Guard District, correct?"

"Yes," I say. "Dr. Newsome did the wrist. Nettie Wolff assisted."

Bollinger lets out a slow, noisy breath. "Well, Eugene Newsome certainly had his faults, but he was an excellent physician. I can't imagine he'd put on a cast without making sure everything was in alignment. And I know Nettie. Even though she's only a med student, she knows her stuff. You all are lucky to have her."

Nettie said she met Bollinger when she did a special mentor program out of this hospital. Then the attacks started, and she ended up stuck in Rapid City. She was moved to our satellite hospital because that was where she was needed.

Bollinger's right about Newsome having his faults—faults that ended up getting him killed. I choose not to mention Newsome's drinking problem. Was he drunk when he set Leo's wrist? I don't think so, but I'm not positive. His drinking was far beyond what I knew about.

"Dr. Newsome did say Leo probably would've had surgery before the apocalypse."

Bollinger slides his stool forward. "It could've been an issue of not lining up the bones properly." He points to the most obvious bulge on Leo's wrist. "This here makes me lean in that direction. But without doing an x-ray or, better yet, a CT scan, I don't know for sure. My guess is this bulge is a twist to the bone."

I grimace. A twist to the bone can't be good.

"Earlier," the doctor continues, "I asked you about your pain level. You said it isn't bad?"

"That's right," Leo says. "There's some pain occasionally, but nothing terrible. I can live with it."

"There's also some swelling." He pokes Leo's wrist slightly, causing Leo to jump. "Obviously, there's some tenderness. We'll splint you, start you on the exercises, and follow up in a few weeks. I'm taking a turn as a roving doctor, so I'll see you when I'm at your hospital."

"Can I go back to work?"

Bollinger gives a slow shake of his head. "Not as a hospital medic. And you aren't ready to join the National Guard. Not by a long shot."

Leo huffs out a breath, but the doctor raises a hand. "I read the note Captain Williams sent about you helping with the new medical school. You said you taught the blood-borne pathogen class yesterday to your local police? You have any trouble with that?"

"No, sir."

I make a tutting noise, causing both men to look at me. "Um, he, um . . . " I look at my husband and mouth *sorry*. "He did have some pain last night."

Leo shakes his head. "In my back. I've been lazing around for months. I wasn't used to being on my feet all day. That's all it was, honey. Truly."

My heart gives a little pitter-patter. A few weeks ago, he would've bitten my head off for saying anything. His injuries took a toll on our marriage. We're doing better now, starting to communicate and put our life back together. Will his wrist not healing properly take us back to where we were? Back to struggling and snapping at each other?

Bollinger looks from me to Leo, his eyebrows raised. "Maybe some full-body strengthening will be in order. No pain in the wrist?"

"Nothing new." Leo shrugs. "You're right about it being tender. It does seem more so with the cast off."

"The splint will help protect it. Teaching at the school will be fine. And you'll have use of your right arm, but I still want you to take it easy. You're still healing."

"Sure, Doctor. I'll do that. Maybe my right-handed writing will even improve."

"Yep. In theory, it's easier for a left-hand dominant person to switch to the right hand. But the theory doesn't always pan out in real life. I'm sure you'll do well enough that someone can make out your scribbles. It worked for me. Anyway, let's get you splinted and on your way. Are you staying here tonight and making the trip back home tomorrow?"

"Correct." Leo flexes his fingers again. "One of our medics and his brother brought us over in a wagon. They're gathering a few supplies, and we're staying in the third-floor dorms. Already checked in. We arranged to keep the horses and wagon at the livery stable."

"It's good you were able to get a room. We thought people might try and stay here for the festival tonight."

Leo looks at me, and I shake my head. "What festival?"

"Kind of an old-fashioned winter carnival. The churches in the area thought it'd be a good idea to help get the community back to right. They had the first one last Friday at the Lutheran church down the road. This one is at the Catholic school, close enough for you to walk. There will be games and food—well, some food anyway. It's every Friday until New Year's. I heard they'll forgo the carnival aspect on Christmas Day for a more traditional celebration."

"We haven't heard about it." I look to Leo, who lifts a shoulder. "We might check it out."

"You should. I didn't go last week, but I heard it was very well done. And well attended. I may go tonight. At first, I thought it was a waste of resources, but perhaps I was wrong. Either way, I'd like to see you before you leave tomorrow so we can make sure the splint is properly fitted. Say, 0800."

"Doctor?" The nurse who's been silently standing by steps forward.

"What?" Bollinger snaps.

I lift my brows at his tone.

The nurse looks embarrassed as she steps back. "I was going to remind you tomorrow's Saturday. We don't have regular— "

He turns on her. "So? You have big weekend plans? Fine. I'll get another nurse to help me." Bollinger turns back to Leo's arm, his demeanor changing and returning to the same calm and friendly man he was before.

I meet Leo's gaze. He lightly flares his eyes, letting me know he also saw what just happened.

Jesse Talbot, the medic who drove us, wants to leave at first light. With the shorter days of November, that's not long before the doctor wants to see us.

Of course, before the EMP, daylight would've been an hour earlier based on our utilization of Daylight Savings Time and falling back in November. We don't bother with that now. Several months back, the president announced the end of Daylight Savings Time during one of his radio addresses.

Other than schedules for workers, time doesn't matter much these days anyway. Most people live by the sun. We do what's needed when it shines and sleep when it doesn't. As a nurse with twelve-hour shifts, this time of year, I go to work in the dark and get off in the dark, whether it's a day or night shift.

"So, see you in the morning?" Bollinger smiles at Leo before sending a scowl toward the nurse.

Leo purses his lips and exhales through his nose. "We'll be here."

It's a good hour before Leo gets his new removable splint. While not fancy, it's an improvement over the stinky cast. The nurse washes his arm and tells him he'll be able to remove the splint to bathe.

He's also given a list of exercises to start with—nothing too difficult or strenuous. Bollinger wants to see how well Leo's progressing before adding anything additional.

Leo's disappointed with the appointment but doesn't seem surprised.

When we arrive on the third floor of the hospital, which has been converted to sleeping quarters, we silently go to our small room. Most of this space has been turned into dormitory-style sleeping, but we were able to get one of the private double rooms. It's nothing elaborate, not by any means, but it'll be great for tonight.

We dropped off our overnight bags and bedrolls in our room before Leo's appointment, so I offer to make up the beds. Lodging in the apocalypse isn't like it was before. There aren't hotel rooms with maid and laundry service—no freshly made beds or clean towels. Instead, we carry what we need. We weren't even sure we'd be able to get beds here since it's on a first-come, first-served basis.

"Let's talk a minute first." Leo plops on the plastic-encased mattress and pats the spot next to him.

I sit rather stiffly, wary of seeming too receptive. I know I shouldn't be like this, but walking on eggshells has almost become a self-preservation mechanism to protect my increasingly fragile heart.

I let out a quiet breath and focus on my memory verse—a promise from God: *Love is patient, love is kind. It is not easily angered, it keeps no record of wrongs.* I quickly realize I've messed it up, leaving out several sentences.

Leo adjusts so our legs touch and wraps his newly freed right arm around my shoulders. His arm brushes against my hair, nudging the elastic band. "Oops. Sorry. I don't want to risk breaking your rubber band."

I smile at him. "Seriously. These elastic bands are among my few prized possessions." Even though I have other hair ties, ones made from old latex gloves, these coated elastic bands are gentler on my thick, curly hair than the homemade ones. I treat them almost like an heirloom.

He leans in and kisses my cheek. "We're going to be okay, honey. I'll do the physical therapy, get some strength back, and then . . . then we'll see where we are. Lieutenant Paul said they aren't expecting me to take my oath until after the new year, same as you. That gives me six weeks to make some good improvement. And with being able to teach at the new medical school, I won't have as much time to sit around and feel sorry for myself."

Leo snorts out a laugh. "Definitely an improvement. We'll see Bollinger in the morning and be home before noon. I bet Gerry will be happy to see us."

I'm sure I get a dreamy look at the thought of our dog, one of the four pups I found shortly after Leo fell from his horse. We found homes for the other three but kept Geronimo, who we almost always call Gerry.

At first, Leo didn't want to keep any of them. Partly because he associated them with the accident, and partly because having a dog at the end of the world is a challenge. But Gerry easily won his heart.

Our next-door neighbors, the Harringtons, were happy to watch Gerry for us while we made this trek to the main hospital in Rapid City. I have no doubt four-year-old Henry Harrington is spoiling our puppy rotten. "Gerry's probably having such a fun time, he'll forget who we even are."

"Don't count on it. That dog is smitten with you." Leo squeezes me closer. "Seriously, though, we're going to be okay. We're through the worst of it. Someday, we'll look back on this time and know God brought us through."

Chapter 3

"Wish I'd known there was a shindig happening." Josiah Talbot runs a hand through his hair before repositioning his worn Stetson.

"The last thing you need, baby brother, is to be wooing some poor girl." Jesse play punches him in the arm. "It's not like you're going to come back here every week for courting."

"Courting? Seriously? Just because we drive a horse and wagon, you need to talk like an old pioneer?"

I stifle a giggle at the banter between the brothers. Jesse Talbot is a medic at our clinic. I've worked with him for several months and have yet to see this playful side that comes out with his brother. Josiah is a deputy with the Citizen Patrol, a branch of the sheriff's department created as part of the rebuilding efforts.

Dozens of people are in line outside the former parochial school, maybe more. I self-consciously clear my throat as my right hand travels to the sidearm tucked into my conceal-and-carry holster.

In today's world, no one goes anywhere unarmed. The Talbot brothers are also carrying. While my weapon is hidden, theirs are on their hips and poking out under their winter jackets. There are plenty of others in line with visible sidearms. Not only the adults but some of the teens too. It's the way life is these days.

Leo's not packing. He didn't even bring a sidearm. In anticipation of his casts being removed, we discussed bringing his 1911 to wear in his ankle holster. But he hasn't shot in months and has lost too much strength. He's ambidextrous but agrees he'll need some practice to feel good about using his right hand again. He gave me a wink and said, "If things go down, I'll just grab for the backup strapped to your ankle."

When we get home, Leo will meet with Lieutenant Paul of the National Guard for target practice, which Bollinger cleared for the now-healed humerus arm only. Surprisingly, the doctor also said Leo can start exercising and can even do basic martial arts training, as long as he's careful with his left wrist.

Hand-to-hand combat and weapons training were a big part of our lives in Bakerville and in the early days of being with the United

Volunteers. When Leo and I first decided to join the Volunteers, I was excited about helping our country recover.

Then our Volunteer unit was ordered to leave South Dakota.

We thought it'd be a good idea to stay here and join the National Guard. Sadly, I somehow missed an important part of the commitment.

The United Volunteers required a one-year commitment. This short time was thought to be a way to get more people to join. I'll admit, it worked for me. Being gone from my family for one year, while being able to help rebuild our country, didn't sound too bad.

The National Guard commitment is a required eight years. *Eight!* Practically a lifetime.

Eight years away from my family.

I was pretty upset when the enlistment requirements were explained to me. Upset I hadn't paid better attention and upset with my husband for assuming I'd be okay with it.

Because of Leo's accident, we were both offered a delay in taking our oath. Him because of his injuries, and me because he couldn't even care for himself in those early days.

Officially, we're still Volunteers under the direction of the National Guard. Since we don't do any policing—the big thing the governor said was an issue—we aren't violating any orders. I'm even told the governor knows about us and chooses to ignore the situation.

But the truth is, I'm not sure I can take the oath. Do I truly want to join the National Guard and become contractually obligated for eight years?

This whole Guard business has been a sore spot between Leo and me, something we're going to have to deal with soon. Especially now that he's out of the casts and is starting physical therapy. We've always believed he'd be well enough by the new year and our National Guard oath would take place in January.

"This is an actual party," Leo whispers in my ear. "It's crazy how excited everyone is."

I glance around and notice this is the happiest group of people I've seen in a while. Each week, we stand in lines to receive our ration vouchers or to collect our food. Sure, these people look much the same—dressed in rugged work clothes and carrying their sidearms and small backpacks or crossbody bags, just like Leo, me, and the Talbot brothers.

But the lines we're used to are quiet and forlorn. Sometimes people will talk quietly among themselves, but we're there to complete a necessary chore.

But in this line, there's talking and smiling, people calling out and waving vigorously to attract attention.

"It *is* crazy," I agree as we take our place at the back of the line.

There's a particularly excited group of young teens in front of us that remind me so much of my junior high years. They talk in excited whispers and point to another group—boys around the same age—and then giggle.

Josiah makes a face and whispers under his breath, "I feel like I've been transported back to the middle school lunchroom. Nothing much changes, does it?"

His words tug at my heart. In some ways, I guess he's right. It's great to see these teens and preteens acting their age. I hope my little brother, Malcolm, who isn't much younger than these girls, gets to do fun stuff like this too.

I received a letter from my stepdad, Jake, a few weeks ago, and Malcolm added a short note at the bottom. He didn't sound upbeat and happy. He said how much he missed our mom and how sad his dad is all the time.

Our mom died in May. She'd been sick for a while, but we didn't know it. While it was terrible, God gave her a blessing toward the end when she fell down a hillside and was paralyzed from the shoulders down. As her body continued to wither away, she was spared from the extreme pain—which we didn't have the medicine to control—until she just shut down.

It's taken me some time to realize that, even if I had noticed my mom was truly sick, the outcome would've been the same. There's no chemotherapy or radiation, and very little surgery in the apocalypse.

Just like Dr. Bollinger doesn't want to surgically rebreak Leo's wrist to repair the malunion, we only do surgery when it's absolutely necessary. Opening up a body can introduce infection. Here, in Rapid City, we have a vastly larger supply of antibiotics and other medicines than we did in our tiny community of Bakerville, Wyoming, but it's still limited.

Until the national infrastructure is repaired with manufacturing and production, along with trucking and transport reestablished, we have what we have. Thankfully, this area was well supplied by the large Monument Hospital, Ellsworth Air Force Base, and Camp Rapid National Guard. Proper and strict rationing has resulted in us still having limited supplies seventeen months after the attacks on our country started.

At first, few people thought the attacks would devastate us. When the first planes were blown out of the sky, it was believed to be an act of terrorism. My mom and Jake were probably some of the few who suggested it could be more. They were what people called preppers and often looked at events with an eye toward how this could affect us in the long term.

Because of their previous planning and diligence, as the attacks continued, my sisters and I were able to realize how our world was changing. We all left our homes and went to Mom and Jake's homestead—or as they'd referred to it many times, their retreat. While safer in the tiny community, we still lost my mom and several others in our extended family.

"Who's that?" Josiah lifts his chin to a group gathered on the lawn. A man stands on an elevated platform with his hands in the air as others kneel around him.

Leo tilts his head. "Almost looks like a church service, but there's too much chitter-chatter to hear what they're saying."

"That's a rough-looking preacher." Josiah shakes his head. "He looks kind of familiar. You recognize him, Jesse?"

Jesse gives a slow bob of his head. "Yup. But I can't place him. I'll think on it. Maybe it'll come to me."

"Katie?" Leo nudges me with his hip. "Looks like they've opened the doors. We're moving forward."

"Oh, sorry. I was just watching them. I caught a couple of words. It sounds like he's saying God is unhappy Rapid City is rebuilding. He wants us to learn to trust Him and to survive off the land."

Leo scoffs. "God does want us to trust Him, that's true enough. Even with the few advances we're seeing here, we're still going to have an agrarian lifestyle for years. The EMP set us back at least a century."

"Still . . . I'd like to listen to him. I miss hearing sermons."

"Sure. Why don't we take a lap around and see what all they have inside, then we'll come back out. Sound good?"

"Yes, thanks."

Inside the building, there are a variety of booths set up. It reminds me of the harvest festivals I attended as a child. The ring toss already has several people, as does the fishing booth.

I watch a little boy around three years old, who reminds me of my nephew Gavin, as he tries to cast the pole over the top of the curtain painted with smiling fish. His mom and dad are at his side, encouraging him to try again.

I wonder what the prizes are for when he finally makes the "hook" over the top? The last time I played this game, around twenty years ago, I think my hook returned with a gift certificate for an ice cream cone. I doubt there'll be ice cream for this boy.

Leo and the brothers move toward the next booth. Josiah takes a deep inhale. "Something sure smells good. I'm surprised they're offering food. Must be the long line at the back, huh?"

"Let's go see what they're serving." Jesse nudges his brother forward.

Leo turns to me with a gleam in his eye. "Hungry?"

Even though we already ate some jerky and biscuits that we brought along from home, my stomach lets out a low rumble. "I had no idea they'd have food."

"If they seem to have enough . . . " He looks around at the gathered crowd. "I don't want to be a pig, but Josiah's right about it smelling good."

We ate communally in Bakerville, and some neighborhoods in Rapid City have banded together to cook all their meals together and share the workload, but Leo and I have been on our own for meals since we moved here. Even when we're at work, our lunches are food we've brought from home. Gone are the days of a work cafeteria or running to a nearby restaurant for a bite.

A smiling man dressed in clerical attire with a white collar around his neck is waving people forward. "There's plenty. Don't be shy. The line's moving fast. You can sit in the hall over there." He points to the double doorway people are moving through, and I catch a glimpse of long rows of tables.

The people ahead of us are as jovial as when we were waiting outside to be let in. When we're close enough to see the front of the line, my anticipation of a hot meal grows.

The servers are smiling and saying hello. It truly does feel like a celebration. I'm overcome with a longing to do something like this in our district. Surely, if the Monument District can organize this, so can we. I'm going to talk to Captain Williams and Lieutenant Paul and see if it's possible to make this happen back home.

Although *home* is only five miles away, the limited number of motorized vehicles makes it feel almost like a different world. These days, the most common mode of transportation is walking. Sometimes people will use horses, bicycles, or as in our case, horses and a wagon or buggy.

We're using the wagon and team housed near the Guard District Medical Clinic and most commonly used when going for supplies or as an ambulance or hearse. We also have a couple of human-powered handcarts we use in the same manner for needs nearby, along with a couple of diesel pickup trucks that run on biofuel.

When we arrive at the front of the line, I greedily accept the bowl. "God bless you. There's biscuits too." The woman tilts her head down the line.

With a bowl and spoon in one hand and a heavy square biscuit in the other, I follow the Talbot brothers into the dining hall. Jesse motions with his chin for Josiah to head toward the back of the already packed room. There must be hundreds of people here. The cheerful mood in the building continues. It's definitely a party.

Jesse chooses a spot in the center of the room, far away from the door we entered by the stage. As expected, he picks a spot with a view of the full bank of glass doors along one edge and the double doors on the other side. Like Leo, Jesse is former military. There's often some good-natured teasing between the two since they're from different branches. Leo's a Marine, and Jesse was in the Army.

We've recently added a new medic to our satellite hospital. She was in the Coast Guard and isn't immune from the teasing either. Both Leo and Jesse have lightly hassled her for being a Coastie. She didn't seem to mind and even joined in.

I'll admit, I didn't follow the name play and was concerned she'd take offense. I asked her later, and she said it was fine and to be expected.

I think Captain Williams is impressed with her. He's brought Merissa on not only as a medic but also added her as a student in our new medical school. While she had medical training in the Coast Guard, and as a wildland firefighter with the forest service, the bulk of her life experience has been gained since the collapse, working with the small clinic where she lived in Montana.

On-the-job training. Same as how I became a nurse.

I'll admit, part of me is a little jealous of Merissa's designation as a medic. Even though the medics mainly work out of the hospital, they're the first ones called when something big is happening.

Not that I want to go to situations like the recent hostage standoff, but it feels like they're more a part of things than we nurses are. Plus, I do have the necessary training from my time with the United Volunteers and the Bakerville Militia.

I take a sip of the still-steaming soup. It's a mixture of vegetables: chunks of pumpkin, potatoes, and starchy kernels of field corn. There isn't any meat in it, but the broth is hearty enough that it may have been made from bones. The biscuit's heavy and crumbly, probably from oats and cornmeal, both grown locally. Overall, it's a wonderful surprise.

Leo comments on how good the soup is. Josiah opens his mouth to say something, then the ground shakes beneath me. My flimsy folding chair topples to the ground and lands me in a heap.

Chapter 4

My ears are ringing. I roll over and try to get to my knees. An earthquake? In South Dakota?

Leo grabs me. "Keep your head down." He looks toward the wall of glass, now shattered. There's smoke, lots of smoke.

"What happened?"

"Explosion."

The word is barely out of his mouth when the gunfire starts. I slide my pistol out of its holster and hold it next to my thigh, my finger indexed along the edge—well away from my jumpy trigger finger.

"Katie." Leo motions to where my backup piece is nestled.

"Here." I hand him the slightly larger pistol I'm holding, then retrieve the Smith & Wesson micro compact from my ankle holster.

"Stay low." Leo motions to the floor, then looks at the Talbot brothers. "Fish in a barrel?"

Josiah looks confused, but Jesse nods. "Sounds like they're shooting people as they run out. Maybe a few snipers positioned on rooftops?"

I glance around the room. "People are injured. They need us."

"We stay low, both when we're moving and giving aid." Leo looks at me and then at the brothers. "Don't go anywhere near the windows or doors."

I point to a woman on the floor a few tables over. "I'll help her."

Jesse motions to a fallen man, indicating he'll take him. Josiah will handle another man nearby.

Leo agrees. "I'll go toward the front and see what I can do."

"Be careful of your wrist," I caution.

The corners of his mouth lift slightly. It's more of a grimace than a smile, but it indicates he'll take it easy.

I duckwalk to the woman. Another lady is next to her, crying as she presses her hands on the injured woman's leg. "Was it a bomb?" She looks around wild-eyed. "And why are they shooting? Who would do this?"

I shimmy out of my backpack and unzip the outside pocket. I grab a strip of bandage and a few homemade squares of several layers of cloth. The woman was cut with some sort of shrapnel.

The crying lady moves enough so I can press the cloth squares into place, and the injured woman cries out.

"Hi, there. I'm Katie. I'm a nurse at the Guard District Clinic."

She mutters something without opening her eyes.

"What's your name?"

"Francine," the crying lady answers for her. "She's my mom."

"All right, Francine. I'm going to try and stop this bleeding while we wait for the doctors." I don't mention the doctors won't be arriving until the snipers stop shooting. I glance toward the daughter. "What's your name?"

"Felisha. Is she . . . will she be okay?"

I don't want to tell Felisha what I really think. The blood puddle around Francine's leg is extreme. Even now, as I'm applying pressure to the wound just above the knee, the bandages are already soaking through.

"Can you dig in the larger part of my bag and pull out my sweatshirt?"

Felisha wastes no time pulling out the lightweight hoody.

"Fold it up, please." She does, then I take it from her and place it over the bandages. "Here. Put your hands here." I motion to the wound. "Press down on it."

She tentatively places her hands on the hoody.

"Hard." I move my knee onto Francine's upper thigh, applying pressure and hopefully stemming the artery. "Keep up the pressure while I put on a tourniquet." Using a tourniquet is a last resort effort, but it's the only chance we have at saving Felisha's mom. The bleeding is out of control.

My tourniquet material is sheeting made into a cravat or triangle bandage. It's something Leo and I both carry in our packs because of its usefulness. The last time I used a cravat was when he fell off the horse. That time, it was a sling opened up to its single layer and triangular. This time, I'll leave it folded in a long, two-inch strip.

I release my hair from my coveted elastic hair tie, slide it along the material, and then tie the strip above the wound with a half knot. I plop a short piece of rebar in as a windlass.

The rebar has been filed to a point on one end—another part of my first aid kit, along with doubling as a self-defense weapon. Now's when it becomes a tourniquet. It'll ratchet down to stem the excessive flow of blood and hopefully buy Francine enough time for the doctors to arrive and fix her up properly.

As I twist the rebar, making sure it's nice and tight, Francine winces.

"Sorry. It needs to be tight so it can stop the arterial blood flow." I remove my knee from her thigh.

From my bag, I grab a strip of duct tape wrapped around an old credit card and a black magic marker. Checking the time on my watch, I scribble the date and 1837.

"What're you doing?" Felisha asks.

"Timing the tourniquet. It's important." I glance around and realize the gunfire has stopped. The room is now filled with the sounds of screams and crying, people begging for help. Where a section of window used to be, there's now a small fire filling the room with smoke.

There's a flurry of new noises, and bodies rush into the cafeteria. "Where's the injured?" someone calls out.

I lift my hand and yell, "Here! Tourniquet in place!"

The man who seems to be in charge points to me. A woman strides toward us. "What do you have?"

I give a brief report as she checks the tourniquet. "You've done this before?"

"I'm a nurse at the Guard District Medical Center."

Her brows shoot up under her stocking cap. "Well, good thing you were here."

"Is my mom going to be okay?" Felisha asks.

"We'll take care of her."

The woman calls out for transport. Seconds later, two men appear with a stretcher. As soon as the woman gives directions on where to deliver Francine, she turns to me again. "Go with them. We need trained people at the hospital."

I glance around for Leo. "My husband's here somewhere. Let me find him. Both my husband and our friend are medics."

Her brows pop up again. "Bonus day. Great." She turns to Felisha. "You can go with your mom, just stay out of the way."

Felisha hugs and thanks me before scurrying off after them.

I scan the room for Leo, Jesse, or even Josiah. It takes me only seconds to spot Leo's tall frame near the side of the room, standing next to a group squatting on the ground. I take off toward him.

"Katie!" His eyes go wide when he sees me. "You okay?"

"I've been asked to help at the hospital. You and Jesse too. Do you know where he is?"

Leo motions to the group he's with. "They're finishing stabilizing our guy, then we're heading out. I just stood up to look for you. There're dozens injured." He steps closer to me. "Not sure they need my help. I'm about as useless as a screen door on a submarine." He motions to his blood-covered splint.

A voice calls out asking for a doctor.

I shake my head. "Let's try and help them."

Leo rolls his eyes before quickly telling Jesse we'll find him at the hospital. The call for help comes out again. Leo and I follow the voice to the edge of the room. Kneeling near the wall is one of the preteen girls that were in line ahead of us earlier.

"Are you okay?" I ask.

She shakes her head and points to her friend leaning against the wall. "She fell or something when we were trying to get away. I don't know what's wrong, but . . . she's not okay."

Leo kneels next to her. "Hey, I'm Leo. What's your name?"

"She's Gina," the friend says. "What's wrong with her?"

Gina gives Leo a blank look. "I don't feel too good. My chest hurts. It's hard to breathe. My back. My throat. And my head feels funny." Her voice is low and raspy.

Leo checks Gina's pulse and watches her respirations.

"What's your name?" I ask the friend.

"Tootie. Is she all right? We got separated. I made it through there— " she points to the double door " —and went deeper into the school, a classroom or something where they couldn't shoot us. I thought she was right behind me. When I couldn't find her and didn't hear any more shooting, I came looking for her. She seemed okay at first, just said she wanted to rest a minute."

"Are you injured, Tootie?" I rest my hand on her shoulder.

"No, no. I'm fine. What's wrong with Gina?"

"Katie?" Leo looks toward me. "She needs stabilization and transport. We may be looking at traumatic asphyxia." He turns back to Gina. "Let's have you hold real still for me, okay? We'll take you to the hospital and check you out. Are your parents here?"

"Our folks were supposed to meet us later," Tootie quickly says. "They're still working."

I scan the room, looking for the woman who helped Francine or someone else who's obviously from the hospital, as I search my memory for traumatic asphyxia.

Breaking down the words, it's a trauma that prevents getting enough oxygen. Compressive asphyxia, maybe? Like when something heavy falls on a person? Or . . . when there's a human stampede and the crowd is so tight suffocation occurs.

Spying the woman who helped Francine, I call out, "Be right back."

When I get close, the woman recognizes me. "Yes?"

"We have a young girl—around twelve or thirteen—we think she has compressive asphyxia, maybe some other injuries too. Can we get a stretcher?"

The woman turns to the man she's treating. "You're going to be okay. Have your wife help you walk to the hospital. We'll get you stitched up as soon as we're able. Keep the bandage in place." She pops to her feet. "Show me."

As we weave our way back to Gina, I ask the lady's name. "Dr. Callahan. You?"

"Katie Burnett." I point to Leo. "That's Leo, my husband."

Leo gives a nod. "This is Gina. She's complaining of a variety of body aches. She has shortness of breath, and her pulse is thready. She isn't sure but thinks she may have lost consciousness."

Dr. Callahan spends only a few minutes checking Gina. She takes a neck brace from her medical bag and gently moves Gina to the floor. "We'll get a stretcher and take you to the hospital. Where are your parents?"

Again, Tootie says their parents are still working.

The doctor's eyes go wide. "They let you come here alone?" She shakes her head. "Fine. You go after them," she tells Tootie. "Send her parents to the hospital."

It takes only a few minutes for Dr. Callahan to get a stretcher to us. She asks Leo and me to go with Gina and give a report when we arrive.

Chapter 5

Merissa

"Merissa, grab all the radios except the one Ryan has and put them on the charger. This is one of those times we should count our lucky stars that we have solar power. Even if it is less than what we truly need to run this place."

As I step away to collect the walkie-talkies from the on-call staff, nurse Jacquie Haley keeps muttering about treating people in the dark.

As soon as the radio call came over about the attack in Monument District, Captain Williams had everyone on-call brought in. Even with a full staff, it still isn't enough to run a proper hospital, especially in an emergency. Just two doctors, two nurses, two medics, and a husband-and-wife janitor team, along with me—brand new and not knowing much about anything.

We also notified all the off-site support staff. Because our building isn't the size of a real hospital, the laundry and kitchen are located elsewhere. It's not ideal, but considering our situation, it seems to work well.

Some of our staff are at the main hospital in the Monument District. Leo Burnett is there to see an orthopedist for his two broken arms. His wife, Katie, who's a nurse here, and medic Jesse Talbot are with him.

This is my second day of orientation—or I should say, it's my second orientation shift. While yesterday was a daytime assignment, I'm on the overnight shift now. I think yesterday went well, and up to now, so did today. But I'm still terribly green.

My work at the clinic we had back home in Livingston is nothing compared to what's needed from me here. There, we did basic stuff only. If someone was seriously sick or injured, they were transported to the still barely functioning hospital in town.

This hospital does it all. There's a surgical suite with an attached recovery room. A large examination room is set up for severe situations, like gunshot wounds, and a slightly smaller room functions the same way. There's a third room used for minor needs.

There are three overnight rooms, which, according to Jesse Talbot, hold three comfortably but can be set up more dorm style if needed. We also have various storage rooms, a break room, a sleeping room, Captain Williams's office, two sink-and-toilet-only bathrooms in the hallway, and full baths in Williams's office and between the overnight patient rooms.

They reworked the existing bathrooms, removing the old flush toilets and replacing them with compost toilets. We even have a compost station in the backyard of the hospital. The full baths have solar showers, which are only used when necessary. There are thermoses for hot water and containers for cold water for hand washing, plus an ample supply of hand sanitizer made in a nearby distillery.

The building has big windows on both sides, letting lots of daylight into the exam and patient rooms. A small solar system provides additional light to the surgical suite, the two larger exam rooms, and the two public bathrooms.

The other rooms use a combination of individual solar lights and battery-operated lights. The rechargeable batteries in the lights and walkie-talkies are replenished when the sun is shining so as not to be a drain on the limited solar system battery bank. Woodstoves provide enough heat to keep us from freezing, but it's still cold after the sun drops.

A serious weakness, not only at the hospital but in our world in general, is water. Rapid Creek flows through Rapid City—which had a population of approximately 76,000 before the EMP, and currently has half that. Many here as refugees, like me. The creek does help considerably with our water needs. Old water wells were also reworked to use with a hand pump, and new wells were hand-dug.

Whether getting water from the streams or wells, it isn't as simple as just drawing the water. Because of contamination upstream and possibly in the groundwater, it all has to be treated before use.

The water crew takes care of that too. They boil water over outdoor fires in large vats and allow it to cool before making it available to the general public. Providing clean water cuts down on the risk of cholera, dysentery, and more. We don't want to risk using contaminated water.

During the summer months, water collection from rainfall was important. Even now, with the temperatures dropping but not yet freezing, water collection is still happening off many rooftops, including the hospital's. There's less concern over contamination with the rainwater, but it's still treated.

Each collection area is responsible for its own procedure. The hospital has a first-flush diverter at each container. As it collects rainfall, the container prevents roof debris from going into the barrel.

There's also a filter barrel connected to the first container. Once the first container fills, the water travels to the filter barrel. The water seeps through a half foot of sand and into a ten-inch bed of charcoal. Then finally, at the bottom of the barrel is about a foot of gravel, with smaller gravel at the top and larger pieces on the floor of the barrel. The spigot is in the gravel section.

Jesse Talbot says they'll probably be taking the barrels down in the next few weeks but are still collecting and storing as much fresh water as possible while the weather allows.

Last winter, the Black Hills had record snowfalls, just like we did in Livingston. The snow melt provided much-needed fluids, but it is quite the job. Depending on how wet and heavy the snow is, it can take up to ten gallons of snow to get one gallon of water.

Like the other districts in Rapid City, the Guard District has a water crew. Our proximity to Rapid Creek is a huge help for them. There's even a water station nearby using ram pumps—something I'm pretty familiar with and was in charge of at my old home—to take water from the creek.

Yesterday, feeling overwhelmed with the whole hospital thing, I considered telling Captain Williams I'd changed my mind. I'm certain I could get a job on the water crew, and it would probably be a better fit for me.

But last night, while writing out my thoughts, I decided to give this position two weeks. If it still feels wrong, I'll resign and find a new crew. I know I could return to the ranch, which would be fine, but I feel the need to make it on my own while doing all I can to help with the reconstruction efforts.

I don't dare tell Pearl my fears and insecurities. She'd have way too much to say about it. She may be my mother-in-law, but we've never been particularly close. It's almost humorous I'm the one here with her. Courtney was always Pearl's favorite daughter-in-law. And with good reason. Courtney was beautiful and poised, and even though I didn't want to like her, she was terribly sweet.

When everything fell apart last year, she showed her fortitude and stepped up. She was an important component of our survival. Her decision to head west to find her family broke Pearl's heart. I'm an only child, and my parents are long dead, so Pearl was the only family I had left after my husband died.

Staying with her was my only option. And I owed it to my husband to make sure she safely reached Rapid City. Part of me thought I'd get her here and figure out what to do with myself. Maybe that'd be an option if winter wasn't starting, and if I wasn't pregnant.

With the handheld radios collected and on the charging units, I search out Ryan, the medic I'm shadowing today. "What do you want me to do next?"

He motions to his radio. "I switched over to the police channel to see if they had more info about the situation. It sounds bad. There was some sort of festival happening. A bomb went off, and as people tried to escape, someone started shooting them." He shakes his head.

"The number of dead is unknown. According to Monument District law enforcement, the hospital is holding up so far. If needed, they'll ship to the closer districts first. We're still on standby. Might as well keep on with your training. Questions so far?"

I probably do have questions, but nothing immediately comes to mind. A lot of what I'm learning today is a repeat from yesterday with Jesse. I'm okay with that. Like Jesse, Ryan is former military, as is janitor Kerry Hendricks. All three were in the Army like my husband; although, neither put in their full years for retirement like Braedon did.

When I met Jesse yesterday, he made a point of calling me a Coastie and giving me some good-natured ribbing. The men started in on each other, with Leo calling Jesse Soldier Boy and Jesse talking about needing to hide all the crayons from Leo. Katie looked uncomfortable and later apologized if they made me feel bad. I assured her it was fine and to be expected.

I'm not entirely sure how to take Katie. She's young, probably only in her early twenties, and smart. Jacquie Haley made a big deal about telling me how Katie isn't a *real* nurse. There were lots of eye rolls and other gestures as Jacquie expressed her strong opinions.

When I told her I'm not a real medic, she was almost speechless—which seems to be a rarity for the woman—and started sputtering about how I must have some decent training to be part of the med school program.

The more the older nurse stammered, the more I realized she was jealous. Jealous untrained nurse Katie Burnett was asked by Captain Williams to play an important teaching role in the new med school. Both she and her husband Leo, along with the other two doctors, Arnetta "Nettie" Wolff and Chastity Morrow, will do most of the teaching in conjunction with Captain Williams.

Turns out, Dr. Wolff and Dr. Morrow aren't "real" doctors either. Believe me, Jacquie had plenty to say about that too. Nettie Wolff was a med student when the first attacks started. She ended up stuck in Rapid City and her dreams of finishing med school were crushed.

It was a few months later when the satellite hospitals were set up, and she was moved from the main hospital to here, functioning as a full-fledged doctor under the supervision of Captain Williams.

Chastity Morrow's only been at this hospital for a few weeks. Before her assignment here, replacing a doctor who was murdered, she worked as a rotating doctor and traveled to the different satellite hospitals to give the regular staff a needed break. Chastity is a physician assistant, or PA.

It's almost humorous how Jacquie went on and on about everyone while also making it clear she's the only real nurse, having a nursing degree and working in the field for the last twenty-plus years. A few more shifts with her and I'm sure I'll know everything Jacquie believes is worth knowing concerning the entire staff.

The only one I've yet to hear her disparage is Captain Williams. She shows a considerable amount of respect for him, even if she doesn't agree with his choice of medical school instructors.

It's about 2330 hours when the radio on Ryan's belt sounds. It's a relay from Monument Hospital telling us we can stand down. They have the situation under control. Captain Williams dismisses the on-call people, telling them to sleep fast. Most are back on at 0600. Those of us still on shift—the captain, Jacquie, janitor Rand Hendricks, Ryan, and me—continue with our duties.

Two of the three exam rooms have people in them. One guy was splitting wood in the dark, and the axe slipped. The other is a woman who's had an upset stomach for a few days. She thinks it may be some kind of food poisoning. I avoid sharing my story of how I also thought I had food poisoning, but it turned out I was expecting.

Because Jacquie was stitching up the axe injury, Williams had me help him with the exam. In the end, her situation mirrored mine. Williams estimates her due date is late June or July. Like so many women these days who have been subsisting on rations and minimal calories, her cycles have been irregular, so it's only an estimate.

She seems rather embarrassed by it. "I'm so, so sorry for wasting your time. So sorry. I'll be sure to follow up with the midwife I heard about."

"Pregnancy is something we treat here at the hospital too," Williams says. "Every Tuesday is clinic day. It's first come, first served. If you ever have a concern, you should come in immediately."

After she leaves, the captain lets out a long sigh. "We've had a hard time convincing people to come into the hospital unless it's a life-or-death situation. There's at least one woman in the community, probably the midwife the woman mentioned, who not only sees pregnant women and helps with childbirth but also treats other ailments with a variety of natural medicines."

Williams doesn't go as far as calling the midwife a quack but does state she's lacking the knowledge needed.

He then goes on to talk about Stella Swenson, whom I've yet to meet. She's one of the other med students and is also a master herbalist and wildcrafter. "If it wasn't for her and her knowledge, more people would die. She'll be a huge asset to the medical team if she can learn to adapt to the hospital's pace."

With only a few hours left on my orientation shift, I'm feeling pretty good about the job and am excited about the medical school. Captain Williams has an easy instructional method, and it's apparent he has a heart for teaching. Maybe accompanying Pearl to Rapid City will turn out to be the perfect choice for me. And for my baby.

Chapter 6

Katie

"You okay?" Leo asks as I fumble at putting the key in the lock of our room.

"Tired." It's just before 0400. We spent the night helping with triage and transporting patients. Even Josiah was put to work. Now the brothers are in the dorm area, trying to get a few hours of sleep before we go home.

Like pretty much every other doctor, nurse, and hospital support staff, Dr. Bollinger was called into work. Seeing Leo, he did a quick exam of his arm and determined the splint was fine, though in need of a cleaning.

I helped Leo with that, and while it doesn't look as good as new, it's fine. We won't need to go in for our morning appointment, but Bollinger did remind Leo to take it easy and do the exercises.

Leo runs his unsplinted hand through his hair. "Four hours of sleep is barely going to make a dent in this exhaustion."

Four hours is a pipe dream. With the noise of people coming and going, plus the plastic-covered mattresses rustling through the night, I'm not sure I sleep for more than fifteen minutes at a stretch. I give up at 0630.

I'm trying to get dressed as quietly as I can when Leo rolls over. "Not the best place for a good night's sleep. Where you going?"

"I don't know. The sitting area, maybe. I thought I'd go for a walk, but after last night . . . " I purse my lips. "I'm not sure how safe it is here."

"I still find it hard to believe someone attacked a gathering like that. It doesn't seem . . . " He shakes his head. "It seems like something that would've happened before, right? You know, schools and concerts. Why now?"

"Why then?"

He cocks an eyebrow at me, but I roll my eyes back at him.

Since we've been married, we've had many discussions that I label as conspiracy talks. Leo's worked to connect the dots of our current situation—coordinated attacks on the country, along with world-changing nuclear detonations, and the current state of our society, which many describe as World War III since we aren't the only country having troubles—to what seemed to be isolated events in the years leading up to the country-wide attacks.

He's particularly focused on the events referred to as lone wolf with a single attacker. We had discussed this before the first planes were brought down and everything changed, but even more so after discovering Lieutenant Commander Sam Mitchell was living in Bakerville.

Mitchell was the doctor who gave Leo his physical when he first joined the Marines. He and his wife were also instrumental in stopping a school shooting in the town of Groyver, Wyoming.

Sam Mitchell's account of what happened during that event—and in the weeks following, when his family fled their home in fear for their lives as others from the school mysteriously died—led Leo down a conspiracy theory rabbit hole.

When we later found out Sam Mitchell actually *was* targeted for murder, and the hit was carried out even in our new apocalyptic world, Leo almost had me convinced he was on the right track.

Almost.

I agree with Leo that the Groyver situation was a setup. It was designed to look like a lone wolf attack when there were several people involved. And I agree there was a hit taken out on Sam Mitchell and the others from the school who stopped the shooting.

But to paint with such a wide brush and say *all* supposed lone wolf terrorist attacks are part of a huge, organized plan to put us exactly where we are today . . . I'm not going there.

"I know, I know." Leo sits up in his twin bed. "Man, this is one of the worst night's sleep I've had in a while—not counting the early days of two broken arms. I'm almost looking forward to the bumpy wagon ride. Maybe I'll be able to doze off. You're right, it's not likely this is related to the *other* events. But why? What were they hoping to accomplish?"

"Does evil need a reason?"

He tilts his head. "I'm not sure it's that simple. They were organized. They caused mass destruction and chaos with the explosion and then sniped people as they ran out. It doesn't even sound like they found any of them. I don't know why . . . " He stretches his hand across the slim aisle between the two beds and touches my leg. "What I do know is you were amazing last night."

My mouth goes into a tight line. "Francine lost her leg. She could still die from infection or something else. Gina will be in the hospital for weeks and will have a long recovery."

"Francine has a chance. She wouldn't have made it out of the cafeteria alive if not for you. You heard the doctor."

I lift my hand. "Yes. Think Jesse and Josiah are up? I'm ready to go home."

His hand tightens on my leg as he pulls me closer. I drop into an awkward stance to hug him. My ear is tickled as he whispers, "I'm ready to be home too."

Leaving at first light, the five-mile wagon ride takes under two hours. We probably would've made it quicker, but there were several security checkpoints—checkpoints that weren't there on our trip to the main hospital.

My hopes of dozing along the way didn't happen, thanks to the chill of the cold November wind and the rough ride in the back of the wagon. As we near the medical clinic and our horses' livery stable, Jesse asks if we'd like a ride the rest of the way home.

Even though my nose is numb from the cold, I shake my head. "I've had enough bumping around. Leo?"

"Let's walk. I'd like to check in at the hospital anyway."

Josiah tilts back his hat. "They let everyone know last night. All the districts were notified about the attack, just in case it wasn't— " he shrugs " —isolated."

"Probably smart." Leo nods. "Guess that'll be the end of their festivals."

"I don't think so. I heard someone tell one of the deputies they'd still have it next week as planned. 'Course, the deputy said that'd be up to the sheriff whether to allow it or not."

I lean toward Josiah and Jesse on the bench seat. "Why would they even want to do it? Wouldn't they realize people won't go? I know I wouldn't, not after . . . " My entire body shudders, not only from the cold but from the memory of last night's carnage.

We don't know for sure but heard dozens were killed outright. Several more died at the hospital. Many more are severely injured and may or may not survive.

Josiah turns in his seat to look back at Leo and me. "Yup. I get that. But at the same time, I understand. If they cancel the rest of the festivals, the bad guys win."

Jesse pulls the wagon to a stop in front of the medical center. "You're on day shift tomorrow, Katie?"

"Yes, the next three days, though I do have to pop over to the school on Monday to introduce myself. Leo's teaching all day."

I glance at Leo, who gives a vigorous nod. "Yep. Hope my old, lazy body can handle it. The pathogens class was only half a day and almost too much for me."

"Got to get you whipped back into shape," Jesse says with a laugh.

The bell above the front door signals our arrival. Kerry Hendricks sticks her head out from one of the rooms. "Hey, how are you?" Her expression is stern. "Do you know about the attack last night? Were you near it?"

My nose burns and my eyes fill with tears.

"We know," Leo says. "We were . . . there."

Dr. Arnetta "Nettie" Wolff steps out of a different exam room. "You were there? Want a cup of tea? We can talk."

Leo looks at me, and I give a slight nod.

Nettie fills up the teacups with steaming water from the top of the woodstove. "Was it as bad as it sounds?"

I plop into a chair. "Worse, probably."

"What'd you hear?" Leo asks.

"There was an attack on some sort of church function. Dozens dead, dozens more injured."

As we clarify the event and what we know about it, including how we worked alongside the first responders, Nettie tsks and shakes her head in appropriate places. As we wrap it up, she asks, "Who's responsible?"

Leo and I shrug in unison. "Didn't hear," Leo says. "I don't even think they found anyone to blame."

"They'll keep looking, I'm sure." Nettie places our cups in front of us.

With the mug warming my hands, the steam rises near my face as I inhale the minty aroma.

Leo takes a sip. After setting it back on the table, he leans back in his chair. "Makes no sense."

"You know what it reminds me of?" Nettie's voice is quiet, nearly a whisper. "Before. When there'd be attacks and— "

I snort out a laugh.

Nettie wrinkles her brow.

"Sorry. It's not funny. Not at all. It's just, well . . . don't get Leo started."

Leo gives a humorless chuckle. "It's not funny. But you're not wrong. It does seem like before. And . . . Katie's right. You probably don't want to get me started."

Nettie's heard the story of Sam Mitchell and his family, but I haven't shared Leo's wild theories. Including how he's convinced what happened at the Mitchells' school is somehow related to the world we now live in.

She crinkles her nose and shakes her head. "I'm sure I've heard it all before. David has some rather strong opinions too." Her cheeks redden at her mention of Lieutenant David Paul. "Some of his theories are really out there, but others . . . " She shrugs. "I can see them."

Leo bobs his head several times. "Lieutenant Paul and I have had some interesting conversations. Speaking of, I'll need to check in with him about my doctor's visit. I'd hoped I would be released and could start training soon. But that isn't going to happen."

A look crosses Nettie's face. "Forgive me. The news of the shooting was so concerning I almost forgot the reason you were there." She points to the new splint on Leo's arm. "How long for this one?"

Leo's tone is matter of fact as he relays the news about the malunion of the left wrist. Nettie assisted the late Dr. Newsome in the casting, and it's obvious she feels some responsibility for the issue. But she does give a bright smile when Leo tells her the other arm is just about as good as new.

I'm grateful when he doesn't mention the ulceration on his shoulder and how even Bollinger said it could've killed him. Leo finishes by relaying the exercises he's to do for rehab and that Dr. Bollinger will reexamine him when he does his rotation.

"What?" She leans forward. "He's taking rotation? Why?" Her jaw tightens, and she visibly swallows.

Leo and I share a look, and both give a shake of our heads.

Nettie visibly relaxes and gives what I can only assume is a fake smile. "I mean, isn't he plenty busy there? Everyone goes to Monument Hospital if they can. It was busy when the lights were still on. That hasn't changed. A prominent doctor like him . . . " She shakes her head. "It doesn't make any sense."

Dr. Bollinger didn't tell us why he was taking rotation and traveling to the satellite hospitals, but the bigger question is, why does Nettie seem so concerned about it?

Chapter 7

"You nervous?" I lift onto my toes and peck my husband on the lips.

He returns my quick kiss before leaning in for something deeper, longer. His unsplinted hand rests on my shoulder while the still-healing hand wraps around my waist. When he finally pulls away, he says, "You sure you can't be late today?"

"Mmm. Tempting. But you can't be late for your first day of teaching either. It seems almost cruel Captain Williams is starting the school at 0600. At least it won't be a twelve-hour class like our work shifts are."

"Right. Only eleven and a half. So much better. Soon, there will be work rotations too. You know on-the-job training is going to be a big focus. The bookwork, though necessary, isn't going to be like it would've been at a medical school in the past. Well, the recent past anyway. He's looking way back and following Dr. William Halsted's residency programs of do one, see one, teach one."

I give a nod. "He's passionate about it. Nettie and Chastity . . . " I make a face. "They're not so convinced it's a good idea."

"You mean Dr. Wolff and Dr. Morrow?" Leo moves his mouth, making his mustache jiggle.

"I hope I can remember that."

Captain Williams made a point of instructing us to call everyone by their proper titles once the med school starts. He says he wants to keep everything professional. Even Leo and I are to be known by our ranks—Sergeant and Private Burnett. Remembering to call Nettie and Chastity *doctor* may be a challenge. Calling my husband *sergeant* may be impossible.

New full-time doctor Chastity Morrow is Nettie Wolff's housemate. The two of them share an adorable three-bedroom with a nurse who works at a nearby long-term care center.

Even though Nettie and Chastity always seem friendly, and Chastity roomed with Nettie before when she'd visit our hospital as a rotating doctor, Nettie seems less than pleased about the permanent situation. She even suggested several alternative houses Chastity could have, such as the one assigned to new medic Merissa Weaver and her mother-in-law, Pearl.

Why Captain Williams decided the two women should house together, I'm not entirely sure. But I suspect it has something to do with the world we live in and, at the time, Dr. Newsome's unsolved murder. After we discovered Newsome was killed for revenge, Chastity was already settled in, and Nettie had accepted the housemate situation.

"I can understand Chastity and Nettie questioning Williams's training method. They're still new to doctoring themselves and are learning in an entirely different manner." Leo reaches for his jacket. "They're concerned about patient safety."

"I know. They've told me. Williams too. But he says he's confident, with proper supervision, it's the right method for today. Especially with our small class size. With the addition of Merissa, there are only seven students."

"Ready to go?" Leo shoves a stocking hat on his head.

I wrap my scarf around my neck. "It's still snowing. I hope it isn't too slick."

"The traction boots will help." He lifts his boot to show the bottom of a screw head sticking out. The reworked soles provide a bit of grip on the ice.

While I already have shoes for work at the hospital, Leo has an extra set of clothes and shoes in his backpack—a larger one than his usual daypack. We'll leave these at the medical school so he has a change of clothes there.

Leo and I walk together as far as the medical school, located in a business complex across the street from the hospital. He kisses me goodbye and says he'll see me in a few hours. I'm working my regular hospital shift today, but I'll pop over to the school at 1300 to give my story and convince the students how wonderful on-the-job training can be.

It almost makes me laugh that Captain Williams thought I'd be a good addition to his teaching staff, especially considering I was an art major seventeen months ago. At least Leo took several classes toward becoming an EMT before the attacks started.

Not me.

Other than a few first aid and CPR classes and reading Leo's EMT books, I knew nothing when our world suddenly fell apart and I found myself as part of the Bakerville medical team. Surprising to say the least. But even more surprising is I'll soon be an official member of the South Dakota National Guard.

After kissing Leo goodbye, I walk the short distance to the hospital. Chastity and Ryan, our medic for the day, have already arrived.

"Good morning, Katie." Chastity gives me a weary smile. "It's going to be a busy one. Three admits overnight, all from the same family."

I wrinkle my brow. "Flu?"

"Maybe. Maybe food poisoning. Vomiting, diarrhea, fever, abdominal pain. They're in the family suite. The mom's doing the best. The little girl is severely dehydrated. The dad . . . " She shakes her head. "He's got it bad. Williams is going to get the students started at the school and come back over. We'll see what to do then."

I change from street clothes to work clothes, feeling thankful for my long underwear on this brisk mid-November morning. The front doorbell sounds, and I quickly stow my things in my locker and dart out to the hallway.

"Put him in exam room two," Chastity directs our medic and another man, who are guiding an obviously ill man as he stumbles down the hallway.

As I step closer, the fecal and vomit odor emitting from the man is almost overpowering.

Always professional, Chastity asks, "How long's he been sick?"

"Don't know, ma'am," the man helping says. "Showed up at his house for work and found him sicker than a dog."

"Work? For what?"

"Wood splitters, ma'am. That's how I got him here, usin' the flatbed cart. I'm gonna need to get it back so we can fill 'er up."

The wood-splitting crew is one of the most necessary work crews. The spring, summer, and early fall months were spent harvesting wood and bringing it out of the mountains. It was left mostly in rounds to be split over the winter. Now, with the cold months upon us, the crew splits and delivers wood to various locations so people can pick it up for use. Or for a few of us with odd work hours, like at the hospital, we get regular wood delivery.

With winter here, we also get water delivery. There's even talk of adding food delivery, but Nettie says they talked about that last year, too, and never did it.

Personally, I'm okay with getting my own food. While standing in line for our ration chips and going to separate locations and lines for our goods isn't my favorite thing, it does give some sense of normalcy and almost reminds me of grocery shopping. *Almost.*

"What're his symptoms?" Chastity asks as he's moved into the exam room.

While Ryan and the wood crew man help the sick man onto the table, I join Chastity at the sink to wash. Without running water, we make do in the exam rooms using a water cooler filled with hot water by each sink. I press the spout to allow water to flow for Chastity.

While she's washing, the woodcutter relays what he knows. "Caruso was fine when I saw him at work yesterday. Said he was gettin' together with some friends last night, a birthday celebration for someone. He wasn't at the staging area this morning, so I went lookin' for him. He houses the flatbed, so . . . " The man lifted a shoulder.

"Anyway, I found him passed out in his own vomit. And it's obvious he's messed his pants too." The man shudders. "Thought maybe he got some bad hooch—ya know, since he went to a birthday party and all. But with as sick as he is, figured I'd better bring 'em on in. Didn't want him to die."

Chastity finishes washing and shakes her hands to dry them, and I move in front of the sink to take my turn. She asks a few more questions about the condition he found Caruso in.

"Caruso lives alone. Was worried he might choke on his vomit or something. The other woodcutters are waitin' on me to bring the flatbed. I'll come back after work to check on him." The man turns and leaves.

We complete Caruso's vitals, and Chastity shakes her head. "Same symptoms as the family next door."

"Maybe they were at the same birthday party?" I take a step toward the door. "Should I go ask the mom if she knows him?"

"I suspect they do. The mom mentioned a birthday party yesterday." Chastity motions with her chin toward the sink. "Wash in and wash out. I know you would've used the hand sanitizer, but let's be extra diligent. Soap and water followed by sanitizer. Take their vitals and give them a quick check while you're in there."

I glance at Caruso, barely conscious and groaning as he cradles his stomach. A terrible rumbling sound happens, followed by a much more obvious noise and an increase in odor.

Chastity shakes her head. "I know you're feeling bad, Mr. Caruso. We'll try and help. In the meantime, Ryan will help you get cleaned up and into a gown."

He moans as I exit the room.

In the family suite, the mom is sitting in the rocking chair holding a toddler while the husband lies curled up on a bed.

"Hi, I'm Katie." I go to the sink to wash.

The homemade lye soap is harsher than what we had before the apocalypse. The hand sanitizer is also harsh. With the combination of the two, and using them every time I enter or leave a patient's room, my hands will be a mess before the end of the day.

As I check the little girl's vitals, I ask the mom, "Do you know Caruso?"

Her eyes go wide. "We were with him yesterday afternoon at a birthday party for another friend who turned seventy. We wanted to do something special. Everyone brought food and played silly games."

"Was anyone drinking?"

She shakes her head. I'm not sure she'd tell me if they were. Prohibition is in full force, with the president of the United States telling us grain is for eating, not drinking. It's obvious the little girl is ill, making bootleg liquor the unlikely culprit of this illness.

When I check the dad's vitals, he comes around enough to ask why he's so sick. The rumble in his stomach sounds like Caruso's. The dad gets a worried look on his face and stumbles from the bed.

I offer to help, but he waves me off and darts to the connected bathroom. I wait in the room until he returns. He's flushed and sweaty but tells me he's okay.

I wash out of the room and step into the hallway. Chastity is there. "They know him, right?"

"Yep. They were at a party for an elderly friend."

Chastity closes her eyes and shakes her head. "Sure hope we don't have a serious outbreak like they did in Montana. That's all we need."

Chapter 8

I let out a noisy sigh. The outbreak in Montana was terrible. We were notified of it on the radio first and then by groups passing through after it happened. Even Merissa Weaver and her mother-in-law mentioned it. They lived in a town near the outbreak.

The details were sketchy at first, but we soon discovered it was ergotism caused by infected rye and other cereal grains. The former college town of Bozeman, Montana, was severely affected and dozens died.

The discovery of the contaminated grain caused a near panic as the Rapid City area grains were examined for the disease. They didn't discover any evidence of the fungus, Claviceps purpurea, but they're still monitoring for it.

"These symptoms are different, though, right? I mean, vomiting is a symptom, but isn't it usually more neurological? Convulsions, numbness, or burning?" We'd all studied up on the symptoms after the news of the ergotism broke so we'd know what to look for.

"Right. I don't think this is ergotism. But it may be an outbreak of some sort. I hope it's not cholera."

"We treat the water and use outhouses. It shouldn't be something so serious."

"It shouldn't be, but that doesn't mean it isn't. There were several cholera outbreaks early on before people got organized. Something may have gone wrong. We need to check on everyone who was at the party. See if you can get a list from the mom. She seems the least sick in the group. I'm going to call Captain Williams on the radio and let him know about this development."

The mom gives me a list of names and addresses, or vague directions to people's homes if she doesn't know their actual address. There were eight families at the party for their friend.

When I leave the family suite, Chastity is waiting for me. "Williams, Leo, and the students are in the office. They're going to make house calls. You have the list?"

I pass it off to her, and she motions for me to follow. She gives a couple of quick knocks on the door to Williams's office before stepping in. "Here it is."

Williams looks over the list, and Leo peers over his shoulder. My husband points at the paper. "Several are on the same street."

"That'll help." Williams bobs his head. "Leo, take three people and go to these addresses." He puts a finger on the paper. "Have someone copy them down. The rest of us will go to the other addresses."

Merissa Weaver, part of Leo's group, copies the addresses they're going to. "What an interesting first day of school."

Within an hour, two of the students who left with Captain Williams return for one of the handcarts, our post-apocalyptic version of an ambulance. They went to the birthday gal's home and found her in nearly the same condition as Caruso and the family.

I make sure an overnight room is ready for her. Chastity and Ryan get the other overnight room put together and make sure all the exam rooms are set up for this particular illness.

I'll admit, I had a small hope this was going to be isolated to the ones we already had at our hospital. I should've known better.

Chastity and I go over symptoms and possible afflictions in our hospital's vast collection of medical books. While we don't yet know exactly what we're dealing with, we're hopeful it's something quick, nonfatal, and will only affect a limited number of people.

While she continues to search out possibilities based on symptoms, I focus my research on Staphylococcus aureus food poisoning. What I read is encouraging . . . at least as far as food poisoning goes.

This illness is caused by eating foods contaminated with the Staph bacteria. Usually someone carrying Staph didn't wash their hands before serving food. While symptoms can be severe, as in the case of Caruso and the dad, it typically isn't fatal and doesn't last long.

Of course, with the way things are, we could have a different experience than when the lights were on. Both men are on the skinny side—as are the mom and their young daughter. It's possible the months of food rationing have left them with a weakened immune system.

The truth is, we aren't sure how a simple illness will affect people these days. Mild illnesses can be fatal in today's world.

By midmorning, all but one of the families are accounted for, and everyone has symptoms to some degree.

In addition to the seventy-year-old whose birthday they were celebrating, a couple in their fifties is also admitted to the hospital. The others can remain in their homes. We set up a house call system, using Leo and the medical school trainees to check on them and take them to the hospital if necessary.

The missing family is a husband and wife who work as transporters. The family living next to them, who were also at the party and are sick, said the couple was scheduled to make a delivery in Deadwood today. Everyone assumes they left as planned.

There's a concern we're wrong about this being a noncontagious foodborne illness and they could spread the sickness. If it's cholera—which we're beginning to doubt, but it's still possible—it could spread through feces.

Williams makes a call on our CB radio, which we use in conjunction with the walkie-talkies carried by our on-call staff, local law enforcement, and the National Guard. While our unit can't contact Deadwood, there are a few ham radios in operation, and he's hoping he can do a relay.

He gives as much info as he knows about the couple, the Glatts, and asks for the message to be relayed to the Deadwood hospitals and clinics, as well as their law enforcement.

Afterward, Williams shakes his head. "Might be making a mountain out of a molehill. Sure hope I am."

"But we don't know, not for sure." Chastity shrugs. "Besides, if they're sick, they may need help."

Williams groans. "You're right. I just don't want to be the doctor that makes a ruckus about nothing. 'Course, I'm sure someone in Bozeman thought the same thing when people started getting sick. You heard they locked down their entire town? They weren't sure exactly what was happening. While ergot poisoning isn't contagious, they were right to do so. They needed to get it under control. They did, and then they went back to business as usual. We'll do the same."

I furrow my brow. "We're going to lock down the town?"

"What?" He crinkles his face. "No. No, that isn't what I meant. We'll keep track of everyone who is ill and keep them isolated. There's no reason to isolate people who aren't sick. Not in our case."

With the first day of medical school turned topsy-turvy, Williams tells Chastity and me he'll move our talks to another day, when we don't have every overnight room in our small hospital occupied.

Ryan's already working on breaking down our third examination room to turn it into a sleeping room. We have a stash of heavy-duty cots for this purpose. While we all hope and pray we won't have anyone else sick enough to stay in the hospital, it's always possible.

Williams touches base with the long-term care facilities, asking them to be on alert and ready to take patients if needed. He also puts a radio call out to Monument Hospital and all the satellite hospitals, letting them know what we have so they can be alert for similar symptoms.

It's midafternoon. Williams, Leo, and the students have gone back to the school building to discuss and learn from today's events before a team will make their house calls to the sick people still at home.

Ryan's radio makes a squawking noise, and a scratchy voice comes through. I'm closest to the base radio, so I run to it to try and understand better. When the voice stops, all I can determine is it was a call for us—Guard District Hospital—but not the contents of the call.

I press the talk button. "Guard District Hospital. Please repeat the transmission. Over."

There's a long pause. I think maybe they didn't hear me. I move my thumb toward the button, but the voice finally comes through— loud and clear this time.

"Guard District Hospital, this is Bethlehem One relaying a transmission from Lawrence County Sheriff. Your missing people have been located. They're being cared for at the Silverado Clinic. More information in four hours via relay."

"Great! Thank you! Um, I mean, copy that. Guard District Hospital expects more information in four hours. Over."

"Copy. Bethlehem One, over and out."

Chastity is leaning a shoulder against the wall. "That's good news. Now, as long as it's food poisoning . . . "

"Yeah. If they're at the clinic, they're sick, right?"

"That'd be my guess. Can you and Ryan handle things for now? I want to tell Williams."

"Sure." I didn't mention she could use the radio to call him. He took one of the handhelds in case we needed him. We use a different frequency for the on-call radios, but it's as easy as changing a channel to call him up.

Like me, I'm sure Chastity is curious about how the school is going, even if it has only been a few hours since we've seen them.

I'm finishing up my shift, and Leo and the students have returned from making the house calls, when the radio relay comes in with an update on the Glatts. The news is good. They're resting comfortably. There's no mention of anything else.

Williams, who is on-site when the call comes in, asks if he can pass on a question: is there an R-naught?

Though slightly coded, there's a good chance those who are listening and relaying will understand what he's asking—is anyone else infected? So far, only those who were at the birthday party are sick.

All are improving and are being rehydrated with electrolyte drinks. These are a simple blend of honey, salt, and a little fruit juice. The honey is wild harvested or from one of the hives being tended.

We still have salvaged salt to use, but salt is being hoarded and is desperately needed. There's some salt in the soil of the Black Hills region, which can be processed for use, but trade is our most likely way to replenish our supply—trade that will need to wait until summer when things are moving again.

Because this illness may be transmissible, everyone at the hospital today, including all the med students, has been ordered to avoid people. While we're not exactly put on lockdown, it's well understood we could be dealing with a communicable disease, and we could be spreaders.

Because of the quick onset of symptoms from the party people, Williams says we'll know more within twenty-four hours. If none of us get sick, we're in the clear. In the meantime, we're supposed to avoid other people. We can go to our homes, but that's all.

There's a light snow shower as Leo and I walk home in the dark.

Leo grabs my hand. "Well, that was an interesting day."

"Did your students do well?"

He clicks his tongue. "For the most part. When we went looking for sick people this morning, Williams gave me the more adept students, the ones he believes will make it through the course."

"It was probably smart for him to take the others."

"Yeah, probably."

"Do you feel . . . insulted?"

"Insulted? No, I figured he wanted to see how his people did under pressure."

"That makes sense. And . . . ?"

"I think he was mostly pleased. They still want to impress him, so they're going out of their way to do so. Everyone knows this is a great opportunity."

I think about what he's saying. Being trained as a doctor is a great opportunity. While our work isn't exactly easy, it also isn't labor-intensive like many of the other jobs. Gone are the days of sitting in an office and typing on a keyboard.

While there are people who make schedules and supervise, those positions are limited. Almost everyone's a manual laborer now. That's the way it has to be. There's wood to cut, food to grow, animals to feed and care for, water to gather . . . it all needs to be done or else none of us will make it through the winter and the days ahead.

Leo squeezes my hand. "Day shift tomorrow, right? Then off for two days?"

"Right. After today, I'm ready."

"I'll get our ration chips tomorrow. I might have time to go during lunch or as soon as school's done."

Many jobs and crews work ten or twelve-hour shifts. To accommodate, the ration office is open from 0400 to 2030 each day. The sixteen-and-a-half-hour window is divided into two shifts of workers, ensuring everyone can get their ration chips on their assigned days. Our day is Tuesday.

While being a ration chip or token distributor is one of the few nonlabor-intensive jobs, it's not a job I'd ever want.

"I don't mind walking with you if you want to wait until afterward. School finishes at 1730, right? Half an hour earlier than when my shift ends. We could go together."

The light of the moon is just enough to pick up the green of his eyes. My heart does a little flip when I see the look of love on his face.

"It's a date, Mrs. Burnett."

Chapter 9

By noon the next day, all our sick patients, except the seventy-year-old birthday woman, are well enough to go home. We decide to keep her an extra day to help her rehydrate.

We heard from the Deadwood clinic about the Glatts. They're still recovering. It'll be a few days before they're well enough to make the journey home by horse and wagon. The best news of all: there have been no other illnesses. Nobody that wasn't at the party has arrived at our clinic, and none of the other hospitals have reported issues.

I'm currently spending a rather awkward hour at the medical school, giving my brief story of how I was shanghaied into becoming a nurse.

Naturally, I don't use the word *shanghaied* and try to make it sound like I was totally on board with joining the Bakerville medical team. But I do mention that I doubt it would've happened if my sister hadn't been injured and I happened to be in the right place at the right time.

Or the wrong time, depending on how you look at it.

Sometimes I wonder how different my life would be had I not joined the medical team. Would Leo have as easily convinced me to join the Volunteer Unit? I knew going in I'd be a medic and not a soldier. Had I thought I'd become a soldier, I may have stayed home. Stayed with my family. Helped my stepdad with my little brother. Helped my sisters with their children. Convinced my husband we could make a difference right where we were.

I don't share any of those thoughts with the med students. Instead, I share how little I knew and how almost all my training was hands-on. Although I did study and read, and still do, I'm the prime example of see one, do one, teach one.

Other than Sheila, my sister Calley's sister-in-law, I was the only one on the Bakerville medical team without any previous experience.

Like me, Sheila didn't ask to be part of the team. She had what was essentially a nervous breakdown and ended up on our version of suicide watch, living in the small cabin we used as our clinic. I guess everyone figured, since she was there, she might as well make herself useful.

When Leo and I left in June, Sheila was doing much better. I wouldn't say she was completely out of the woods, she definitely still had issues, but I don't think she was a threat to herself at that point. Mental health is a big deal these days. Many people didn't have a situation like Sheila's where she was put under care to help her.

I haven't heard any firm numbers but know there were a lot of suicides in the early months following the nuclear bombs—when food was running low and the prospects of things returning to normal were shattered. Even now, there are still attempted and successful suicides.

In many ways, the attacks that started our downfall were excessively cruel. Few believed the original attacks could be world changing. As attacks continued day after day, people started to pay attention. For many, a kind of fight-or-flight mechanism was activated, and they chose flight.

People fled the cities in the hope of finding safety elsewhere. The interstates, freeways, and small highways turned into giant parking lots.

People ended up stranded. The smaller towns couldn't support the number of people suddenly at their doorstep. The resources—food, fuel, lodging, and more—were ravaged.

Leo and I lived in Manhattan, Kansas, and the population of our town practically doubled overnight. That's when we decided to go to my mom and Jake's home in Bakerville, Wyoming. I guess our flight response was also activated.

At first, I didn't want to go. I wanted to stay and wait it out. But when a shooting happened down the road from us, it seemed like the right decision. Like so many others, I thought the country would be safe. While it was probably safer than huge cities, we still had troubles.

We were certainly not immune from bad things. Our little town was attacked more than once, and not only by outside forces. It was an inside force that caused the death of several. Sheila's mom was one of them. That incident resulted in Sheila's downward spiral.

While talking to the med students, I briefly touched on psychological well-being and how that was a focus in Bakerville. It only makes sense it was since one of our medical team members was a psychiatric nurse.

When I'm finished, I give a rather awkward shrug and then look over at Captain Williams. "Um, was there anything else you wanted me to mention?" I'd warned him public speaking wasn't my forte.

He grips my hand and gives it a firm shake. "Thank you, Private. Ready to take some questions?"

I'm sure I give him a deer-in-the-headlights look.

He lets out a small laugh and whispers, "You'll be fine."

While most of the class seemed interested during my talk, Geoff Landers rolled his eyes more than once. I try not to take it personally, but . . .

Merissa gives me an understanding smile before raising her hand.

"Um, yes, Merissa?"

"Are you happy with your decision? To join the medical team, I mean."

"Decision?" I laugh. "It wasn't exactly a decision. It was more like . . ." I glance at Leo. "I'd say I was, um, nominated for the position."

Leo gives me a wink.

I raise my eyebrows at him before looking back to Merissa, just in time to see another eye roll from Geoff Landers.

Captain Williams takes a step toward the students. "Mr. Landers, did you have a question for Private Burnett?"

"Nope, not really. It's just . . ." He shrugs.

"Just . . ." Williams prods.

Landers looks from Williams to me and squares his shoulders. "Seems a little odd to me is all. Katie— "

"Private Burnett," Captain Williams interrupts. "Even though none of you will be part of the National Guard, we'll still adhere to proper titles, as already discussed. You'll address me as Captain Williams." He points to Leo. "Sergeant Burnett." Then to me. "Private Burnett."

Landers's already ruddy cheeks deepen. "Uh, yep, sorry . . . Captain."

Geoff Landers was most recently on the firewood crew. I heard it was the fourth or fifth crew he'd been on in recent months. When he heard rumors of the medical school opening, his dad petitioned Captain Williams for a spot for Geoff.

Geoff had just finished his first year of college at Black Hills State University as a biology major when the attacks started. According to his dad, he was on the premed track.

Chastity told me Williams declined him after the first interview. It took an intervention by someone else—Chastity wasn't sure who—to get Geoff a second interview and a probationary spot in the medical school.

Landers clears his throat and looks at me. "You were, essentially, in the right place at the right time?"

I paste a smile on my face. "Pretty much, yes."

Captain Williams makes a popping noise with his mouth. "One thing you, Mr. Landers, can and will learn from Private Burnett is humility." He pierces Landers with a stare.

Landers leans back in his chair and crosses his arms.

"Her story is the basis for this school. I toyed with the idea of training laypeople after Dr. Wolff joined our hospital. But it was Private Burnett joining our group that convinced me. If someone who had almost zero medical knowledge could become so proficient in such a short time, well, so could others."

Williams glances over at me again. "Another area in which Private Burnett is proficient is her ability to empathize. She seems to understand how people are feeling. Many times, medical professionals forget about the person they're caring for. They're on a mission and want a specific outcome. When you start doing your rounds, pay attention to how Burnett interacts. And not only with the patients but with her coworkers as well."

Again, Landers rolls his eyes, though he's discreet about it this time. He's not the only one. Several others make a face or show some sort of response.

My cheeks burn. It's nice to hear compliments from Captain Williams, but it's also embarrassing.

There are a few other questions and conversations before the captain shakes my hand again and thanks me for my time. I meet Leo's gaze on my way out.

He gives me a wink and mouths, "See you soon."

Back at the hospital, I finish my shift. I'm grateful it's a somewhat quiet afternoon. Our elderly patient is doing much better and says she's ready to go home. Chastity convinces her to stay one more night. I'm finishing up my notes about her when Leo and Captain Williams arrive.

"Almost time?" Leo gives me a peck on the lips.

"Give me fifteen minutes. Did it get any colder out there?"

"Nah. It's not too bad. I was thinking about putting in a doggie door for Gerry. Right out of the laundry room and into the backyard, that way he can come and go as he pleases."

I purse my lips and consider this. "Maybe. I'm sure he doesn't like being home alone."

"True. He's always had his littermates and me there until recently. Now . . . " Leo lifts a shoulder.

"Maybe we could see if Henry could go over during the day? He could take Gerry out in the yard and play with him a bit."

"That's a good idea. With Oscar doing better, it might be good for the boy."

Henry Harrington is the little boy of our next-door neighbors, Oscar and Kirstie. A few months ago, they had a middle of the night break-in at their home. Oscar's dad was killed during the event, and his mom was injured. There'd been a string of robberies before that, but this was the first time someone had been killed or hurt.

When Leo and I heard the shot, I went out our back door and Leo the front. The robbers came out the back, too, and I caught a glimpse of them in the moonlight.

A few weeks ago, Oscar, part of the Citizen Patrol, was on the squad that thought they'd found those responsible for the break-in and his dad's death. There was a shootout, and Oscar was injured. The guys they were after were killed. While those two may have been part of the robbery crew, they weren't the ones I'd seen.

As we walk to the ration office, what used to be a small strip mall on Main Street, we talk about the options for our little dog as well as how medical school went today.

"I don't know about Geoff Landers." Leo shakes his head. "He's smart enough, I guess. But he has an attitude."

"Yeah." I blow out a breath and watch as the condensation billows in front of me. "That's why Williams declined him the first time. He came in all . . . all pompous."

"That hasn't changed. He's sure had a lot of different jobs. Can't seem to find something he's good at. Maybe this will be it. Merissa did well today. She's smart, too, but doesn't flaunt it in the same way. And I think she has even more experience than she lets on."

The line at the ration office is out the door—nothing unusual. As always, people pretty much keep to themselves.

I'm surprised when a woman with a baby falls in behind us and gives me a cheerful hello. "Wow. My husband said there'd be a line, but this is crazy." She lets out a laugh while bouncing her baby. She's got him wrapped up well in a fabric sling carrier.

I turn so I can talk with her. "This isn't as bad as usual. During the summer months, the line will stretch around the block. In winter— " I shrug " —people have different shifts, maybe?"

"Maybe so. My husband always gets our ration chips, but he's out of town. He's a drayer—you know, one of the delivery people who go between towns? Anyway, he had to take a different shift because one of the other couples got sick. So, here we are."

I don't say anything, but I suspect the Glatts are the sick couple.

"Kind of fun to do something different, though I'd much rather have stayed home by the fire." She tickles the baby under the chin, and he gives a hearty laugh.

"How old is he?"

"Almost a year."

"I have a nephew around the same age. I miss him like crazy." I tug on Leo's arm. "Leo, take a look at this cute little guy."

Leo turns and gives a nod. "What's his— "

The next words are lost as a percussion fills the air and I find myself flying, slamming into the woman and her child.

Chapter 10

I let out a groan and roll off the woman and her baby. She isn't moving, but the baby is sitting on his bottom, still wrapped in the fabric carrier, and flailing his arms. His mouth is open, screaming, but it sounds too far away. Almost like we're underwater. I move to untangle the little guy and yell for my husband.

He's on his knees, cradling his splinted arm. Behind him is a gaping, wide-open hole where the ration building used to be. What's left of the building is on fire and putting out both light and heat.

Leo blinks a few times. "Are you hurt?" His lips form the words, but his voice doesn't sound right.

"What?"

"Can you hear? Open your mouth and work your jaw. See if that helps."

I do what he suggests and am rewarded with one ear popping and a loud ringing.

"Better?"

I nod. Everything still seems underwater and far away, but at least I can hear on one side.

"Are you injured?" he asks again.

"I don't— " I take quick stock of my body. My hands and knees are scraped from the pavement. "I'm fine. We need to help." I continue to untangle the screaming baby from his mom. She's still flat on her back, eyes closed.

"The building is gone." Leo is looking behind me. "Don't try and go in there. We'll help people out here."

I shudder as I think of what I saw—the gaping hole and more. Too much more.

I swallow hard. "I'll start here." I motion toward the mom and baby. "Be careful with your arm."

His mouth is in a tight line. Other people are moving around, some slowly, like they were knocked off their feet like Leo and me, and others quickly. Maybe people who were far enough away to not be affected by the blast have arrived to help.

I turn my attention back to the crying child. "You're okay, baby," I croon, wishing I would've asked his name. "Stay right here with me while I check your mama."

His mom lets out a low groan before her eyes pop open. She gasps and mutters, "Johnny?"

"Hey. Hey." I give her what I hope is a comforting look. "You're okay. Your son—he's here."

Her eyelids flutter and she moans. "He's okay?"

I look over the baby. I haven't had time to examine him yet. "I think so. He's—can you hear him? He's got a great set of lungs."

She gives a weak smile. "Always . . . has."

I move the baby near her shoulder and slide closer to the woman. "What hurts?"

"Mmm. Head. Back. What happened?"

I glance again at the now-destroyed building. A bomb? What else could've done this damage? A sinking feeling begins in the pit of my stomach. A bomb set on purpose just like at the festival. Can there be any other explanation? Will they shoot at us too? I duck my head in anticipation.

"Katie? Katie Burnett?" A man squats next to me. "You hurt?"

"Bowski?"

He nods. "Are you hurt?"

I shake my head, sending a jolt of pain through it. "I'm okay. Are there snipers?"

"Hope not. Doesn't seem to be, anyway."

"Leo's here . . . somewhere."

"We've put out a call for help and let the hospital know. It looks— " He glances toward the destroyed building, then his eyes travel to the parking lot and what used to be an orderly line of dozens of people. How many were already inside?

Bowski turns back to me. "If you're okay, I'm going to see where I'm needed. We'll start transporting, so if she needs it— " He points to the woman.

"She does. Can you send someone over?"

"Yup. On it."

"Thanks, Bowski."

The woman's eyes are closed again, but she stirs when I touch her wrist. "Try not to move."

I check her vitals and then slide out of my small backpack. She has a few cuts on her face, but there's a bit more blood on the pavement around her than I think there should be.

I gently put my hands on her neck, feeling around without moving her. The way she landed, with me practically on top of her, and with complaints of her back hurting, she could have a spinal cord injury.

She lets out a deep groan when my fingers touch the back of her head. There's wetness. Blood.

I stifle a groan of my own. "You're okay. We'll get you to the hospital." I remove a square of cotton from my pack and press it lightly against the base of her skull.

"Mmm." She winces. "Johnny?"

"He's here." With my free arm, I move the child—who is now merely sobbing instead of screaming—closer to his mom.

She rests a hand on the boy's snowsuit-covered leg. "Hey, sweet boy. Mama's here."

He lets out a blubbery sob. "Ma-ma-ma-mama."

The woman starts to roll to her side, but I put a hand on her arm. "Let's have you hold still until we can give you a proper checkup. They're bringing the handcarts and, um, probably the wagon and pickup truck too."

The words are no sooner out of my mouth when Merissa Weaver appears at my side. "Is she ready to go?"

"Who's helping you?"

Merissa motions to two men by her side, one holding a wooden board we use as a stretcher. I recognize both from the neighborhood around the hospital.

"My exam was limited. She's complaining of back and head pain." I motion to where I'm applying the bandage. "She's bleeding. Lost consciousness and isn't completely alert now. Let's wrap the cloth in place, then she'll be ready to move. Do you have a cervical collar?"

With a nod, Merissa kneels next to me and plops a large duffel bag on the ground. It's one of the medical kits we keep at the hospital for exactly these situations. Situations where there may be mass casualties.

After the shooting by Monument Hospital, we went through our four bags, cleaning and organizing, even beefing them up a bit.

Once we have the collar in place and have secured the bandage, Merissa motions to the men. "Get her on the stretcher. Take her to the pickup. Leave her on the board. Then hustle back to me. Give me five minutes. We'll fill the wagon before it leaves."

She turns to me. "Can you take the baby? Bert's wife is there." She motions toward one of the men now taking his place at the injured woman's feet. "Give her the baby. Can you stay at the wagon and make sure everyone's stable before we transport them? They'll need you at the hospital. The urgent cases are being transported immediately with the handcarts."

I give a nod and pick up the baby. The handcarts are suitable for a single person to pull with one person in the cart; they move as fast as foot power allows.

"Be sure you don't jostle her," Merissa tells the men as they put the woman on the stretcher. "Hustle back with another board." She turns to me. "I'll see you at the hospital." She gives a quick look around at the chaos and destruction. "Sometime, anyway."

The woman in the truck purses her lips when I hand her the child. "What's his name?"

"Johnny."

"And his mom?"

I shake my head. "I'm not sure."

She gives me a curt nod. "Well, I'll do what I can."

"I'll stay with you. I work at the hospital. As soon as we have a few more people, we'll leave." I hoist myself up on the wheel and throw my leg over to climb into the bed of the pickup truck.

Three people arrive within a few minutes. One is carried by Bert and the other guy, with two limping alongside. Merissa is walking with the limpers, one of them leaning heavily on her shoulder.

As the people are loaded into the bed of the truck, Merissa motions for me to talk with her. I hop down so we can huddle.

She gives me a report on each of the injured, none are immediately life-threatening issues. "Another head injury." She motions toward one of the limping men. "Broken femur on the stretcher. The walking woman has some cracked ribs, maybe more. There're still dozens to be tended to. It's going to be a long night."

I touch my hand to her forearm and connect with her gaze. "Don't be lifting the stretchers."

Her face remains stern, leading me to feel like I've overstepped.

"I won't." She turns to Bert and the other guy. "Got the last stretcher? We'll have it staged when the truck returns."

"Who's driving?" I look around.

"I am." Bert's wife is already moving toward me. "You riding up front or in the back? You'll hold the baby."

I think I should stay in the back with the injured, but Merissa tells me to get in the cab and get moving. We'll be at the hospital in minutes.

The truck has barely stopped when I hop out of the cab, baby Johnny in my arms. There are a couple of people already at the back of the truck—more volunteers from the neighborhood.

"Who's running triage?" I call out.

"One of the nurses. She's set up in the lobby—where it's warm," a guy wearing a bright yellow beanie says. He turns to one of the injured. "Can you walk, buddy?"

The man, face covered in soot and wearing similarly dirty clothes, winces. "Yeah, Chuck. I can walk."

Yellow Beanie Guy steps back. "Warren? Sorry. Didn't recognize you."

"I look that good, huh?"

The other guy helps the woman with the broken ribs down out of the truck. She lets out a loud moan, which makes Johnny cry. His mom calls from the stretcher, "Johnny? What's happening?"

I smile, knowing her alertness is a positive sign. "He's fine. Just lots of excitement. I'm going to hold him close. As soon as possible, he'll be at your side." I turn to Yellow Beanie Guy—Chuck. "I'm Katie, one of the nurses here. I'll walk these two in and see you inside."

Nurse Jacquie Haley oversees triage. She instructs me to have the ambulatory patients sit in the waiting room. It looks like every chair we have in the hospital, and possibly even the new medical school building, has been arranged in auditorium-style seating.

After I have them seated, I turn to Jacquie. "Where do you want me?"

She gives me a strange look. "Katie? Is that you?"

I lift my hand and slide off my stocking cap. My rubber band broke at some point. My crazy curly brown hair springs out in all directions. "Um, yes."

"You're a mess. Get washed up. And where'd you find the baby?"

Holding the baby on my hip and my cap in my other hand, I take a swipe across my cheek. My red glove comes back covered in black. I probably look a lot like Warren, the man with the head injury.

The bell above the front door dings. The men from the parking lot bring in the stretcher with Johnny's mom on it. "The baby belongs to her." I motion with my chin. "I'll, uh . . . should I keep the baby with me?" In the bright light of the hospital, I can see the baby is also covered in soot.

Jacquie lets out a sigh. "Is he injured? If he's injured, that changes things."

"Doesn't seem to be, but he needs an exam. I landed on him and his mom. Mom hit her head. She's bleeding but is mostly alert."

Jacquie orders the men to put the baby's mom on one of half a dozen tables lined up in the hallway. These tables were specially made to receive a stretcher for this purpose. They're usually stacked and stored in one of our storage sheds. Since I've been in Rapid City, we haven't had a mass casualty event with a need for this setup.

I swallow the lump in my throat and report on each of the people in the pickup with me. As soon as the last injured man's stretcher is brought in and placed on a table, the men acting as orderlies say they're going back for another load.

"Better get cleaned up, Katie." Jacquie shakes her head. "It's going to be a long night. Not that we ever have anything but long nights around here. One thing after another. It's exhausting."

"Are they sending help from other hospitals?"

"You haven't heard?"

I shake my head. "Heard what?"

"We're not the only ones. Other districts had their ration centers hit too. Maybe all of them. I don't— " Her voice catches. "I don't know how many. But lots. We're on our own."

Chapter 11

Merissa

"Hey! Hey! Are you with the hospital?" A man kneeling next to someone calls from the far edge of the disaster zone.

"Yes, I'm a medic." I rush to his side and visually evaluate the woman on the ground. In the dark and with her positioning, I'm surprised she was found. "Has she been out since you found her?"

"Yep. She's got a pulse, weak but there. Looks like a broken leg too." He motions to the oddly contorted extremity. "You're new here?"

"Yeah. One of the medics." I give the woman a quick assessment. "I'll go back for the stretcher board. We're expecting one of the pickup trucks to return shortly."

"I'll go after the stretcher board. At the staging area?"

"Should be. If not, wait for the truck. They'll bring one back." I don't add the number of wounded may surpass the number of simple stretchers the hospital has on hand.

As the man stands, my head follows him up. He's tall. Probably a foot taller than my height of five-six. Even under his winter coat, he still looks well built, though I'm sure his body is a completely different shape than it was before the EMP. Obesity is no longer common, even being overweight is rare. Most people are skinny. Some are too skinny.

He hustles off, his long legs eating up the ground.

I continue my quick exam of the woman—ensuring her airway is clear and then checking for bleeding and other broken bones. As I check her arms, she squirms. She squirms again and lets out a sigh, then gives a pain-filled cry.

"You're okay. You're okay. I need you to hold still."

Her breathing turns heavy. "What . . . what happened?"

"There was an explosion. I'm Merissa, I work at the hospital. We're going to get you taken care of."

"Where's my husband? He was right next to me. We were waiting in line."

"I'm not sure. There are a lot of injured people, and many of them have already been taken to the hospital. Your husband may already be there."

"Okay. If you think he's okay."

As she closes her eyes and seems to relax, I don't want to tell her I'm not sure whether he's okay or not. The number of dead is high. They're just now starting to go inside what's left of the building. So far, there have been no survivors. They aren't even finding bodies. The detonation seems to have vaporized those nearest it.

To add to the tragedy, a policeman told me we weren't the only ones that were targeted tonight. Each of the other district ration centers also had bombs go off. The number of dead . . . I can't even imagine how high it's going to be when it's all said and done. Not to mention, all the hospitals will be overwhelmed with injuries.

"Hey!" The raised voice nearby draws my attention. "I said I'm looking for my wife."

One of the guys who's been helping—I didn't catch his name but think of him as Yellow Hat because of his apparel—raises his hands. "Dude, everybody's looking for someone."

"I don't care about everyone else." The yelling man steps closer to Yellow Hat and pokes a finger into his chest. "I want my wife. Are you gonna help me find her or not?"

"Look." Yellow Hat takes a step back and puts his hands out to his side, attempting to defuse the situation. "We're doing the best we can and are taking people to the hospital. You should go there."

As Yellow Hat turns away, Yelling Man grabs him by the sleeve and pulls him close. From this distance, I can't hear the exchange but watch as Yellow Hat shrugs off the man's hand and takes a step away.

Yelling Man shoves Yellow Hat hard enough to send him to the ground. He wastes zero time pouncing on Yellow Hat, his fists flying in all directions.

The tall man who went after the board comes striding over, backboard in hand, seemingly without a care in the world. He places the backboard on the ground and yanks the assailant off Yellow Hat. "What exactly is it you two think you're accomplishing here?"

Yelling Man is now sitting on the ground half a dozen feet away. He points to Yellow Hat. "All I wanted was to find my wife. He wouldn't help me." His voice comes out in a nasally whine.

"I told you to go to the hospital. I'm going to tell the deputies about you. You're out of control and should be locked up."

"Knock it off, Chuck," the tall guy says. "Emotions are running high tonight. This isn't helping anything."

Chuck—Yellow Hat—scrambles up from the ground and points at the other guy. "You need to calm down, dude." He picks up his stocking hat that fell off in the fray and then stomps away.

The tall man picks up the backboard, easily holding it under one arm. He turns to the other guy, "Like Chuck said, your best bet is to go to the hospital. You might be able to catch a ride with one of the pickup trucks."

Yelling Man starts to say something else but apparently decides better of it. He gives a weary shake of his head and then slowly gets to his feet, thanks the tall man, and walks away.

When the tall man reaches me, he says, "Saw the headlights from the hospital truck creeping down the street. Let's get her over there."

We carefully move her onto the backboard. I'm concerned not only about her leg but also her back. The way she landed, she could have a spinal cord injury. She stirs a little but doesn't wake up again.

The man takes the feet while I take the head. "Did you see anyone else near her? She was asking for her husband."

He stares intently at the woman. "I think I know her. Hard to tell with her face covered in soot. But I think her name is Susie. I worked with her and her husband on the garden crew last summer. I'm thinking she was probably closer to the explosion and got thrown."

"Sounds about right," I agree. "I'm surprised you actually saw her."

"I heard her moan."

As we pass by one of the small fires caused by the explosion, I ask him if it's common for a husband and wife to be on the same work detail.

"Some are. Some aren't. Depends on how well they work together. Same detail can be nice so you have time off together."

Noticing his wedding band, I ask, "Are you and your wife on the same detail?"

A cloud passes over his face. I instantly feel like a heel. It's stupid of me to presume he works with his wife or that she's even alive. I'm still wearing my wedding band, even though my husband's been dead for over a month now. A month. Sometimes it feels like yesterday, and sometimes it feels like a lifetime ago.

Pearl and I have only been in Rapid City for a little over a week. So much has happened during this short time, it almost feels like we've been here forever.

I'm beginning to wonder if this is the place for us, though. While the hospital and med school are good opportunities, the violence here is concerning—the attack at the Monument District festival a few days ago and now this.

And not only us but every district being hit. There's little doubt this is an organized event and was most likely perpetrated by the same people responsible for the festival attack.

Pearl was practically beside herself after the festival bombing. I can only imagine what she's going to say about this. She might want to pack up and go home.

Even though that isn't an option.

We're here until spring or whenever the transports we used to get here determine they can start running again.

Who am I kidding, even in the spring, there's little chance we can leave. I'll have a newborn, and we don't have any place else to go. With our Livingston home destroyed and no relatives there, we'd be homeless and on our own. Staying in the Black Hills, with Opal and her family nearby, plus my work opportunities, is our only option.

"You okay?" the man asks.

"Fine." I grit my teeth and keep moving. My arms ache from carrying the woman. It's only a few more seconds before we arrive at the waiting truck-turned-ambulance.

"Merissa?" Jesse Talbot moves to my side and takes my end of the stretcher. "What do we have?"

"This gentleman— " I motion to the tall man.

"Bowski," Jesse says. "Heard you were helping."

"It's a mess." He motions with his chin for me to continue as the men move Susie into the bed of the truck.

I finish the brief report and tell Jesse I'm going to walk the perimeter. I want to see if there was anyone else thrown out of the immediate area.

"All right. We'll finish loading." Jesse gestures toward the ambulatory injured people sitting alongside the edge of the staging area, being tended to by a nurse from one of the care centers. "Is this it?"

"Unless we find more in our search."

Jesse climbs in the bed for the ride back. "Ryan will be on the next truck. Should only be a few minutes."

As the pickup carefully pulls away, the tall man turns to me. "I'll help you with your search. By the way— " he offers me his massive paw " —I'm Ritchie Kasubowski. People just call me Bowski since it's a mouthful."

Grasping his hand, I dip my chin. "Merissa Weaver."

"Let's grab a few more people." He lifts his chin to where Chuck— the guy wearing the yellow hat and now also sporting a puffy eye—is standing with a few other guys. Bowski goes over and talks to them, gesturing with his long arms about what he needs. They totter off to do his bidding.

Back at my side, Bowski says, "They'll go clockwise around the building. Figured we could go counterclockwise. I had to explain to the youngest guy what clockwise meant. Not even sure Chuck and the other one knew, but they were too embarrassed to admit it."

"Seems right with the way things used to be. Digital clocks were the norm."

"Yup."

Bowski and I walk the perimeter in silence, taking it slow and stopping often. Before long, we meet the three men.

"How'd you cover your area so quickly?" Bowski asks.

"We just did. We're sure we didn't miss anyone," the younger man says.

To be certain, we recanvas the ground they've already covered. In the end, there are no new victims.

"Nice meeting you, Merissa Weaver," Bowski says when we're back to the staging area. "Sorry it was in a place like this."

I agree and then turn to the nurse who's monitoring the patients. The roar of the pickup carries through the quiet as it drives toward us. This is the last load to take to the hospital. Even though I'm exhausted, we've still got a long night ahead of us.

Chapter 12

Katie

Jacquie was right. It was a long night that morphed into a long morning. It's midmorning, and we're still treating and stabilizing. There are a few still needing surgery and others who have minor injuries we're taking care of. Some have been released and sent home. Others, like Johnny's mom, were kept for observation or treatment.

Five people died after being brought for emergency treatment. Many more, dozens at least, died at the scene. We don't know exactly how many people were in the building when it exploded.

According to the ration office supervisor, there were half a dozen workers. She estimated there to be around thirty people inside the building, based on what Leo and I reported we knew about the line outside and where we were when the building blew up.

Among the injured, the talk is of little but the explosions, not just the one here in our district but the rest of them too. Through the radio relay system, we've now heard from each of the Rapid City districts. All were hit. Each ration center was destroyed. Each one resulted in numerous deaths and injuries. All hospitals are overloaded.

The district my friend Opal Maher lives in has a small clinic. It's a three- or four-bedroom house with a single doctor, two nurses, and two medics. When the relay radio reported on them, they said the entire community came out in droves, much like what we have here with everyone in the neighborhood acting as transport.

I'm sure Opal is among those helping. I'm praying no one from her extended family was at the ration center yesterday. I know Opal's day is Friday, but they have so many relatives, friends, and workers living on their ranch that it's certainly possible they were directly affected.

I glance over at Merissa, a relative of Opal's by marriage. She's stitching up a woman's forehead wound. We're so overloaded, there's no way to move the injured woman to a private space. The best that could be done was to set up a treatment chair in a corner somewhat shielded from others.

I don't even have that for the sprained ankle I'm treating. My patient, a boy in his late teens, is part of a row of people with similar injuries. I'm working my way down the line. Chastity Morrow already triaged everyone and set up this system. It's awful, but it's the best we can do.

I turn my head when the front doorbell sounds. Deputy Shaw is there with an older man I don't recognize, dressed in a proper county sheriff uniform. Like the hospitals, the sheriff set up satellite offices for each district. A few pre-disaster deputies or city police were put in charge of the satellite offices and staffed mainly with Citizen Patrol—men and women who've been deputized to help during the apocalypse.

Shaw is our main deputy. Leo and I have gotten to know him fairly well after he interviewed me when Dr. Newsome was killed. Shaw asked if he could have one of our puppies. Tank, the largest puppy from our litter, has been living with Shaw and his wife for a few weeks now.

Shaw walks next to the other man and gives me a curt nod. "Is Captain Williams here?"

"Um, yes. Operating room one, I think."

"Can we stick our heads in?"

I scrunch up my face. "In an operating room? I don't think so."

The older man huffs. "It's urgent."

Shaw lifts his eyebrows. "This is Sheriff Melvin Cabal. He came over from the Public Safety building."

With the ration centers being hit last night, I have little doubt it's related. Why else would they be here? "I'll see what I can do." I turn back to my patient. "I'll be back in a minute. Keep your foot on the stool, okay?"

"Yup." He lifts a hand in Shaw's direction. "Deputy."

Deputy Shaw crinkles his forehead.

The boy clears his throat. "You, uh, interviewed me for the Citizen Patrol a few weeks ago."

"Ah, yes. Sorry. It's been a long night."

"Yeah . . . it has."

Shaw points to the boy's ankle. "Nothing too bad?"

"Nah. Just a sprain." He looks to me for confirmation, and I nod.

At least Chastity thinks it's a sprain. Without x-ray capabilities, she's only going by the clinical appearance. It presents as a sprain and not a break. We'll need to wait and see how he heals.

"My, uh, dad—he's here too. He was hit by a piece of the building or something. Shrapnel. They had to operate on him."

Shaw takes a few steps closer. "I'm sorry to hear that. He's doing okay?"

"Yeah, I guess. I'll be able to see him after my ankle gets taken care of."

"I'll be right back," I tell the boy, then motion for Shaw and the sheriff to follow me.

Back from the disaster site and washed up, Leo's tending to the line of people in the hallway. These are people who've received their initial treatment but remain for observation or secondary treatment. Leo's going from person to person, giving them water and snacks, if they're allowed food and drink, while checking mental status and pain levels.

He raises his eyebrows when he sees us, and I give a slight lift of my shoulders.

At the door to the operating suite, I instruct the men to wait here. I step into what's been set up as the scrub room. I use hand sanitizer before placing a mask over my face and cracking open the door to the actual operating room. "Captain?"

His eyes lift from his work. "Yes?"

"The sheriff is here."

"Shaw? What's he need?"

"Shaw and the *actual* sheriff."

"Humph." Williams shakes his head and mutters something too low for me to hear, then looks at Dr. Nettie. "Can you finish closing?"

"Yes, sir. We still have . . . how many waiting, Katie?"

"Two, I think."

Williams removes a glove. We have a small supply of sterile gloves reserved specifically for the operating room. Before the apocalypse, sterile gloves were used once and tossed. That's no longer the case. Now nothing is disposable. They're washed and reused, though not for operating.

With this disaster, I know our already limited supply will take a hit. They'll soon be operating barehanded. Even now, certain procedures are done glove-free.

He flips the other glove off and puts it in a wash basin. "I'll be quick. I'm sure this is about the attack . . . not only the one here but if it's the *actual sheriff* then the rest of the attacks too."

In the scrub room, Williams asks me to work the foot pump for him. I must give him a strange look. He shakes his head. "My left foot is killing me. I think I have an ingrown toenail or something."

My lips form a tight line as I start working the foot-operated water pump. "We'd better take a look."

He rubs his hands under the now-flowing water. "Agreed. Let's see what these guys need first, then maybe find Dr. Morrow and have her check me over."

"She's on a break in the sleeping room. I can wake her up."

He shakes his head. "It'll keep. Feels like the water's running a little slow. Better get someone on refilling it."

"The Hendricks are here. I'll let them know." Rand and Kerry Hendricks are husband and wife, both part of our janitor crew. Kerry is also one of the students from the medical school.

"All of my med students are still here?" he asks as I hand him a towel.

"Um . . ." I furrow my brow. "I think so. Well, Geoff Landers may have gone home."

He straightens his back. "That so?"

I shake my head. "I saw him gather his things and go out the back. Merissa asked if he was leaving, but he didn't answer. I don't know. Maybe something happened, and he was needed at home?"

"Hmm. Well, let's go see what's happening with the sheriff."

In the hallway, I take a step in the direction of my young patient, but Captain Williams raises his hand. "Join us, Katie."

I glance from Williams to Shaw, who gives a barely perceptible lift of his shoulder. "Uh, sure. Yes, I can. I was about to wrap an ankle."

"I'd like you to take notes," Williams says as he shuffles toward his office, walking awkwardly on his left foot. He glances at Shaw. "At least, I assume this will be information that should be recorded?"

"Not a bad idea." Shaw says. "But we're also looking for information from you."

"I'm sure Burnett can give us what we need."

I hide my face so none of the men can see my apprehension. While I do have a good idea of what has taken place tonight, I'm not sure

I'm the best person to deliver the report. Captain Williams probably has a better grasp on our patient count than I do.

Jacquie Haley handled the official patient list, but I've kept a number tally.

In Williams's office, he motions to a notebook on the desk before he slides behind it. "Pardon me, gentlemen. But I'm slipping out of these shoes. My toe is killing me."

"Problems?" Shaw asks.

Williams waves his hand as his pungent foot odor wafts through the room. Shaw and the sheriff both react with faces.

"Sorry." Williams shrugs. "An ingrown toenail, I think."

A feeling of dread runs through me. The foot odor is strong, and I think it's from more than simply being in the same shoes for so long. There's a concerning foulness to the stench.

Shaw glances toward me and then back at Williams. "Need to get it looked at?"

"I will, I will. Let's get this wrapped up first. What's up, gentlemen?"

The sheriff leans forward. "You know the explosion you had here wasn't isolated?"

"Of course. We tried to call for help on the radio and . . . " Williams tilts his head. "That's when we found out."

"Hundreds are dead. Several hundred injured. Every ration distribution center was destroyed. Their staff are among the dead. The detonations were effective at what they were intended to do—mass destruction and casualties."

Williams rubs his temples. "Do we know who's responsible? Same people as the explosion in Monument District?"

The sheriff shrugs his entire body. "We have no idea. I mean, that'd make sense. There wasn't any shooting this time. There's a lot we don't know. Anyhow, we're looking for numbers of wounded and dead. You have those for us?"

Captain Williams looks at me.

I unzip my fanny pack and pull out my scratch paper. "These are from the notes I took. Jacquie Haley kept the official record. Mine should be pretty close, if not exact."

The sheriff flairs his nostrils. "Where's Haley? She should be the one in here."

I look at my shoes while Williams says, "She's not here, Burnett is. If Sergeant Burnett says her records are close, you should assume she's underestimating and her records are right on."

My eyes dart to Williams. Why'd he refer to me as Sergeant Burnett? Is he confusing me with my husband?

Williams's cheeks are flushed, and there's a light sheen of sweat on his forehead. Even though it's warmish because of the small woodstove burning merrily in the corner, it's not hot. I glance out the window at the falling snow. Definitely not hot.

Williams clears his throat. "Burnett, your report."

I share the information I have on the dead, the couple of people we have in critical condition that are unlikely to survive, the seriously injured, the ones still awaiting treatment, plus the ones who have been treated and discharged. I also share the number of dead that Merissa and the other medics reported when they returned from the scene—the ones who never made it to the hospital.

"The dead at the scene matches our number," Shaw says. "We believe there are more, but they were too close to the blast to have remains. We have reports of missing persons."

"We have a list of missing also. My count is eleven."

"Also the same."

"Well," Williams says, sitting up in his chair, "is there anything else?"

The sheriff steeples his hands. "We're going to post guards at the hospital. We'll be coordinating with the National Guard to rotate shifts with them. No one in or out unless they have a reason to be here."

Williams lets out a noisy sigh. "Can't say I'm surprised. You'll be guarding other places too? Food distribution? Water?"

"Those, among other places. We're adding additional personnel specifically for this task."

"Almost feels like we're back to the early days of the troubles. Seems we were guarding everything then too. You're increasing the guards at the dams?"

"That's out of my purview. I'm sure you're well aware the National Guard was tasked with dam protection by the governor."

The sheriff's snotty tone catches me by surprise. The laugh from Captain Williams surprises me more. "Still upset about that, Melvin? You really do need to learn to let things go."

The sheriff's face tightens as he colors from pink to red to almost purple. He quickly gets to his feet, knocking over his chair in the process. Without bothering to set it to right, he strides toward the door. "We're done here. You've been notified of the additional security. Let my men do their job, and we won't have any troubles."

With a gleam in his eye, Williams gives a sloppy salute. "Right-o. See you around."

Shaw shakes his head as the door to the office slams. "Sorry." He sets up the overturned chair and slinks out of the room.

"Fool." Williams shakes his head. "I've known that guy since middle school. He's as much of a jerk now as he was when we were teens. But he's what we're stuck with until the elections return. Too bad."

I glance at the shut door. "Well . . . someone must have liked him to vote him in, right?"

"Humph. You didn't hear? The prior sheriff, who was voted in and doing a fine job, had a heart attack a few days before the attacks. He was in the hospital. When the cyberattack happened, he didn't make it. One of the chief deputies was out of town when it all started. The other was killed in a car wreck the same day the sheriff died. Someone at the county level brought up Melvin's name and . . . "

He throws up his hands. "Here we are. Good thing we've got Deputy Shaw. At least he knows what's up. Well, better get these shoes back on."

"Should I go see if Chastity can look at you first?"

He waves me away. "Nah. Let her sleep. Just getting out of the shoe helped."

"It's, uh . . . I think you may have an infection. The smell— "

"My wife has always complained about my feet too. Sorry."

"No." I shake my head. "It's not just that. It's more than foot odor. You're also flushed. Can we at least take a look?"

He huffs out a breath and bends over to remove his sock. "Fine, fine. I was mentioning to your husband the other day how you rarely miss a thing. We should put you in our school."

"Um . . . okay? I can always use extra training. Are there certain classes you think I'm lacking?"

He stops midmotion. "Not what I meant. You know the plan is for the ones who complete the course to work as doctors? Not nurses or medics. Doctors. You could be a doctor."

I feel my cheeks redden. "Uh, maybe. Would that work with my National Guard commitment?"

"Perfectly. By the way, I'm not sure if you heard the way I referred to you in front of Melvin, but I couldn't bear to call you private with him here." Williams straightens up without having removed his sock. "You're getting a field promotion. It'll be coming through any day."

"I am? To sergeant? How?" I can't stop the grin from taking over my face.

"How? I recommended you. Leo's getting a bump too. He'll move up to Staff Sergeant."

"But we're still part of the Volunteer Unit, not National Guard."

"Right. Under my command. The rank will hold when you take your oath."

"I thought I needed to be a private for a certain amount of time, then a corporal, and— "

"Things are different during times of war. Congratulations on your promotion, but let's keep it quiet until it's official. I'll be giving Leo his news later today. I wouldn't expect you to keep such news from him." He wiggles his foot toward his shoe.

"Your toe, sir?"

He huffs out a breath and mutters, "As bad as my wife." He leans over and peels off his sock with a wince. The putrid smell increases. I tilt my head and squint to look at it. "See? Ingrown toenail."

"Are you sure? From here, it doesn't look like it originates from the nail. The inflammation is there, sure. But the center seems to be lower."

He squints his eyes and bends over farther. "Well . . . I don't know. You may be right. It does look pretty nasty, doesn't it?"

"Let me wake Dr. Morrow. I don't think we should put this off."

Chapter 13

The crunch of the snow under our boots provides a soothing cadence. Even Gerry's too-large-for-his-body paws add to the music.

We've been working with Gerry to get him to walk alongside us and not pull on the harness or leash. Every few yards, he looks up at me as if to ask, "How am I doing?" Sometimes, I swear he wants to communicate. And I'm sure he smiles.

"Good doggie. You're a good walker on the lead."

Now that Leo only has a splint on one arm, he's able to walk Gerry too. It does help that we only have one dog now and not four. The multiple dogs were too much, and they were too young, weaving around his feet and causing him to trip. Gerry's easy for him.

We both know how fortunate Leo was not to have hurt himself worse than a broken nose and loose teeth. I wondered if the malunion of his wrist was from his fall, but based on my research, the fall was much too late in his healing to be blamed.

Since we're walking together, I offered to take the leash so we can walk hand in hand. The flashlight in Leo's splinted hand bounces along the path in front of us, giving us enough illumination to see our way through the darkening night.

I'm tired—more tired than I think I've ever been. Other than the short time we were in line at the ration center, right before the place exploded, we've been working nonstop for over thirty-six hours.

Thankfully, after Leo finished triaging at the explosion site, he took a few minutes and ran back to our house. He gave Gerry a quick walk before leaving him with the Harringtons next door. We know young Henry spoiled him rotten.

Leo gives my hand a squeeze. "Are you glad you're on night shift tomorrow?"

"Mm-hmm. I don't know how we're going to do it—the school, all the wounded. Chastity, Jacquie, and Jesse are all still on."

"They'll do it. All of them got naps today in the on-call room. Jesse even went home for a bit to get cleaned up. Plus, Williams enlisted several from the neighborhood to stay on tonight too. They'll help monitor people. It's not ideal, but it'll work."

"Yeah. I hope his toe heals okay."

"So weird. What do you think it is?"

I snort out a laugh. "You're asking me? It's not like anything I've ever seen before."

"But Williams thought it was an ingrown toenail, right?"

"Before he really looked at it. Seems he has a history of them, so when it started to ache halfway through the night, he assumed that was the trouble. After he looked at it . . . " I shake my head before I realize Leo can't see me. "He knew it was something else."

"But what?"

"That is the mystery. When Chastity—I mean, *Dr. Morrow*—came into the office, she suggested it was a spider bite, but then decided that may not be it. They talked about gout. Even I was skeptical of it being a spider. The urine test didn't show any uric acid increases—nothing out of the ordinary anyway. None of the limited testing we can do resulted in anything."

"So, they're treating it as an infection of unknown origin with topical and oral antibiotics? It's the only smart thing to do. Williams is in excellent health. He'll be fine."

"Should be." I ignore the fear in the pit of my stomach that it could be something truly serious.

"Lieutenant Paul's pretty stressed."

"About Williams's toe?"

Leo lets out a low chuckle. "No. I don't think he even knows about the toe. About the explosions and needing to set up round-the-clock protection at so many locations."

"But he's working with Shaw and the Citizen Patrol, right? It's not just the Guard?"

"That's the plan. But he says it'll stretch them too thin. The Guard already has patrols at the dams and a few other locations, and it's not like they're all at Camp Rapid just waiting on things to do. They're already stationed all over the Black Hills, doing what's needed. He wishes the governor wouldn't have booted the Volunteer Units. They need the help."

"Did he say anything about who they think did this?"

"Not really."

I tilt my head in his direction. "*Not really?* What's that mean?"

"Oh, you know. There're theories, plenty of theories. Could be the same group that shot up the festival." Leo tenses, and I'm sure I do also as I recall the carnage of that night. "But they don't know for sure. Different MO since they didn't shoot at survivors—at least, that's what the sheriff keeps saying, so he doesn't think it's the same group."

"But both used explosives."

"Yep. I don't know how much investigating they can do to find out if it's the same people. I mean, they haven't even been able to stop the burglary ring. There was another break-in the night of the explosions."

Sadness over the loss of our neighbor, Mr. Harrington, sweeps over me. His son Oscar was shot when they raided a house they thought the robbers were holed up in. Oscar looked good tonight when we picked up Gerry. He seems to be recovering well but is also irritated he's still laid up and unable to help with the current situation.

Captain Williams has been making regular house calls to monitor Oscar. But with his foot problem, he's going to be on crutches now, making almost everything more difficult. I can't imagine he'll be able to continue house calls and visits to the long-term care centers. Maybe that'll be something the medical students and Leo take over.

"I just wish it'd all stop and we could have some peace."

"Well said, Staff Sergeant." I bump my hip into Leo's leg.

"Why thank you, Sergeant."

I let out a girlish giggle. "Can you believe it?"

"Does the promotion make you feel better about joining the Guard?"

I puff out a breath of hot air. Joining the National Guard, and the secrecy surrounding the details of our commitment, has been a sore spot between us.

Leo not being fully honest and telling me we'll likely be staying in Rapid City for the entire eight years happened before he fell off the horse and broke both arms. His surliness during his convalescence seemed to compound the deceit.

We're doing better now, talking and communicating about our difficulties. And I've tried to be honest about my concerns over such a long commitment and how I've never seen myself as a member of the military.

One year in the Volunteer Unit is certainly not the same as joining the professional military people at Camp Rapid for eight years, though I'm assured by Captain Williams and Lieutenant Paul that little will change for us. We'll still be working out of the hospital and medical school, likely for the duration of our enlistment, and can even stay in our little house.

But my family will still be in Wyoming, and I'll be in South Dakota.

"I'm not sure if it does or not. It doesn't change much for me."

"That's true." Leo's tone is calm. A few weeks ago, he would've flown off the handle at me for even suggesting I didn't want to join the Guard.

"We still have time to discuss it. We won't take the oath until after the new year." I hear him swallow hard. "Provided my arm is healed."

"Your arm will be fine," I say with complete conviction. "But, uh, Leo, what if . . . what if . . . "

"What if you still aren't good with it? I've thought about that."

Now it's my turn to swallow hard. "You have?"

"Lots. I've known . . . " He lets out a sigh. "I've known you were upset since the decision was made to let us join the Guard, since the day Lieutenant Paul came over and told us and you realized I hadn't been entirely truthful with you."

Anger wells up in my belly. I pull my lips together. *Love is patient. Love is kind. It does not envy, it does not boast, it is not proud.* I let out a slow breath as the verse I've been focusing on for the last several weeks grounds me. It'd be easy to blurt out an angry response. Too easy.

I keep my tone even. "Why'd you lie to me?" It's a risk asking this. Is our relationship well enough to have a rational conversation? And can we even be rational after the days we've experienced and lack of sleep?

I see the motion of his head out of the corner of my eye. I twist my head to look at him full-on. He gives my hand a squeeze. "Watch your step. It looks slick here." Safely past the icy patch, he urges me to a stop.

As I face him, he takes me into his arms. "I was a jerk." His words tickle my neck. "I had it in my head that if you knew the truth, you'd say no."

He takes a step back, and our eyes meet. "You can still say no. If you really don't want to join the Guard, we can finish our Volunteer commitment, be done, and go home."

"They'd let us?"

"Lieutenant Paul thinks so. He hasn't made any official inquiries, but he thinks they'll let things continue as is. A year from the day we took the oath ends our commitment. We'd be free to return home. Back to your family."

I bite my upper lip, and a shiver runs through me. "We should turn around. It's getting colder." Gerry lets out a low whine, which I take as his agreement.

We walk about half a block before I get up the nerve to respond. "I'd like to go home."

"We can. If that's what you truly want, we will."

I squeeze his hand as I mull over his offer. It's the first time he's made such an offer, except the one time he shouted out in anger that I was welcome to pack up and go home. Then, the way he said it, wasn't an offer for *both* of us to go home. Just me. Alone. Without him.

But this . . . this is new.

He's offering to finish out our commitment to the Volunteer Unit and be done. *Go home.* My heart does a little flip. Things have been rough between us. Even before he fell off the horse, we had issues—issues that started shortly after we left Wyoming with the Volunteers. At first, it was little things. He'd snap at me, or I'd snap at him. Those little disagreements expanded when we settled into our home in Rapid.

Even though we'd been married for almost a year, we hadn't lived alone as husband and wife. In the weeks following our wedding, we lived in an RV on my parents' land, surrounded by our family. We took our RV up to the ski lodge where most of the community relocated to for the winter. There, our friends who'd shared our wedding day with us became our housemates—or RV mates, as it was.

A small smile flitters across my face as I remember our perfect wedding. Well, as perfect as a wedding could be in the wake of an apocalypse. It wasn't just a double wedding, but a triple. With limited resources, it only made sense to have one celebration.

The wedding was at Mom and Jake's place by their swimming pond. The weather was perfect. The food was more than adequate. And the company was amazing. Everyone had a great time and was able to forget the predicament we were in for a short while. Well, not completely. But it was still nice.

Here, it seems we're surrounded by the apocalypse every day. There's rarely a time we can just be. Getting away to the mountains and camping with the hunting group was supposed to be a semi-vacation for us.

Then Leo fell. Any fun we were supposed to have was gone. The things we see at the hospital, the robberies, the shooting at the festival, the explosion . . . it never lets up. What will be the long-term effects on our bodies—on our minds—of this continual stress?

I think back to Leo's offer of going home. I want to answer him and tell him yes, let's do it. Let's go home. But is home truly the right choice for us? I don't know. I need to pray. *We* need to pray. "I think— "

"Wait." Leo's voice is quiet and soft. "Hold up." He quickly shuts off the flashlight.

"What is it?" I mimic his timbre, not whispering but speaking low.

He tugs my hand, moving Gerry and me to a clump of sparse brush—brush that'd make a fine hideout in the summer, but the naked branches do little on this cold November night.

"Look. There." Leo points to a man scurrying from a similarly sparse bush. He tucks in behind a pole, trying to make himself invisible. A few seconds later, a second guy slinks out of the brush and moves behind a couple of decorative landscape trees.

My eyes narrow. The first man pops out and hustles to another copse of brush. The second guy moves again. When he glances around, the moonlight shines on his bearded face. The beard is an odd shape, almost too perfectly groomed. And even in the dark, it has a reddish-orange tint to it.

Could this be? Is that the man I saw the night Mr. Harrington was killed? Are these the robbers?

Chapter 14

"Look, Leo." I point to the bearded man.

Leo steps closer and moves his mouth near my ear. "I see 'em. What do you think? Is it them? The ones who broke into the Harringtons' house?"

"The bearded one . . . I think so. But the other, he's not tall enough. What do we do?"

Leo keeps his eyes forward, watching the men move again. "I'm going to keep an eye on them. You take Gerry. Go get Shaw. His house is only a few blocks from here." He points in the direction of Deputy Shaw's home. I know where he lives from when we delivered Gerry's littermate Tank.

I take in a deep breath as I continue to stare at the men. "You'll be careful?"

"I'm going to keep eyes on them. Nothing else."

"Okay, I'll— "

"Whadda ya folks doing lurkin' in the bushes?" My hand immediately goes to my pistol, nestled in a belly band near my appendix. "Ah, ah. Keep your hands where I can see them. Both of you."

Gerry lets out a low growl, the coarse hair on his back standing up straight. He moves in front of me and bares his teeth.

I tighten my grip on the leash and make a noise deep in my throat to quiet my dog.

Leo lifts both hands, moving them away from his body. "We aren't doing anything. Just out for a walk and saw . . . " Leo's still using his low tone of voice as he glances up at the man. "We saw a couple of guys moving from bush to bush. We're just staying out of their way. That's all."

The man lowers his voice and steps close enough I get a good whiff of the onions he had for dinner. "What're they doing?" he whispers as he scans the area.

Leo shakes his head. "We're not entirely sure. We think . . . maybe . . . "

"They're the robbers?" Onion man's breath comes out in a gasp. "Whadda we gonna do?"

Leo and I share a look. I give a slight shake of my head.

Leo responds with a grimace. "My wife is going after the deputy sheriff. I'm going to keep eyes on them." Leo lifts a hand in the direction of the men. They're by a house half a block away.

"Good idea." Onion Breath steps closer to me.

Gerry lets out a warning growl.

The man shoots a look at my dog. "Protective, isn't he?"

"Very," I mutter before shushing Gerry and looking at the skulking men again. While we can see the men's outlines and movements, they're no longer near enough to make out their features. "You'll be okay?" I raise my eyebrows at my husband.

"Same plan as before. Get Shaw and hurry back."

"Deputy Shaw?" Onion Breath asks. "Good plan. He'll bring them all."

I glance at Leo, who shrugs, then at the man next to him. He's slightly taller than Leo and has broad shoulders.

Onion Breath smiles at me, showing off his perfectly straight and shiny teeth. "You want me to go after Shaw and you can stay with your man?"

My skin prickles, and the little hairs on the back of my neck stand at attention. Something doesn't feel right about this.

When I was a young girl, my dad died of a heart attack. One minute he was alive, the next he was gone. My mom, widowed with four daughters, struggled for a while. She had to take time off work, and my sisters and I took time off school.

When we started getting our life back together, something Mom suggested we all do was take a self-defense course. I didn't understand at the time why she wanted to do it or how it'd be a good idea, but it was.

The self-defense class was an in-depth course where we spent a weekend at some kind of summer camp. We had food and training all weekend long. My memories of that weekend aren't so much the things we learned but how we started to get better. How mom finally smiled, and my sisters and I did too.

I do remember sitting in a room for a talk from a woman who kept talking about our intuition or our gut feelings and how we should never ignore them. For years afterward, Mom would ask, "What does your gut tell you?" By the time I reached high school, Mom shifted to saying, "Have you prayerfully considered this?"

During my last years of high school and most of my time in college, I was on fire for God. Mom knew this and tried to help me keep my gut instincts in line with what I believed God's plan was for my life.

In the last couple years of her life, my mom also had a huge growth in her walk with God. She and my stepdad had their struggles, and it was only through turning to God and putting Him first in their life that they were able to salvage their marriage.

In the days after the EMP, their trust in God became even stronger. When I was shot while my mom, two sisters, and I were being kidnapped, it was not at all uncommon for me to wake up from my injured stupor to find my mom praying by my side.

But it wasn't just the prayers during the bad times that showed Mom's belief. It was the praises during the good times and her always being thankful. Thankfulness was what I remember most.

Thankful that before things fell apart, Mom followed her gut instincts—or as she'd come to believe, the leading of the Holy Spirit— to prepare when times were good to help us get through the rough times.

Mom and Jake's basement storeroom, backup systems, and supplies not only helped our family but also much of the Bakerville community. Their instincts were good, and aligning their desires with what they believed was God's will made a difference for many.

In the time since my mom died, I've tried to hone my skills of discernment. It hasn't always been easy. My gut is often emotional, as in the case of my marriage to Leo. While I believe God's will is for us to be together, sometimes my own flesh takes over and I think it'd be easier for me to go home and let him stay here. Even if that isn't what I truly want.

But things like this . . .

When there's an imminent danger, I know I need to pay close attention. To listen as the Holy Spirit leads and guides me. His wisdom is given to guide me in truth. Perhaps to indicate things to come. The little hairs on my neck can be a vehicle He uses.

"I'll go." I give a tight smile, then direct my gaze at my husband. As our eyes meet, I cock one eyebrow. "Get this wrapped up and get home. I can't wait to warm up by the fire."

Leo's eyes narrow. "Yeah, babe. A hot fire sounds good. Be careful, and I'll do the same."

My stomach tightens. I'm sure Leo understood my message, my concern *something* may not be right. My mention of the word *fire*, a word we use as a war cry when it's time to strike, didn't go unnoticed. He'll stay alert, not only for the two sneaking up on the house but also for Onion Breath.

"We'll run. We'll be right back."

"Want me to stay with you?" Onion Breath tugs at his stocking cap, decorated with half a dozen souvenir pins along the fold.

I start to say he should go back to his house when Leo lifts his hand slightly. "Yeah, help me keep an eye out."

With my upper lip between my teeth, I give a slight shake of my head.

Leo kisses my cheek and whispers, "Keep your enemies close." He pulls back. "Hurry. I'm ready for a hot *fire* and a warm meal."

I take a quick look at the house where I last saw the robbers . . . before they walked in the front door like they own the place. Maybe they do. Maybe this is a huge misunderstanding.

The quickest way to Shaw's would be going forward, but I'd have to pass by the robbers. Gerry and I move cautiously as I try and keep the sparse winter foliage between us and the crooks.

When we've passed a couple of homes, I glance over my shoulder. The house the potential robbers went into is out of view. I scratch Gerry behind the ears. "Let's go for a run, boy."

His entire body shakes in response, and he lets out a low whine. Training Gerry and his littermates not to bark was something we started almost as soon as they moved in with us. It's definitely paying off tonight.

Gerry's run is more of a lope, with his big feet bounding on the snow. I let him set the pace for the first bit and then urge him to increase his speed. Gerry and I have run together a few times, but hard runs are something I tend to do alone. It's easier. Much easier.

When we're about half a block from Shaw's place, Gerry puts his nose up in the air and gives a big sniff. He seems to get a second wind and makes a beeline straight for Shaw's house and his littermate Tank.

I urge him to slow down. "We'll walk up, Gerry." I gasp out the words. "Catch our breath so Deputy Shaw can understand me."

Even though I'm in good physical shape and am used to running, the cold of the night has made breathing more difficult. I cough, another side effect of running in the cold.

My hand is positioned to knock when a voice from the other side of the door demands, "Who's there?"

I take a step back so I'm fully visible in the peephole. I put my hands out to the side to show only a leash is being held. "Katie Burnett. You got Tank from us. I'm married to— "

The door opens a few inches. "Something wrong?" Deputy Shaw's head isn't visible, but Tank's nose pokes out. Gerry lurches forward to greet him.

"Yes, maybe. Leo and I saw the guys we think killed Mr. Harrington. He's— "

The door opens the rest of the way. "C'mon in. Carol?" he hollers over his shoulder. "It's okay. It's Katie Burnett and her dog. There's trouble."

Carol Shaw steps around the corner and into the entryway, her pistol along her thigh. "Hi, Katie."

Deputy Shaw ushers me in. Standing in the entryway, I tell him all I know. When I'm done, he looks at his wife.

She walks toward the base radio on a table. "I'll call on the radio for you. You don't know the house number?"

I shake my head. "Not where the robbers are. But I know the house number closest to where I left Leo and the other guy."

"Okay. We'll use that."

"I need five minutes," Shaw says. "Tell them we'll meet on alternate channel three to coordinate. I don't want everyone converging on Leo and giving us away. Katie, you can stay here."

"Um, I can help."

Shaw looks toward his wife, and she tilts her head. "Might need her in case things have changed. If Leo moved . . . "

The deputy doesn't look at all happy. "Can you keep her dog?"

"Of course. And I'll call the hospital so they're on alert also."

It's less than five minutes before Shaw is ready to go. I'm truly amazed at his speed and organization. I give Gerry a rub and tell him to be a good dog while he plays with his brother.

The trip back to Leo is a fast-paced walk. Shaw's long strides eat up the pavement. I take two for his one, putting me at a near jog—or at the very least, the pace of an Olympic speed walker, though without the perfect form. As he walks, he gives directions over his radio to those on the other end.

When we turn onto the block nearest where I left Leo, I put my hand on his forearm. "Almost there."

He slows as we make a cautious approach and asks those on the radio to check in. Their responses arrive through his earbud. "A few are close to their assigned positions, but many are still some distance away. We'll get in position and wait."

As we get near the bushes where I left Leo, my stomach drops. I scan the area, and the sinking feeling increases. My husband is gone.

Chapter 15

I put my hand up in a stop motion, keeping us behind a scraggly-looking line of brush. I do another quick scan and look from the brush Leo was hiding behind to other likely spots between there and the house the robbers were casing.

My gaze lands on what was once—before the electricity went out and our world changed forever—a nicely landscaped yard two doors down from where I'd last seen Leo. During the summer months, there was a lovely willow and several Japanese maples in this section.

Something catches my eye, some sort of movement. I concentrate on the area, watching for another flicker of motion.

"What is it?" Deputy Shaw asks, his voice the perfect timbre to keep it from traveling through the still of the night.

"Leo isn't where I left him." My gaze doesn't waver from where I saw the movement.

"Okay? He may have needed to move to get a better perspective. Where's the house?"

I point out the house we last saw the guys at. Shaw relays the info and gives directions to his team through the radio.

My eyes dart back to the willow tree. There's another flash of reflection in the moonlight. "Over there. Look at the willow."

He tilts his head and narrows his eyes. "Got it. Let's wait here a minute." He turns his mouth toward his radio, positioned on the collar of his heavy winter jacket, and relays that Leo isn't where we thought he was.

Shaw gets updates from his team as to where everyone is. Once he determines they're where he wants them, he tells me to stay put while he checks out the willow tree.

With my heart pounding wildly in my chest, I purse my lips. "I've trained for this. Not only in the Volunteer Unit but as part of the militia we formed back home."

He looks me up and down before making a slight clicking noise with his mouth. He gives me a single nod. "All right. Stay behind me. I'll move first while you cover me. When I stop at cover, you get to me. I'll cover you." He removes his sidearm and mirrors it along his thigh.

I repeat his motion with my own pistol.

"You have a backup?"

I shake my head, wishing I had my ankle holster on, but I'm not wearing it today. I usually only carry it on nonwork days, figuring my main pistol and the on–site weapons have me covered. "Just the 9-millimeter, but I do have two additional magazines." I motion to the left side of my waist.

"Let's hope we don't need 'em."

"Pray," I murmur. "*Pray* we don't need them." I let out a long, slow breath and form a silent prayer. *Please, God, please watch over us. Keep my husband safe from harm.*

"Ready?"

Shaw doesn't wait for me to respond before he moves from our hiding spot to a new location twenty feet away, much the same way Leo and I witnessed the two alleged robbers move earlier.

Before I move, I glance at the willow tree where I saw the movement. I narrow my eyes. Nothing. No movement or anything else that catches my eye. I dart to Shaw's location. I'm barely in place before he gives me a nod and moves again.

We continue our leapfrog moves until we're in the yard next to the willow tree. Shaw's made it to the next set of bushes. He motions me to move. When I reach him, he puts out his hand and signals me to move closer. With our heads together, he lifts his chin toward the willow. "Know that guy?"

My eyes follow as he lifts his pointer finger. Leaning up against the tree, with his chin to his chest as if he's asleep, is Onion Breath Man. His stocking cap with the souvenir pins must have caught the moonlight and caused a reflection.

"He's the one I told you about. Is he . . . dead?"

Shaw tilts his head and purses his lips. "I don't think so. Looks like his chest is fluttering. But look at that . . . " He motions with his hand. "There's tape around his wrists and rope around his arms, connecting him to the trunk of the tree."

I narrow my eyes to better take in the view of the man. Even his ankles are bound, with tape over the top of his heavy work pants. My stomach sinks. "Where's Leo?"

"Is this his work? Binding the guy up?"

My lips pull into a tight line. Leo carries duct tape in his daypack, the same as I do. And he carries a couple lengths of twine. But the rope around this guy's arms isn't the same as what we have.

I shake my head, and my nose begins to burn. The tears will come next. I straighten my shoulders and will the emotions away. "I don't think so."

Shaw talks into his radio, alerting his team of the man tied to the tree and that Leo isn't in sight. He tells them to keep alert, that this may be a trap. He gives new directions as to what will happen next. Part of the team will keep their eyes on the house, the rest will move to a closer location.

The burn in my nose and sting in my eyes increases, as does the hollow feeling of my stomach. I swallow hard.

When he finishes on the radio, he says, "We'll wait a minute while everyone gets into position."

The wait seems to stretch on forever. I continually scan the area, looking for any sign of my husband.

Shaw touches his hand to his ear. "Status?" After a pause, he says, "Copy."

He leans toward me. "One of my guys sees your husband. He's bound to the same tree as this guy." Shaw lifts his chin in Onion Breath's direction. "Looks to be unconscious."

The beat of my heart increases and my mouth goes dry. He's okay. I'm sure he is. He must be, right? Shaw said he could see Onion Breath's chest moving. Surely, Leo's also fine.

Please, Lord, let Leo be okay.

I shake my head to clear my concern and then shimmy out of my backpack.

I kneel and pull out the supplies I think I'll need to treat Leo and the other man. What exactly I'll need, I won't be sure until I evaluate them. I also take out a couple of emergency blankets and a cravat.

Shaw requests a check-in from his team. With everyone in position, the plan is to have some of the team hit the house while two others simultaneously retrieve Leo and Onion Breath. The rest of the team will provide cover. Shaw and I are staying put, with Shaw acting as cover for his man that's checking Onion Breath.

After several tense minutes, as I'm beginning to wonder what the holdup is, Shaw finally gives orders for them to go. Within seconds, the silence of the night is interrupted by the splintering sound of a door. Two men appear out of the darkness and rush toward the willow tree.

I stare wide-eyed as one of the men runs a knife through the rope holding Onion Breath to the tree. The second man, the one helping Leo, is out of view except for his right shoulder. My knees feel weak, and I'm holding my breath. The man finally hoists Leo onto his shoulder. Leo hangs limp, looking like dead weight. The man struggles, falling to one knee.

"Cover me," Shaw says into his radio as he starts moving. "I've got Burnett. Reeves, help with the other guy."

Please, Lord. Please.

My breath is coming in shallow bursts as Shaw helps the other man with Leo. Shaw points in my direction before they head toward me. I see his lips move as he says something to the men helping Onion Breath. Soon, they're also headed in my direction.

I let out a slow breath through my nose and think about my treatment options. While I want to focus on Leo, I know I'll do my professional duty and check on the other man too.

I quickly spread a mylar emergency blanket on the snow-covered ground. Shaw and the man he's helping gently put Leo down. "Reeves, assist her. I'll call for a handcart to be on standby."

Before Shaw can touch the button on his radio, it sounds off. Someone from the house is reporting the place as all clear. The two men carrying Onion Breath put him down. He lets out a moan.

I quickly check Leo's breathing. It's good but maybe a little shallow. His pulse is slow and steady. He lets out a groan when I feel the back of his neck. "Leo? Can you hear me?"

"Mmm."

My eyes travel the length of his body, looking for anything out of the ordinary. They land on his splinted wrist . . . or where the splint should be.

I move my hands to the sleeve of his coat and gently slide it up. The bulge on his wrist is worse than before, and it's swollen and changing color. What happened here? Where's his splint?

"Okay, babe. Good. Just . . . just hold still. We'll get you to the hospital." I turn to the man who was ordered to assist me. "Monitor his breathing. I'm going to check the other guy." I turn toward Shaw. "Handcarts?"

"Ready. We need to make sure the area's secure before we bring them in."

I scoot next to Onion Breath. He's groaning and turning his head from side to side. "Hey, there. I'm Katie. We met earlier. Can I get you to hold still?"

He lets out a colorful string of words and bats his hand at me. "I'm fine. Just . . . man. Who clobbered me?" His eyes narrow, and his voice raises an octave. "Oh, hey. It's you. Where's your husband?"

He turns his head. "Oh. Got him too?" He releases a few more words, letting me know exactly what he thinks of not only whoever clobbered him but also the world in general.

Leo is also starting to come around more. I hear him ask what happened, followed immediately by, "Is my wife okay?"

I turn back toward him. "I'm here, honey. I was with Shaw. I'm fine."

"Okay. Good." He closes his eyes. "My wrist?"

"Not so good. Your splint is gone. It's probably broken again. I can wrap it or— "

"I'll keep it still. It's only for a few minutes, right?"

"Let me at least put it in a sling."

Within a few minutes, Shaw gets a report from the men checking the house. It's empty. Shaw determines the area is secure. Both men are talking and coherent when Jesse Talbot brings over the handcart.

He raises his eyebrows when he sees me. "Going for a record?"

"Huh?"

"Seems wherever the trouble is lately, you and Leo are smack-dab in the middle of it."

I shrug. "Not a record I'm interested in setting."

I give a quick report on both men. Leo fills in the blanks with what he remembers. They were watching the house when Onion Breath, who Shaw seems to know and says his name is RJ Kittleson, went down with an *oomph.*

Leo turned and put his arm up, the one with the splint on it, and blocked getting hit himself. But there must have been another guy because the next thing he knew, he was tied up. He was punched again, knocking him out.

RJ Kittleson adds a few details about being hit several times. I check where he says it hurts. There isn't a bump, but he does wince when I touch him. He complains of a headache and keeps moaning.

Leo also has a headache and a visibly swollen jaw. When I check his head, he has a goose egg where he was hit.

If the assailants were with the guys we watched go into the house— the one with the beard that I'm almost positive is the same man I saw the night Mr. Harrington was shot and killed—we're truly blessed Leo only has a few bumps and bruises.

I glance at the wrist again . . . and a rebroken left wrist.

Chapter 16

I walk with the handcarts. Both men are now quiet, the bumpy ride doing little for their pounding heads and aching bodies.

Leo cradles his slinged wrist close to his body. His tightly clenched jaw and pale lips speak volumes about his condition. One of the policemen found Leo's splint, busted in half from the blow. We brought it along in case it needs to be reused.

I put my hand on the side of the cart. "We're almost there. Half a block or so."

Leo gives me a strained smile. "Sorry, babe."

"You're going to be fine. This is just . . . just a minor setback."

He snorts out a breath. "Stupid. I don't know how they got the drop on us, how we didn't hear them."

"Really?" I raise my eyebrows. "You haven't been hearing right since the explosion."

"Maybe not. But Kittleson?"

I glance at the other cart. The big man is sitting up, leaning against the front boards, his eyes closed. The man hefting the cart is breathing like a freight train.

Deputy Shaw walks alongside the cart. He wants to go to the hospital and get proper statements from both Leo and Kittleson after they're checked out. I look back at Leo and shake my head. "I don't know."

At the edge of the parking lot, Shaw tells the National Guard sentry who we are. The sentry says they've been expecting us.

Chastity Morrow is waiting outside, her arms wrapped around herself as she pulls her long sweater tight, the portico of the building keeping the lightly falling snow off her.

Jesse slows Leo's handcart to a stop, trying to recover his ragged breath. "Katie will report."

I give my report on Leo first, stressing his arm isn't splinted, only in a sling, because of the short trip. Then I report on Kittleson. Since both men are somewhat ambulatory, they're taken in by wheelchair instead of a gurney. Good thing since the gurneys are still in use by those injured in the explosion.

The hospital is still overly crowded, with every room filled to capacity and people sleeping in the hallway. Chastity, Jesse, and Jacquie Haley are officially on shift, along with janitor Rand Hendricks. A few of the medical students were also tasked with spending the night, along with people from the neighborhood. They're taking turns resting in the on-call room.

Because of the explosion and Williams's injury, classes will be suspended for the rest of the week. The students will work in the hospital and the long-term care centers, where many of the injured have already been transferred.

Only one exam room is not being used as a sleeping room. Both men are taken in there. Chastity orders Kittleson—or as I continue to think of him, Onion Breath—up on the exam table. "Leo, keep your arm still. We'll take care of you next."

"Mm-hmm. I'm definitely keeping it still."

As Chastity examines Kittleson, she asks about his family. He says he lives alone. He was out for a walk when he saw Leo and me sneaking around. She lifts a hand. "Wait." She glances back at Jesse, who's standing by the door, ready to help as needed. "Can you get Shaw in here?"

"W-why?" Kittleson stutters.

"He wants to get your statement. I told him I needed to check your mental clarity first. You seem good, so . . . " She shrugs.

The man pales. "Uh, yeah. Sure."

With Deputy Shaw in the room, RJ Kittleson suddenly seems less chatty. As Shaw asks him questions, easy ones like where he's living these days, the man seems to become confused and clutches his head in his hands.

"C'mon, counselor. You don't remember where you live? I know that big house you had burned down. Where are you staying these days?"

Kittleson shakes his head and grabs his temple.

Chastity says maybe they should wrap it up and talk later, after he's had a chance to rest.

Shaw slaps his small notebook closed and strides toward the door. With his grip on the handle, he turns back toward the exam table. "I'll be right outside if the urge to talk returns."

With his head in his hands, Kittleson mutters something I can't hear.

Leo leans toward me. "Can you go with Shaw? Ask him about the house?"

I shake my head. "It was empty."

"Empty as in abandoned? Or empty as in no bad guys?"

I scrunch up my face. "I don't know."

He lifts his eyebrows. "Mind finding out? Also, where's Gerry?"

"With Shaw's wife and Tank. He's fine."

Leo gives me a brief grin. "No doubt."

I scurry out of the room, telling anyone who cares that I'll be right back.

"Need a hand?" Jesse asks as he follows me from the room.

As soon as we're in the hallway, with the door shut behind us, Jesse asks, "You know that guy?"

"Kittleson? No, you?"

"Seen him around. Never talked to him, but I think . . . " Jesse looks down the hall where the sleeping patients are. He motions me to step closer. In a low, secretive voice, he says, "I think he may be part of the black market."

I step back and flare my eyes. "Really?"

He tilts his head. "Bowski would know."

Of course he would. Ritchie Kasubowski, called Bowski by most, is a nice enough guy. When Leo broke his arms—the first time—Bowski provided a few items to help with the pain. I discovered he's deep in the Black Hills black market.

I'd heard about the market but expected those involved in it to be the shady and thieving types. Bowski doesn't seem like that. He seems more like someone you can depend on. Sure, it's against the rules to trade on the black market as opposed to using ration chips, but there seems to be a lot of looking the other way.

Especially where Bowski is concerned. Although he isn't officially part of the Citizen Patrol, he's sometimes called on by Shaw and the department to help with situations; he even helps the National Guard. He was part of the group responsible for a raid on what was thought to be the house of the robbery crew a few weeks ago.

"He was here earlier. Helped at the explosion site and worked as an orderly."

"Yep." Jesse nods. "Haven't seen him for hours, though. Let's talk to Shaw. That is what you were going to do, right? Get an update on what's happening?"

"That's what Leo asked of me."

We head toward the waiting area at the front of the hospital. Shaw and two of his deputies are there. I recognize one as Reeves, the man who assisted me with the initial treatment of Leo and Kittleson. The other is Jesse's brother Josiah.

Now that Reeves has his stocking cap off and fewer layers of clothing on, I also recognize him from the blood-borne pathogen class Leo and I did for the department last week.

Last week . . .

So much has happened in such a short time: the explosion and shooting at the festival, the people with food poisoning, the explosion at the ration center, and now this. It certainly seems longer than the few days it's been. A wave of exhaustion rushes over me. How long has it been since I've slept?

Shaw raises his chin. "Katie? Is Kittleson talking?"

"Not yet. We just . . . " I motion toward Jesse.

"You know him?" Jesse asks.

"Oh yeah, we know him all right."

"You called him counselor." I point back toward the exam room. "Is he a therapist?"

"Lawyer," Shaw scoffs.

I wait for Shaw to say more. After a few beats of uncomfortable silence, Jesse says, "Uh, yeah. I think he's part of the black market with Bowski."

Josiah Talbot shakes his head and widens his eyes at his brother.

Reeves chuffs out a laugh. "With Bowski? What are you talking about, dude?"

"That's enough." Shaw gives Reeves a pointed look, then looks back at me and Jesse. "Is there a private room Kittleson can go in after he's treated?"

"Private?" Jesse motions to the people sleeping in the hallway. "Uh, no."

Shaw rubs a hand across his bearded cheek. He looks at the ceiling and shakes his head. "Any way you can do some rearranging? I know I'm asking a lot."

Jesse looks down the hall again. "I don't see how. We're full up. And it's the middle of the night. People are trying to sleep."

"Why do you want him to have his own room?" I ask.

"I think it may be better for him. Better for his . . . let's say comfort."

Jesse grunts. "Comfort? Seriously?"

I touch Jesse's arm. "What about the firewood room? Is anyone in there?"

"That isn't a patient room."

Bobbing my head up and down, I agree it's not. "But . . . what if it is, just for tonight? Do we have any cots left?"

"Maybe, but he may not need to stay. The guy didn't look too bad. Chastity will probably— "

"He needs to stay," Shaw interrupts. "For tonight, at least."

Jesse shakes his head. "I'll set up a cot in the firewood room." He trudges down the hall, continuing to shake his head.

"Good thinking," Shaw says. "Was there . . . did you need something?"

"Leo wanted me to ask you about the house, the one we saw the men go inside. He was wondering if it was empty, like deserted, or if someone is living there."

"Living there. We think we know who. He works an overnight shift at the water plant."

"Was it burglarized?"

"Maybe." Shaw bobs his head several times. "We think so, yeah. We'll know more when the resident can do a walkthrough. I'll come in and chat with Leo once Kittleson is out of the treatment room. For now, let's keep it quiet, okay?"

"Yeah, sure. I'll let Dr. Morrow know about Kittleson staying overnight . . . for observation."

"Thanks, Katie."

When I step into the treatment room, Chastity is obviously wrapping up with RJ Kittleson. I clear my throat. "Um, Dr. Morrow, can I see you in the hall?"

She glances toward me, a question in her eyes. "Give me a moment." She steps to the sink, washes and sanitizes her hands, and then asks nurse Jacquie to clean the abrasion on RJ Kittleson's elbow.

Leo looks at me with his head tilted and his brows furrowed.

"It's okay," I mouth.

I glance at the exam table and see RJ staring at me. His eyes are narrowed and his mouth is pulled tight.

I lift my lips in what I hope is a smile, or at least not a grimace. "Feeling better?"

He lets out a moan. "Not much."

"Sorry. Hopefully, with a little time, you'll feel okay."

Out in the hallway, I ask Chastity about his diagnosis.

"Humph. Other than a skinned elbow, I can't find much wrong with him." She waves a hand. "Oh, I'm sure getting knocked on the head left him feeling bad, but clinically? He seems fine."

"Shaw wants you to keep him overnight."

"No reason." She shakes her head. "Someone can walk him home and make sure he gets there okay, but he doesn't need to stay."

"Shaw insisted. He even wants Kittleson in a private room."

She looks down the hallway past the sleeping patients and toward the waiting area. "I'll let him know *that's* not happening."

I put my hand on her forearm. "Um . . . I thought maybe we could put him in the firewood room. I asked Jesse to set up a cot."

She flares her nostrils and gets a hard look. "That's not a call for you to make."

"I know. I didn't . . . I wasn't making the call as a medical, um, professional. But as an option to help Shaw with his, uh, his investigation. You know?"

She leans against the wall and crosses her arms. "No, you made the call as a wife. You're upset about what happened to Leo and think RJ Kittleson may have some answers."

I look down at the toes of my boots. "You're not wrong."

"You stepped outside of your authority by asking Jesse to set up a cot. By even suggesting the firewood room. You should've brought this to me."

"I know." My voice is a whisper.

She lets out a sigh. "I suppose, since you've already made the arrangements and it's what Shaw wants, we'll go ahead with it. But, Katie . . . " She shakes her head.

"I've noticed a lot of improvement in your confidence over the last few weeks. And maybe, if I wasn't so dad-gummed tired, I'd be less snappy about it. I probably wouldn't have thought about using the firewood room. And I definitely wouldn't want to use it for a patient who needs actual monitoring. But in this situation, it *was* good thinking."

I'm not sure if I'm being reprimanded or complimented. I decide to go with complimented. "Um, thank you."

"Did you ask Jesse to check the mousetraps? Never know when a mouse is going to come in on the firewood." She gives me an exaggerated wink followed by a girlish giggle.

A few days after Chastity started working here full time, I grabbed some wood to refill the wood box in the break room. I dropped my load when I noticed a mouse staring at me.

Knowing this was an issue, we had traps set up in the room, but they hadn't been checked and were sprung. Now we're discussing not only using traps but also getting a cat to live there. We can't have mice running around the hospital.

Mice are something I never would've considered to be an end-of-the-world issue. But they're definitely here. And not just in the hospital. Mice and rats are becoming an issue throughout the city.

I'm glad there weren't more people like Dr. Newsome and his brother-in-law Bruce Blake who wanted to eliminate all pets. While we have mousetraps, cats and dogs are also needed to help keep the pests under control. The last thing we need is some kind of disease spread by rodents to sweep through our area.

I shudder. "I'll remind him."

I start to walk away, but Chastity stops me. "You know Leo rebroke his wrist?"

"I wondered."

"It may be a blessing in disguise. We might be able to repair the malunion."

My eyes go wide. "You're going to operate?"

She lifts a hand. "No, no. That isn't what I was thinking. I'll perform the initial exam and confirm what I'm seeing. I'd like to ask Dr. Bollinger to come over and reset it. His expert skills may be all we need to fix up your husband, provided Bollinger can get away. With the explosions, I'm not sure."

Chapter 17

RJ Kittleson balks about staying, insisting he's fine and is going home. Although medically Chastity agrees with him, she plays her part and asserts the need for observation.

"We've even set up a private room for you." She delivers an award-winning smile. "I'll admit, it isn't much. But you saw how many patients we have when you came in. Some of them would love a private room."

"Then give it to them. I'm going home."

"I can't force you to stay, but . . . " She looks at the floor and shakes her head.

"That's right. I'm out of here." Kittleson straightens his shoulders, puffs out his chest, and narrows his eyes at Chastity. "But what?"

"Pardon?"

"You said you can't force me to stay, then you had a funny look and said *but.*"

"Well, it's true. I can't force you to stay. There's just . . . when someone's hit on the head, even a slight hit, they can have delayed reactions to things. People can be fine and talking one minute and then—" she snaps her fingers " —*poof.* They fall over."

While Chastity is relaying an actual medical condition, something I witnessed when my neighbor Crystal Harrington was hit on the head with the butt of a handgun, I'm not sure RJ Kittleson is at risk of this.

In Crystal's case, she was talking and seemed normal, only complaining of a minor headache. We were following the handcart her husband was in, and she suddenly went down.

At that time, we only had one handcart; her injury was the deciding factor of our need for a second. A couple of neighbors carried her to the hospital. Doc Nettie saved Crystal with a minorly invasive procedure to relieve her brain bleed. It was still a concerning few days. We weren't sure if she'd live or join her husband, who died from his gunshot wound.

It's possible Kittleson's hit to the head could result in the same Talk and Die Syndrome Crystal experienced, but somehow, I don't think it's likely. Like me, Chastity was unable to find any bump or indication of the strike.

Leo's injuries are prominent, with visible bumps and bruises. Leo should probably stay the night for observation. Where Kittleson is given a private room—even if it's in a less-than-desirable space—my husband will likely join those lined up in the hallway.

I close my eyes and let out a breath through my nose. When I open them, Kittleson is putting a hand on his head. "You think that could happen to me?" he asks. "That . . . that . . . *poof?*"

Chastity gives an exaggerated shrug. "There are plenty of things in the medical world we aren't entirely sure of. Anything's possible."

Kittleson lets out a muttered string of profanities and then groans. "Fine, I'll stay."

Jacquie and Jesse get Kittleson situated in his sleeping quarters while I tidy the exam table and set things up for Chastity to look at Leo. He's been in the chair, quietly cradling his slinged arm, for the time it took for Kittleson to be checked over and convinced to stay.

While his staying was deceitful from a medical point of view, I can only hope it helps Shaw and his team with whatever it is they're doing.

Shaw didn't say much, but I can only assume he suspects Kittleson is part of the group responsible for all the break-ins we've been having. They thought they'd found the group's headquarters before. The two people there put up a fight and ended up dead.

But they weren't the same people I'd seen the night of Mr. Harrington's murder. And though the break-ins did cease for several days, they started up again last week.

I stare at the exam room wall as the memory of the night and the men I saw by the light of the moon come into view. The man with the beard looked to be one of the men we saw lurking outside the house tonight. The second man was taller than the six-foot-high fence surrounding my backyard.

I don't think he was the second man tonight. The bearded man seemed right, but the second man wasn't tall enough.

My eyes shift to RJ Kittleson as he slides off the exam table. He's a tall man with wide shoulders and a long, unkept medium-brown beard with threads of silver poking out at odd angles.

My heart pounds in my ears as I think back to when Kittleson scared the daylight out of me a short while ago. He was standing next to Leo, his head a few inches higher than my six-foot-four husband. I swallow hard, and the hair on the back of my neck rises to attention again.

This is him.

RJ Kittleson is the second man from the night Mr. Harrington was shot and killed. His beard is longer and wilder now, but his height and body shape are the same.

Josiah Talbot recently mentioned there's a rumor that the original robbers left the area after the raid on their place that killed their buddies. They say the break-ins happening now are from a copycat group.

I was leaning toward believing him until I saw those two men tonight. The one with the orange beard is the same one I saw that night. Kittleson was probably acting as a lookout while the bearded man and an accomplice did the break-in.

If Kittleson is part of the robbery team—and I'm pretty sure he is—then who hit him, and who hit Leo? Did the two men go in the house, out the back, and circle around? Did they clobber Kittleson first as a distraction—only hitting him hard enough to register—before unleashing their full fury on my husband?

I glance at Leo. He's sitting perfectly still with his eyes closed. His chest is moving in a regular rhythmic motion. Is he sleeping? My heart swells with love for him. The familiar sting of tears burns my nose and eyes.

Chastity lightly drops her hand on my arm. "You okay?"

I swallow the lump in my throat, knowing I need to tell Shaw what I think may have happened. Who I think RJ Kittleson really is. I glance at the man as he leans on Jesse and they make their way toward the door.

"Just tired," I croak. I swallow again. "Exhausted."

Chastity lets out a sigh. "Yeah. Have you slept at all?"

I heave out a breath. "Not since . . . " I shake my head. "I don't even know. I had a day shift, and then the explosion happened. Leo and I had just got off, and it was already after dark the next day. Took Gerry for a walk and— " I motion to the room " —here we are." I glance at my husband again. "At least he's getting some rest."

"Not for long. I think we're ready to check him out. You heard me ask Jacquie to make rounds, check in with the students and make sure everyone's fine?"

"I did. I assumed you'd have me assist you?"

"Exactly. I need a bathroom break. Can you wake up Leo and get him on the table? I'll be right back."

I bite my lip, wanting to tell her my need to talk to Shaw. As the exam room door shuts, I decide I'll let Jesse get Kittleson settled in the firewood room before finding Shaw.

Waking Leo is as easy as always. One of his skills, which is terribly useful during the apocalypse, is to be able to fall asleep without any trouble and wake up with only a touch. He doesn't jump or make any noise. His eyes open, and he's ready to go.

I'm nothing like him. Even exhausted, it takes me many minutes to settle into sleep, and waking up is like coming out of a fog. I'm slow and groggy. Sure, there's the rare occasion when I'll wake up and be ready to go, but that's definitely the exception rather than the norm.

With Leo on the table as we wait for Chastity, I share my suspicion about Kittleson.

"I wondered that too," Leo says. "Shortly after you left to get Shaw, I realized Kittleson fit the description you gave of the robbers. I was thinking of an excuse to separate from him when Kittleson went down. Then my lights went out. How are you holding up, honey?"

I laugh. "I should be asking you that. I'm not injured."

"C'mere." Keeping his injured arm tight to his side, he opens the other one. I step close to the table as he pulls me in tight.

"I love you." His breath tickles my ear and sends shivers all the way to my toes. "I'm glad you went after Shaw. I'm glad you weren't there when— " His voice cracks. I feel him shake his head as he positions it closer to me.

"Let's . . . do you want to pray?" I ask.

Leo moves his head back to meet my gaze. "Yes. Absolutely." He keeps his arm around me.

I reposition so my hand can find his, resting at my waist. Our fingers intertwine. He clears his throat and bows his head. I watch as his long lashes flutter as he closes his eyes.

When he begins to speak, I quickly close my own eyes. "Father God, we thank You for who You are and all You do. Thank You for pulling me back to You. For Your soft voice that kept calling to me even when I was so sure I could handle things on my own. Thank

You for giving me Katie and letting her love me through it all. I know I certainly didn't deserve it." He squeezes my hand.

"But You made a way for us. I know we still have issues and things to work out, and my injury from tonight may make life more difficult. Please, God, help keep me from going to the dark place I was in before. Keep me focused on You. Focused on the good I can do even while I'm healing. Focused on my wife. And please help Shaw and his team put an end to the burglary ring before others are injured or killed." He releases a sigh before squeezing my hand again.

With this squeeze, I know he's signaling to me it's my turn to pray. I take in a breath and let it out slowly. "Thank you, Lord, for the blessings You've given us. Thank you for Leo not being injured worse than he was. I— " The emotions swell up within me as my eyes and nose sting.

Leo pulls me tight.

When I speak again, my voice comes out as a squeak. "We've been through some tough times, but with You, we can come out stronger. You know the plans You have for us. We may want to do our own thing, but trusting in You, and believing in You, is what we need to learn to do.

"I'm putting my faith in this latest, um, injury that this is what will be best for Leo. You'll use it to heal his arm. You'll give Chastity the knowledge she needs. You'll make a way for Bollinger to fix Leo properly. Soon, we'll look back on this part of our life together as nothing but a blip."

I pause as I think of my mom and Jake. They went through a tough time in their relationship after the death of their friends. They were to the point of planning how to separate when they realized what they needed wasn't to be apart but to have God as the center of their marriage. Things didn't change overnight, but they did change. When my mom died, they were the couple God meant for them to be.

"Help us, Lord. Help us put You first in our marriage. Help us focus on Your Word and Your desires so they become our desires." The creak of the door stops my words. I rush on to finish. "We pray these things in Your Son's Holy name, amen."

I lift my eyes to meet those of Chastity. She caught me reading my Bible one day in the break room. While she was nice enough about it, she did make a point of saying she's not a "churchgoer" and didn't want me trying to convert her.

"Probably a good idea. With all we have going on around here, maybe you can ask the Big Guy Upstairs— " Chastity points toward the ceiling " —to lay off on us for a bit. While you two were in here praying, I've been on the radio. I managed to contact Dr. Bollinger. Like us, they're spread thin and exhausted. The explosion in their district resulted in more deaths and injuries than we have."

"No surprise," Leo says. "More people live in that area, right? Their ration center is larger?"

"Yep and yep. Anyway, Bollinger was there. He just finished a surgery. He's going to get some sleep, and if everything is stable when he wakes up, he'll come here and take care of your arm."

My eyes go wide. "Really?"

"That's the plan. I'll put on a temporary splint, and he'll do what he needs when he gets here, which may be as soon as tomorrow but probably not until the next day. He'll radio when he's leaving. Now, let's get on with the exam. How's the head?"

She pokes and prods Leo for several minutes, asking about the injury and what he remembers.

Although he did lose consciousness from the original strike and again from the secondary hit—he has two goose eggs on his head along with a bruised jaw showing the points of impact—he's lucid and has excellent recall. A few of his memories are fuzzy, but that's to be expected.

"I'm not seeing anything I didn't expect to see." She looks from Leo to me. "You're going to have a whopper of a headache for a few days and— " Her assessment is interrupted by the ring of the bell on the backdoor.

When the back door sounds, we assume it's a hospital employee. When the front door sounds, it's likely a patient.

Chasity grins. "Whew. Thought we might have another emergency on our hands. I want to keep you here tonight."

Leo gives me a wink. "Shocking."

"Just a precaution." Chastity lifts a hand. "I'm sure you'll be fine. But I also don't want you walking around much with a broken arm. Katie, do you want to help me splint it?"

"Sure, yes."

"Great. We'll— "

The door to the exam room pops open, and Jesse comes in. "Hey, that Kittleson guy took off out the back door."

Chapter 18

Chastity rolls her eyes. "Of course he did. I knew Kittleson had no interest in staying. Deputy Shaw still here?"

Jesse's head goes back and forth on a swivel. "Nope. He's gone. The sentries are out there. Two in the front and at least one in the back, but I'm not sure they'd stop him. Their job is to keep people from getting in, not prevent them from leaving. I'll grab my coat. Jacquie's calling Shaw on the radio."

From the hallway, we hear, "He's on his way back," as Jacquie relays their conversation.

Chastity lets out a noisy sigh. "This is a hospital. Not a jail. He'd better not say anything about anything or else— " Her lips go tight, and she shakes her head. "Go on out, Jesse, but be quick about it. I'm going to finish with Leo."

"Um, Jesse?" I call out. "Can you tell Shaw I think Kittleson might be the second man I saw the night Mr. Harrington was killed?"

Jesse raises his eyebrows. "You sure?"

I shake my head. "No, but . . . " I lift a hand.

"You heard her description, right?" Leo asks. "It fits Kittleson."

Jesse looks to the ceiling, pausing a minute before nodding. "Yeah, maybe. But Kittleson—he's a lawyer, not a thief."

Chastity snorts out a laugh. "A lawyer, not a thief. That's funny. What kind of lawyer?"

"Don't know. Contracts or something maybe. I'll tell Shaw."

The splint Chastity fashions isn't the same as the one Leo got at Monument Hospital. That was something to give a little extra support in the final days of healing. This is one to completely immobilize him until a proper cast can be put on.

The splint makes sense. His arm is so swollen it may not cast well anyway. Part of me wonders had Dr. Newsome splinted Leo and allowed the swelling to subside a few days before applying the cast, would it have healed properly the first time?

We're close to finishing Leo's arm when there's a soft knock on the door followed by Jacquie's head popping in. "Deputy Shaw's here to see you. Can he come in?"

Chastity meets Leo's gaze. "You mind?"

"Nope. That's fine."

"Send him in."

Shaw enters the room with Josiah Talbot on his heels. "You heard?" the senior deputy asks. "About Kittleson?"

Chastity continues working on Leo without looking up. I watch as her jaw tightens, and she speaks through clenched teeth. "I heard."

"Yeah, well, can't say I'm surprised."

I shoot a look at Shaw and Josiah. "Did the sentry see him?"

Josiah gives me what may be a wink.

Shaw smiles. "Oh yeah, the sentry and our man. Everything went as we'd hoped."

Chastity meets my gaze and then turns to Shaw. "As you hoped?"

"Yup. We figured Kittleson would take off. We have eyes on him. He went straight home. Which, in case you all didn't know, is nowhere near where he was tonight."

I look to Leo, who raises his eyebrows. "Is that right? Where does he live?"

"Several miles from where he was supposedly out for a walk."

"Did you know where he lived before you followed him?" I ask.

"Not exactly. We didn't know where he'd been living since his house burned down." Shaw leans against the wall and directs his gaze toward me. "Jesse told us about what you think. We had him on our list of potential suspects, but he had an alibi."

"Really?" I furrow my brow. "He has an alibi?"

He scrunches up his face. "An alibi we're seriously beginning to question. I think we may have our man, plus a good idea who the other one is. It's all coming together nicely. About time. Thanks for your help, Chastity. We appreciate your cooperation."

"Uh, Deputy?" I lift my chin toward him. "Have you talked to your wife? Is my dog okay?"

Shaw waves a hand. "Perfectly fine. Tank and Gerry spent some time running around the house and have both settled down." Shaw motions toward Leo. "You being admitted?"

Leo rolls his eyes. "Kept for observation."

"Try to get some rest. I'll see you tomorrow. You don't need to worry about Gerry. He's fine at my house until you're able to get him." Shaw and Josiah stride out the door.

Chastity looks at her watch. "It's almost 0100. Since the firewood room is now empty, it might be a good spot for the two of you to get some rest."

I shake my head. "Nope. No way. That room gives me the heebie-jeebies."

"The mouse memory is still too fresh?" Leo laughs.

"Yes. I probably shouldn't have even suggested the room for Kittleson." I let out a soft laugh. "Maybe he left because a mouse ran up his leg." The vision of a mouse scurrying around combined with my exhaustion takes my soft laugh into something I can't control. Within seconds, I'm laughing uncontrollably, and tears are streaming down my face.

Chastity joins me while Leo looks on.

As we're trying to regain control, Chastity wipes her eyes. "Can you imagine?"

I can, and that sets me off again.

"You two need some sleep." Leo shakes his head.

"That's for sure," Chastity gasps between giggles.

Twenty minutes later, Leo and I are in the break room. We're added to the half dozen patients already sleeping in here, ones who are also being kept for observation only.

The room has been rearranged to allow for cots. The two couches are also in use. While I get a cot—the same one Kittleson used in the firewood room, which I diligently inspect for any sign of vermin—Leo sleeps in the recliner, which helps keep his slinged and splinted arm stable.

Even on the less than comfortable, possibly rodent-tracked cot, I sleep like a log. I'm sure Jacquie or Jesse came in at some point during the night to do their rounds, but they didn't wake me. I stretch and turn over to look at Leo. He's still in the recliner, and Jesse's squatting next to him. They're talking quietly.

Leo smiles at me. "Hey. Sleep well?"

"Mm-hmm. Time'zit?"

"Just after shift change," Jesse answers. "I'm taking off but wanted to give Leo the news."

I rise to an elbow. "What news?"

"They found them. Kittleson. The two you saw. Half a dozen others."

"What? The burglary ring?" I swing my feet to the floor. "All of them?"

"Maybe. They aren't talking much, so Shaw isn't sure it's all of them. He wants you to see if you can ID any of them as the guys you saw either last night or from the Harringtons."

I bob my head. "Okay. Uh, they're alive this time?" The last time I was asked to make an identification of Mr. Harrington's killers, they were dead.

"They are."

"Are they at Camp Rapid?" Although the county jail is only a few miles away, they've set up a makeshift jail at Camp Rapid. It's designed to only be temporary while they await transport to the secure jail. These days, crimes have to be pretty bad to warrant incarceration. Murder qualifies.

"They are. Josiah is on his way to walk you over." Jesse tilts his head in Leo's direction. "Chastity would prefer Leo not go with you. The less he moves around, the better until Bollinger can see him."

"I understand. I'm fine going with Josiah."

Leo purses his lips. "I hope they'll have it set up so you can see them but they can't see you. I don't like the idea they may know you."

"Well, it's not like RJ Kittleson wouldn't recognize me. And we did tell him we thought we were watching the robbers." I lift my hands. "It'll be fine, Leo."

Jesse tells me I have a few minutes until Josiah arrives. After giving my husband a peck on the lips, I excuse myself to visit the restroom. My daypack contains the bare necessities I need to start my day: a wide-tooth comb to try and tame my unruly mane, a bar of soap kept in a little plastic container, and a toothbrush.

While we still have soap, thanks to a crew who makes it, toothpaste is rare. Leo and I still have a tube we brought with us from Bakerville, but it's nearly empty. We're to the point we save it for special occasions, choosing to brush only with water.

I heard someone's making toothpowder out of some kind of clay. It was supposed to be part of our rations after the first of the year. Now, with the ration distribution centers destroyed, taking out many of our nonfood supplies, toothpaste may be the least of our resupply worries.

When I decide I'm presentable enough for the day, I return to the break room. Merissa Weaver is the medic on duty today. She's evaluating each of the patients in the room. I overhear her tell one of the women she'll probably be released to go home soon.

The woman begins to cry. "What for? My husband was killed in the explosion. I have no reason to return to my home."

Listening to her makes me think of the woman and her baby we were next to when the building exploded. Before we ended our shift yesterday and took our dog on the fateful walk, her husband showed up. The lady is still here, but her husband was able to take baby Johnny home.

She's expected to make a full recovery, but it's going to be a while. She'll be transferred to one of the local care centers while she heals. Captain Williams suspects several broken ribs and possibly a small break in her vertebrae from landing so hard on the cement. She isn't the only one. Many will need long-term care and rehabilitation.

There are a handful of houses that were turned into long-term care facilities and nursing homes within a three-block radius. Just like our hospital, they're understaffed. They're set up as a residential type of facility, with people living on-site to provide round-the-clock care along with shift workers coming in.

When Leo and I first arrived in Rapid, we were told we'd probably be given a nursing home assignment. While working in a nursing home is fine, I'm grateful we ended up at the hospital instead. The death rate in some of the homes is high, with them functioning as hospice, and I was still so deeply in grief over losing my mom. I can't imagine how it would've been. I struggled enough at the hospital.

When we'd lose a patient, it was devastating. I close my eyes as the memory of Elizabeth and her preterm baby replays in my head. I hope, by the time another woman arrives to give birth, those memories will have faded.

I glance at Merissa. We've established a tentative due date of late March to early April for her. Because she has lost so much weight off her already lean frame from the food rationing in her Montana town, she suffered from amenorrhea. She'd had only a couple of menstruations in the year since the attacks. The last was in May, but based on her clinical observations, we're assuming a later date for fertilization.

When Nettie and I first examined Merissa, she asked us to keep the pregnancy quiet. She didn't want her mother-in-law to know. Now that she's on our medical team and part of the first batch of medical school trainees, I think she should at least tell Williams about it. Maybe she has; I don't know. Merissa is nice enough but keeps to herself. I guess we all do these days.

While Nettie and I are friendly, and I've shared some of my life before the apocalypse, we mostly talk about things happening now. I don't even know much about her. Other than saying she's from a small town in Kansas, she doesn't share about her life before coming to Rapid City.

I do know a little about her time at Monument Hospital. She was there on a short-term rotation when our world fell apart. She hinted something wasn't right there, and she was reassigned to our Guard District satellite hospital instead of remaining at the main hospital in the Monument District. She was less than pleased when Chastity was given a permanent assignment here too.

Merissa and her secrets. Nettie and hers. And Chastity . . . something's going on there too.

Not that it matters. All that matters is today. Getting the robbery ring stopped and bringing Mr. Harrington's killers to justice. Taking care of the people injured in the explosion. Making sure my husband is fixed up properly.

I glance toward him, and he gives me a smile that melts my heart.

Chapter 19

Merissa

"I need five minutes," I say to Jacquie Haley as I stride by.

"Okay, Merissa, but only five. It isn't your break time yet, and . . . " As always, her words continue. I'm far enough away to easily block out the shrill sound of her voice.

Both bathrooms are full. I let out an angry breath at the lack of a private space here and notice the door to the wood storage room. I quickly slip inside. The room has a soft glow from an outdoor solar light hanging from a bracket on the wall.

These lights are great for rooms not hooked up to the large solar system. That convenience has a limited lifespan, though, like everything in this world. Eighteen months into the apocalypse, the batteries in the solar lights are weakening. Even with a full charge, we get only a few hours of use from them. There's already discussion about what to do when the garden solar lights no longer work.

Closing the door, I lean against it. Solar lights aren't my concern at the moment. These last few days have been hard. The explosion and deaths have been terrible. The aftermath is almost worse. I've barely been able to keep my emotions in check. Especially this morning.

Susie, the woman Bowski and I found thrown far from the explosion, is recovering well enough to return home. She has a few friends who'll help her while her broken leg heals. Her husband was found the next day—or I should say, his *remains* were found.

They were near the front of the line, close to the ration center. Where she was thrown clear, her husband probably died within minutes of the blast, right where they stood.

Physically, Susie may be ready to go home. But mentally and emotionally, she's a wreck. So much so, I'm concerned for her. When I spoke to her earlier about her release, she totally lost it and started raving about how she had nothing to live for. Her husband was her life, and now he's dead; she said she might as well be too.

Chastity Morrow was still on duty, covering for Nettie Wolff who was doing care center rounds before starting her shift. I went to Dr. Morrow about my concerns and what Susie said. It did little good. Not only was she less than sympathetic, but she also said, "Things are tough all over. Got to be strong to survive in this world. If she's not up to it, she'll die."

I felt almost as if Dr. Morrow had slapped me. While the woman isn't exactly warm and fuzzy, she's always seemed to care deeply for the patients and what was best for them. I don't know if she's simply exhausted and irritable like the rest of us or what exactly.

I've seen her whispering and laughing with my fellow med student Geoff Landers. Landers is a piece of work. I can't come close to understanding why Williams added him to the program. He has zero practical skills with even the most basic first aid. He says he was premed in college, having finished his freshman year only weeks before the attacks started. Maybe his inexperience with life in general is part of the problem.

At nineteen, I was probably just as cheeky and headstrong as he is. The difference is I was already in the Coast Guard and learned real quick that cheeky and headstrong would not be tolerated.

Geoff Landers would benefit from joining the National Guard and developing some discipline. He could even learn basic medical skills and catch up with the rest of us. As it is, Williams gives him extra homework and duties, which he doesn't seem to do.

Instead of dropping Landers from the program, which is what I think should happen, Williams is slowing the rest of us down so Landers can catch up. I guess reviewing the basics doesn't hurt, but it's still frustrating. Especially when what we desperately need is more trained people. With the craziness of our world, we can't afford to delay training new doctors.

Dr. Morrow's shift ended, and Dr. Wolff is the only doctor on right now. She's been busy, but I plan to talk with her about Susie. Dr. Wolff is only a few years older than Landers, having already completed premed and her third year of medical school when the attacks happened.

I've liked the young woman from the beginning. She doesn't waste words on needless conversation. She's got a quiet strength about herself that's reassuring not only to the patients but to the staff as well.

But I do think there's something more to Dr. Wolff than she lets us know. She's tight-lipped about her life before. From the brief introduction she gave during med school orientation, I know she's from Kansas and went to med school at the University of Kansas in Kansas City. Katie Burnett also went to college in Kansas, but she went to K-State in Manhattan.

One of the men in school with us suggested the two women are from rival colleges. Dr. Wolff shrugged and said, "Maybe in the past, but we're all on the same team now, working together to save lives."

I swear Captain Williams beamed with pride at her statement.

Taking a few deep breaths, the scent of the firewood room almost reminds me of a forest. The earthy aroma is nearly therapeutic as I imagine sitting on a log surrounded by tall trees.

I need a day to get away. To ride my horse and go. Take a picnic lunch and find a stream to enjoy it by. Hear the soft babbling of a creek, the rustle of wind through the brush and trees. Braedon and I often spent a Saturday like that. We'd pack a lunch, take the horses, and just go. It was almost magical.

The flutter in my stomach reminds me my horse-riding days are on hold until after the birth. And riding with my husband is something that can only happen in my memories and dreams. I whisk away the tears traveling down my face and pull myself together. I take a few more deep breaths before I straighten my back and slip out of the firewood room.

When I let Jacquie know I'm back, she asks me to go around and make sure everyone has what they need. In overnight room one, which has four women in it, including Susie, one of the women says all she needs is to go to the bathroom.

"I'd be happy to help you," I say, as I glance around the room and notice Susie isn't in her bed. Maybe Dr. Wolff has already evaluated her and sent her home?

"Will you take me to the hall bathroom? Susie's been in ours for about an hour now."

A sinking feeling starts in my bowels and travels up to my chest. Moving quickly to the bathroom door, I knock and call out her name. When she doesn't answer, I try again while turning the doorknob.

Locked.

I turn back to the patient who needs to use the room. "You're sure Susie went in here?"

"Yeah," she scoffs. "Can you take me out to the hall bathroom?"

"Susie?" I deliver three solid knocks. "Susie, if you don't open the door, I'm coming in." I wait a couple of beats. "Step away from the door."

The doors are cheap, hollow-core slabs salvaged from the office building we now use for our medical school. The lock is also nothing special, the kind on a bedroom or closet door in a home.

I step back from the door to give myself enough space to kick and breach it. Braedon gave a crash course in breaking down doors when we worked on our hometown security team. He'd told me, "You never know when you need to get in a room quickly."

I know to kick near the doorknob and follow through with the motion. In position, I lift my foot and immediately feel my center of gravity shift in an unhelpful way. *The baby.* I let out an aggravated sigh.

"Hold on, Susie. I'm going to get some help."

"What's wrong with her?" the other woman who needs the bathroom asks as I rush out the door.

Anger and irritation surge through me. As the medic on duty today, this is something I should be able to do. Not being able to do what's needed for the job is an issue. I search through my mind to think who can help. Nettie is the doctor, Jacquie is the nurse, and Kerry Hendricks is the janitor.

Kerry. She can help. She's physically strong from her work. Plus, she was in the Army before moving to Rapid City. She's my best bet.

Not seeing any of the staff in the hallway, I yell out Kerry's name. After my second call, she steps out of one of the storage rooms. Leo Burnett also pokes his head out of the break room.

"Need something?" Kerry asks.

"Yes, come quickly."

"Can I help?" Leo asks.

"Maybe. Hurry."

At the bathroom door, I quickly relay my concerns.

The roommate who needs to use the bathroom pipes in with, "That Susie is awfully upset about losing her husband."

"I'll do it," Leo says. Before I even have time to protest, he yells for Susie to get away from the door and gives it a solid kick. The flimsy door immediately yields. Leo, who's made sure to keep his splinted and slinged arm tight against his body, quickly steps out of the way.

Susie's slumped on the floor, surrounded by a puddle of blood. The decorative mirror above the sink is in pieces, and several shards are near her body.

"I'll get Dr. Wolff," Leo says.

Kerry and I crowd into the bathroom. Susie's much too pale. I check her pulse at her carotid since her wrists are the source of all the blood.

"Anything?" Kerry asks. She grabs a few clean rags that we offer as toilet paper and wraps the wrist nearest her, gently pressing her knee into it to stanch the bleeding.

"Barely."

Kerry grabs another rag and awkwardly applies pressure to the left wrist. "This one looks worse. Should we straighten her out? Get the board?"

"I'll go after the backboard. You keep the pressure up."

As I clumsily get to my feet, Dr. Wolff appears at the door. "Status?"

"There's a faint pulse at the carotid. I haven't taken any other vitals. Kerry is applying pressure."

"I'll get the backboard. Kerry, you'll help me move her. Merissa, I'll need you to keep the pressure up."

In almost record time we have Susie in the exam room. The cut to her right wrist is deep but not life-threatening.

"She probably did this one first," Dr. Wolff says. "There are hesitation marks. Not so on the other wrist." She lets out a sigh. "Looks like there could be damage to the ligaments . . . and who knows what else. Merissa, call Captain Williams. I need him to evaluate. Kerry, you stay and help me. I'm going to start an IV."

"Will she make it?" Kerry asks.

"Yeah. I think so. She lost some blood for sure, but . . . yeah, she should survive. *This time.*"

With the intravenous fluids and the bleeding slowed, Susie starts to come around. When she realizes we're treating her, she cries and mutters about how we should've let her die.

When Captain Williams arrives, she won't allow him to look at her wounds, arguing she didn't consent to treatment and is going to make us pay.

With her stabilized for the moment, he assigns Kerry to stay with her while the rest of us leave the exam room.

In the hallway, the captain asks what happened. I tell him what she told me earlier. He asks Dr. Wolff if she'd spoken to her.

"I hadn't. Chastity did rounds this morning, while I checked the care centers. Chastity's report said she was ready for discharge and could go as soon as someone showed up for her. When I poked my head into the room earlier, the other three were asleep and her bed was empty. I thought she already left."

Williams lets out a sigh. "We've known mental health care is an issue. Sometimes, I think we'd be better off focusing on psychiatry more than physical medicine. That's what we need. A school just for mental health. We have too many people teetering on the edge."

Chapter 20

Katie

"Katie, I appreciate you doing this. I know it's not an ideal setup." Deputy Shaw motions to the door with an elongated peephole.

"But it's the best we can do here. We want you to see if you know the man in the room. Then we'll take him out and add a new man. It's not a lineup like you may have seen on television. We'll make sure that happens once they're taken to the county jail. This is just preliminary."

I glance from Shaw to a woman standing next to him. I don't know her, but she was briefly introduced as JoAnn. She gives me a nod as she taps her pen on her clipboard. Shaw said she'd be recording my observations.

I let out a breath. "I understand."

"Good. Can you step up to the viewer and take a look? Tell me if you recognize the person in the room."

With my heart pounding loudly, I clasp my hands in front of me. My nervousness is almost overwhelming as I take a few steps forward. I tentatively put my eye up to the hole. What I see on the other side makes me pull my head back and whip it toward Shaw. "What? Why— "

"Just to test the position. We want to make sure the view is exactly as needed, and Lieutenant Paul was kind enough to be our guinea pig."

"You could've told me it'd be him."

"Probably, yes. Go ahead and line back up again. Make sure you see him clearly. Do you need him to move at all?" Shaw motions to my feet. "I noticed you stretched up onto your toes. How about a step stool?"

It takes only a few minutes to get things arranged properly so I can see Lieutenant Paul clearly as he sits on a chair in the small room. Shaw asks him to stand and turn around, making sure my view of him continues to be acceptable.

When we're done, Lieutenant Paul gives me a small wave before going out the side door. I get off the step stool and look around. There's a small pile of sawdust by the wall next to the door. "Is this new?" I motion to the peephole.

"Put in an hour ago. We'd discussed this as a lineup room but hadn't moved forward with it since we had no need. The peepholes were in storage in case we needed them."

"Peepholes? There's only the one."

"Right. But we can put in others. Our original plan was to do a series of three holes and try for a five-man lineup. We couldn't figure out how to make that work properly, so we only did one hole. One person. It'd never hold up in court, but it'll help us know if we have the right people. Then the regular lineup will be at the jail. Make sense?"

I shrug. "I suppose. And you're sure they can't see me?"

"Positive." Lieutenant David Paul strides around the corner. "I couldn't even make out your eyeball from where I was. But I can hear your voices. The room isn't soundproof. Keep your voice low, and let Shaw know with silent signals if you recognize the person in the room. If you're ready, I'll have the first man brought in."

Lieutenant Paul hustles around the corner. The first man is RJ Kittleson. After viewing him through the peephole, and nodding I know him, he's ushered out of the room.

"We can talk now," Shaw says.

"Why bother with him? You know I know him."

JoAnn quickly scribbles on her paper. "Did you know him before last night?" She raises her head to meet my eyes.

"No." I shake my head. "I mean, maybe. He snuck up on Leo and me when we were, um, when we were watching the other men sneaking up on the house. I'm one hundred percent sure about that— he's the same guy. But I think he's also one of the men I saw at the Harringtons' house the night they were robbed."

She asks a few more questions, which ends in me basically repeating everything that happened from the time Leo and I left the hospital and took Gerry for a walk to when Shaw and I found Leo and Kittleson tied to the tree, along with recounting my memory of the night Mr. Harrington was killed.

JoAnn taps her pen on her paper again. "What was causing the glint of light?"

"Hmm?"

"You said you saw something shining. What was it?"

"Oh. He had a couple of different pins on his beanie. I guess, when he moved his head, they reflected the moonlight. That's all I can figure."

"But wasn't he unconscious when you and Deputy Shaw found him?"

"Yes, he seemed to be."

"So why were you seeing the illumination?"

I look to Deputy Shaw, who shrugs. "Did I mention JoAnn's an attorney?"

A sinking feeling starts at the base of my gut. "Am I . . . is there a question as to the, um, the validity of my statement? Because he was with me." I point to Deputy Shaw. "He saw it too."

Shaw gives a single bob of his head. "I did. Katie pointed it out, and after a minute or so, it sparkled again."

JoAnn gives a slight smile. "What you saw isn't in doubt. Why you saw it is the question. Was he unconscious? Or were you seeing the shine because he was moving around?"

My mouth forms an *O* shape when I realize what she's getting at. I close my eyes as the image replays in my head. "He could've been faking. Did you talk to the man who reached him first?"

"I have. I just wanted your impression. Especially with your medical training."

"He seemed to be coming around when I checked him. After he was moved, I kind of expected it. But . . . " I chew on my top lip. "I, uh, I checked my husband first, so . . . " I lift my hands.

"You do know he didn't show any bruising or contusions? My husband, Leo, has a palpable bump on the back of his head and a noticeable one on his forehead, along with a bruised jaw. RJ Kittleson . . . nothing."

"Yes. Thank you." There's a bite to her voice. She looks toward Shaw. "Shall we continue?"

The deputy lifts a hand. "It's your show, JoAnn."

"Wait." I clear my throat. "I was wondering, you're an attorney. Kittleson is an attorney. Did you work together?"

She shakes her head. "No, not usually. He was a desk lawyer. Contracts, land deals, business stuff. He made quite a name for himself and was, quite honestly, very successful at what he did. Had his pick of clients. He was in court a few times supporting clients but not usually arguing. He wasn't a trial lawyer."

"So you weren't, um, friends?"

She makes a scoffing noise. "Royal James Kittleson had few friends. He had a collection of acquaintances, people riding on the coattails of his success mainly, but that was all. Shall we continue?"

I agree I'm ready while I mull over what she's said. It's weird to me that a successful attorney would turn to a life of crime. Even if it is the apocalypse.

JoAnn pokes her head around a corner and directs the men there to bring someone else in. Within a few minutes, I'm back at the peephole, staring at a stranger. I step off the stool, shake my head, and whisper, "I don't know him."

The process continues with the next person, a woman, also a stranger. When they're ready for me to look at the fourth person, my first impression is to laugh. My second is to shrink away from the peephole to ensure he doesn't see me.

In the brightness of the room, lit up with an LED lantern, is a man in a costume. His bright orange-red mustache and beard are perfectly shaped into a triangle. It's hanging slightly wrong, though, so the whisp of an actual mustache is showing above the bright one.

Shaw has him stand up from the chair and turn in various motions. I'm completely positive he's one of the men from the night Mr. Harrington was killed and also from last night, lurking around the neighborhood we were walking in.

"Take off the beard," Shaw says.

The beard hooks over his ears with loops, something like the kind we have on our face masks at the hospital. With his fake beard off, his natural beard and mustache show fully.

My hand goes to my mouth when I realize I know this man. He was one of the men who went on the hunting trip with us in September, the excursion where Leo fell and broke both arms. He was with Bowski when Bowski came over to check on Leo and give him a handful of painkillers.

A sinking feeling sweeps over me. I'd wondered if it was possible Bowski was part of the robbery crew. I'd asked about it several weeks ago when I was asked to identify the dead men after they'd raided what they thought was the robber's hideout. Bowski was injured in that event.

I'd asked again last night after Leo was hurt. Jesse Talbot was with me, also questioning if Bowski could be involved. Shaw and his deputies—including Jesse's brother—told us we were wrong.

But now . . . were we wrong? I've seen this man with Bowski before. Could he be part of the burglary ring without Bowski knowing?

Or is Ritchie Kasubowski, a black marketeer, involved in the robberies too?

Chapter 21

"So, the beard really was a fake? Kirstie Harrington was right?" Leo's voice drips with disbelief as he shakes his head.

"And can you believe who it was? I'm telling you, Leo, I think Ritchie Kasubowski is involved in this."

Leo's headshake continues as he puffs out a sigh. "I like Bowski. You've heard the stories about him?"

"Of course. The stories of how he's deep in the black market? That's how he was able to give you the painkillers and booze, right?"

He tilts his head. "He *is* the black market. He organized the entire thing. You know why Shaw and the deputies like him so much?"

"I . . . no. I thought it was because he's nice."

"He's a big reason so many people survived last winter. He's, um . . . " Leo leans closer and lowers his voice. "He's like your mom and Jake. A prepper."

I let out a soft laugh. "I don't think you have to be so secretive about it now. With my mom dead and Jake in Wyoming, no one would care if they were preppers. Besides, what they stockpiled before the EMP is essentially gone."

They'd planned a year's supply of food and essential goods for our entire family, along with setting up their thirty-acre farm to produce food. Even with all their planning, though, it wasn't enough. They quickly realized security was an issue. When they banded with the community of Bakerville to move up to the ski lodge for the winter, most of their personal goods were used for the entire town.

Both Mom and Jake had some serious misgivings about that and almost decided to keep the family separate and on their own. In hindsight, it's good we didn't. There was a group that stayed behind, and they were slaughtered when a neighboring town wanted what they had.

"You're probably right. If I know Bowski's story, so does everyone else. He's a lot like your folks. He spent years gathering supplies, preparing for the end of the world as we knew it. But he didn't have the support of his partner—his wife. According to David Paul, she thought he'd lost his mind. Got tired of shelves full of junk and how he'd keep buying more and more food and supplies instead of letting them get a new car or stuff she thought they needed. One day, she took their daughter and left."

"Ah . . ." I nod, remembering him telling me Mr. Harrington was the principal at his daughter's elementary school. When I mentioned I didn't know he had a daughter, he didn't elaborate. "Where'd they go?"

"West Coast. California, according to Lieutenant Paul. It was only a few months before the attacks. Long enough for her to divorce him and start a new life with their daughter. He said Bowski called her as soon as the planes crashed, begging her to come back to Rapid. Lieutenant Paul heard she was on her way when the freeways turned into parking lots. But . . . I don't really know."

"California." I let out a sigh. My stepdad's brother, sister-in-law, and two nieces lived in California. My grandparents kept hoping they'd show up in Bakerville. But now, almost eighteen months after the attacks began, it's unlikely. Possible, I guess. But unlikely.

Thinking so much of home makes me hope for a letter soon. I mailed one off a few days before we went to Monument Hospital for Leo to get his arms checked.

With it being full-on winter, I'm not sure if the letter has even left town. While there's still travel happening locally with the drayers and others, I'd be surprised if people are going far enough west for mail to make it to Bakerville. More than likely, it'll be spring before they receive it.

I plan to keep writing anyway. I'll mention important events in each letter. That way, if one of the envelopes goes missing or gets delayed, they'll know what I'm talking about. Even with the weather, I'm still hoping I'll hear from home soon.

So much has changed since I left. My sister Sarah, who we suspected was widowed when her husband and father-in-law went missing last fall, is now officially husbandless with the bodies being found. Husbandless for now, anyway. She and Jason Hatch plan to get married on Christmas Eve.

I wish I could be there, not only to witness the blessed event but to draw it too. With the loss of electronics, photography is now a relic. My family does have a tablet they use for photos; it was in a homemade Faraday cage in the basement when the EMP hit. But because they're strictly digital, they're stuck forever in the tablet. From those photos, I'd sketch or paint images.

The last photo I sketched was of my mom. I finished it shortly before Leo and I joined the Volunteers. I haven't drawn anything since. I didn't have it in me. Lately, I've been feeling the desire to draw but have been too busy to make it happen. Plus, I need to find supplies, which is not an easy task.

Thinking of photography reminds me of the newspaper and photographers in the Rapid City area. Getting a newspaper up and running was one of the things that set the Black Hills apart from the rest of the country. Even though it's only weekly and is just a slender report on rough-crafted paper, news is news. This, combined with the radio system, helps people feel connected.

Other industries, such as Sanford Underground Research Facility, have made the Black Hills a leader in our country's rebuilding efforts. Not that I know what's happening at the Research Facility. I only know that, with their depth underground, they were unaffected by the EMP.

"Katie? Did I lose you?"

I shake my head and snort out a laugh. "I guess you did. I was . . . thinking."

"I could tell. You had a cute little furrow between your brows."

I subconsciously massage the spot. "Terrible about the patient who tried to harm herself. Does Williams think she'll have the use of her arm?"

"Arm, yes. It's the left hand he's concerned with. There may be a loss of mobility in some of her fingers and her thumb. Thankfully, the other wrist was not deep."

"It's good Merissa found her when she did. I mean, I know cutting usually has a high survival rate, but it sounds like she was serious about it."

"Once she finally calmed down a bit after talking with Kerry, she allowed Williams to examine her and it came out she'd had other attempts. When she was younger, before she met her husband, and even once after the EMP. Once he determines she's stable, Williams is going to move her to one of the care centers. Hopefully, she can be monitored enough to prevent a reattempt."

"Is he really going to add a psychiatric school in addition to the regular med school?"

Leo lets out a low laugh. "Wouldn't surprise me. He was on the radio with someone at the main hospital talking about it. The med students will probably have more mental health training, and he might train one or two of them to be specialists. My guess is Kerry would be good at it."

After a few moments of silence, I ask, "Are you sure about Bowski? That he isn't involved? I mean, you know how things can change. What if he started off good, but not knowing about his ex-wife and daughter sent him over the edge?"

"I don't know, maybe. Lieutenant Paul says he pretty much shared everything he had. Set up soup kitchens and did lots of good."

"And everyone loves him, right? Perfect cover to . . . to get away with . . . " I throw my hands up. "With anything. See? And the guy wearing the fake beard is his *friend.* It seems a little suspicious to me."

Leo smirks. "I think instead of pursuing medicine, you may want to become a detective."

"Hardy-har-har. What a great idea. I'll start an agency . . . um, Detective at the End of the World." My face falls. "Then maybe I could solve not only the burglaries but the new terrorist attacks. People could stop dying." I straighten my back as my eyes fill with tears. "Who do you think is behind it?"

Also suddenly solemn, Leo shakes his head. "I don't think anyone knows. Other than it probably being the same group that blew up the ration centers and targeted the festival, there's little info on exactly who it is."

"Not everyone thinks they're related. The county sheriff— "

"Who both David Paul and Deputy Shaw think is an idiot."

"Williams too."

"Yep. These people *know* the guy and say he has no business being sheriff. But we're stuck with him until there's some sort of formal election."

"Which is something they're talking about, right?"

"Seems so. But nothing will move forward until spring. Maybe then they'll discuss the logistics of elections. The governor is the one pushing for it you know, insisting it's important to return to a semblance of normalcy, continuing our constitutional republic, and get out of this martial law."

"They don't call it martial law."

"Humph. If it walks like a duck . . . "

"Knock, knock." Doc Nettie pushes the door to the break room open. The other patients that were under observation were released while I was with Deputy Shaw, so we've been enjoying having the space to ourselves. Nettie looks surprisingly happy as she enters the room with Dr. Bollinger on her heels.

Leo and I both stand to greet him, but Bollinger waves a hand. "Please. Well, Leo, when I said rebreaking was one of the ways to fix a malunion, I wasn't suggesting you go out and do it."

Nettie lets out a girlish giggle.

My head swivels toward her. Girlish giggles are not a common response from my friend.

She covers her mouth and looks at her shoes, redness creeping up her neck.

Bollinger puts his hand on the small of her back. The gesture seems a lot friendlier than physician colleagues.

Leo seems oblivious to their interaction. "Believe me, Doctor, it wasn't my choice."

Catching a rolling stool with his toe, Bollinger slides it to where Leo's sitting on the recliner. "Well, let's take a look." He tests Leo's fingertips for circulation and looks over the splint. "Well done. This your work, Nettie?"

She clears her throat. "Chastity."

The doctor's face splits into a wide grin. "Oh, yes. Spoke with Ms. Morrow earlier. She's a good addition to your little hospital."

A muttering noise escapes from Nettie. Even though the two are housemates and were friendly when Chasity used to be a visiting doctor, things are strained between them now that Dr. Morrow's here full time.

"What's that?" Bollinger looks expectantly at Nettie.

"Uh, yes. Dr. Morrow is a welcome addition. Especially with Captain Williams needing a few days off."

Bollinger clicks his tongue. "Too bad. I was planning to visit your medical school to see how it's working out. I admire the captain for taking this on. It's something we all know is needed but none of us had the gumption to go for it. Leave it to Chris. He's always been a go-getter." Bollinger returns his attention to Leo. "You taught a day or two?"

Leo scoffs. "Barely. It's been a little crazy here." My husband gives a brief overview of the food poisoning and how it took up a full day as we tracked down everyone we thought might be affected.

He also mentions how it was fast-acting and, while we don't know exactly the source or specific toxin, we're glad it was limited to only those at the party. Unfortunately, not knowing the cause means it could happen again.

"Heard about that. Glad it wasn't something more widespread. We had the flu go through Rapid last winter. It was bad." Bollinger pokes at Leo for another minute. "Let's take you into an exam room, get this brace off, and see exactly what we're dealing with. Since I'm here, I think I'll still take a gander at the classroom and maybe meet some of the students."

"Merissa Weaver and Geoff Landers are both working today," Nettie says. "I'm sure they'd be happy to answer any questions."

I suppress a smile. I'm sure Geoff will be more than happy to talk Bollinger's ear off. Merissa . . . not so much.

The four of us move from the break room to one of the open exam rooms. Between last night and this morning, the exam rooms have been cleared of patients and the halls have been emptied.

The sleeping rooms are still occupied, giving us a full house for our limited staff, but it's getting better. Many of the patients have been moved to long-term care facilities, leaving them overloaded and short-staffed. It's truly a mess.

"Dr. Bollinger, great to see you." Dr. Morrow steps out of one of the patient rooms.

"Chastity! I thought you were off shift." Bollinger pulls her into an embrace.

I catch a glimpse of Nettie as her shoulders slump. She quickly recovers and plasters a serene smile on her face.

"Oh, I am. Just popped in to check on someone." She bats her eyelashes. "And to see you, of course. It's been too long."

"Mm-hmm. It has."

"Doctor?" Nettie takes a step toward the pair, who are still standing much too close to each other. "Shall we get Leo taken care of?"

"Indeed." Bollinger nods, his eyes still on Chastity. "Nice work on the splint. Care to join us for the unveiling?"

In the exam room, the tension between Chastity and Nettie is evident. When Chastity moves to assist, Nettie shoots her a look. "You're off duty. Act like it."

Bollinger appears to ignore the snipe, but I have a sneaking suspicion he not only heard it but enjoyed it. There's definitely something going on between these three doctors.

When Leo first broke his arms back in September, Williams suggested a consultation with Bollinger at one of the early appointments. The late Dr. Eugene Newsome thought they were simple breaks and would heal fine. But even then, the captain suspected something more.

Nettie seemed excited about the prospect of Bollinger coming to our hospital. But Williams wanted Leo to go to Bollinger, saying they were better set up for orthopedics there.

Before the EMP, Nettie was doing a special med school rotation with a doctor who worked at the Monument Hospital. I guess that's how she came to know Bollinger. Chastity was also at Monument Hospital and, up until recently, was there at least part of the time as a rotating doctor, bouncing from hospital to hospital to help lighten the load of the on-staff doctors.

I ponder the interaction between the three as Leo's wrist is unwrapped.

Bollinger makes his now-familiar tongue-clicking sound. "Yep. Looks like quite the break." He puffs out a sigh. "If the world was back to normal, we'd probably be looking at surgery and hardware. Of course, without x-rays . . . " He shakes his head. "Plus, opening up anyone is the last thing we want to do. Nettie, what do you think?"

Nettie steps a little closer. She chews on her top lip for several beats. "External fixation?"

Chastity lets out a laugh. "No. Bad idea."

Bollinger leans back and sends Nettie a look of pride. "External fixation. Well done, Dr. Wolff. Exactly what I was thinking."

Chapter 22

I lean my head against the back of the couch and let out a breath. Gerry moves against my ankle.

Leo drops a hand on my thigh. "Is the tea okay?"

"Mm-hmm. Fine. I'm just . . . " I shake my head. "It's all catching up with me."

"Let's get you a good night's sleep. You're on at 0600 tomorrow, right?"

I straighten myself and rebalance the mug that's been doing little more than warming my hands. "How's your wrist?"

"Hurts some. Not terrible."

"Have you ever seen an external fixation, um, cast?"

"Not in real life. Just the images and sketches in medical books. I may look a little robotic." He waggles his eyebrows at me. "I guess we'll know in a few days."

I shake my head at Leo's quip. I've seen the same sketches of external fixation. Hippocrates, who systemized medicine and gave us the Hippocratic oath, among many other things, used wooden rods along the outside of the leg to immobilize fractures.

While external fixation devices have changed drastically in the time since Hippocrates, Bollinger says the principle is much the same. It's similar to internal fixation, where surgery is performed and hardware such as screws, plates, or pins are used to hold the bones together.

The big difference is this doesn't require opening Leo up. There's less chance of infection, and the fixation device is only left in place while he heals.

Bollinger sent us home with Leo's arm put back in a splint. He said he wants to give it forty-eight hours for the swelling to reduce. He's used external fixation a few times since the EMP and has found waiting a few days gives the best results. Plus, it'll give time for the hospital to empty out a bit after the mass casualty from the explosion.

Leo's surgery will take a few hours, and he'll stay overnight. Bollinger will use a local plus, as he put it, something to help Leo relax before drilling holes into undamaged portions of the arm above the fracture and in the hand bones.

He'll install bolts into the holes. The bolts connect to rods, which attach to some sort of metal frame that will circle his arm. Robotic is right!

But the risk of infection is much lower than full-on surgery. The first few days will require extra monitoring. For the duration of the time he's in the device, we'll need to clean the pins and check the puncture wounds. What neither Leo nor I are talking about is Bollinger's statement of another three months of healing.

It's already been over two months since he fell off the horse. Two difficult months. Will Leo go back into the depression he's finally coming out of?

Leo leans forward on the couch to rub Gerry behind the ears. "Bollinger seems pretty excited about our med school."

"Part of me thinks he's putting off your arm so he can come back and see the school in action."

"That's a definite possibility. Plus, he said he didn't think to bring a device with him."

"You believe him?"

Gerry whines and moves closer to us. Leo spends several moments telling him what a good dog he is, his voice rising a few octaves.

After loving on our dog, he says, "I have no reason not to believe him. It's plausible he wouldn't bring something like that with him. I'm grateful, with everything happening at all our hospitals, he took the time to come see me. You heard him say he's on-call tonight? Said he'd nap on the drive back. Although, how he's going to nap in a wagon, I don't know."

I take a sip of my lukewarm tea. "What do you think is going on with him and Nettie? And Chastity too, I guess."

Leo stops petting Gerry and sits up. Gerry lifts a paw and rubs it against my leg. I run my foot along his back.

Leo tilts his head at me. "What's going on with him and Nettie, um, or Chastity?"

I snort out a laugh and shake my head. "You didn't see it?"

"I . . . " He lifts his unsplinted hand. "No. Was I supposed to see something?"

I giggle. Where Nettie doesn't giggle, it's a normal reaction from me. But the sound still reminds me of Nettie and how she almost seemed to be someone else around Bollinger. She was still her usual competent self, but there was something else about her—something softer.

Until Chastity magically appeared. The softness immediately evaporated and was replaced with rivalry. Or maybe, more accurately, it was jealousy.

If I had to guess, Bollinger knows exactly what the issue is between the two women and is fanning those flames. He wasn't oblivious to the friction between the two like Leo is.

"Katie? Was I supposed to see something?"

I give him a smile and shake my head. "Maybe, but it's okay you didn't. I think Nettie might have a thing for Dr. Bollinger. Or at least had a thing in the past."

"Lieutenant Paul won't be happy to hear that, though it may explain a few things."

"What things?"

"You know . . . about them. Or how there isn't exactly a *them*, even though he'd like there to be."

"What do you mean? They see each other, right?"

"Yeah, some. It isn't serious, though. He wants it to be, but she keeps pulling away. If she has a thing for Bollinger—which seems odd considering he's, what, twenty years older than her? But if she does . . . well, too bad for Lieutenant Paul. What do you mean Chastity too? You think *she* likes Bollinger also?"

"Maybe."

Leo snorts and shakes his head. "What is it about the guy? The fact he's a doctor? He's not good looking, is he?"

I purse my lips and look toward the ceiling. I can't say I see the appeal of Bollinger. He's not unattractive, but his demeanor is slightly off. In some ways, he reminds me of Dr. Newsome: brash and arrogant.

The way he snapped at his nurse when Leo and I first met him told me a lot about the man. Newsome would do that, too—talk down to nurses. I'd feel about two-inches tall when he finished with me. "No, I definitely don't think he's good looking."

After taking Gerry out to the backyard for a few minutes, I tell Leo I'm ready for bed. "Do you need something for the pain?"

"Took my usual herbs," he answers. "Those along with the lavender tea should be enough. The new break doesn't hurt much. In fact, it may even feel a little better than it did. Strange, huh?"

I scrunch up my face. "The malunion was bothering you that much?"

"I don't know. I guess. You know, I just sort of got used to the pain. Well, not exactly pain, more like discomfort. Bollinger may be right. Breaking it again was the best thing I could've done." He tilts his head and shrugs, which reminds me we need to check the abrasion.

"How's your sore?" I point to his shoulder.

He dips his head. "Nettie checked it this morning while you were doing the lineup. I must have hit it last night and not realized it. The scab opened up, and the bandage was soaked."

I draw in a sharp breath. "We . . . I . . . " I shake my head. "I didn't even think it may have been reinjured too."

"Neither did I. It wasn't hurting. Still isn't. She cleaned it up again. We'll keep an eye on it. I'm sure it's nothing."

I step closer to him. "You're sure?"

He stares at me, a twinkle in his eye. "With the best nurse in Rapid City? I'll be fine."

I furrow my brow. "Nettie's a doctor."

He scoffs and laughs. "I meant you. *You, Katie.*" He steps closer to me. "What am I going to do with you?"

"Love me forever?" I step into his embrace.

"No doubt." He drops a kiss on the top of my head. Gerry waddles his little dog legs, wrapping himself around our ankles. Leo lets out a light chuckle. "Yes, Gerry. I love you too."

Chapter 23

"Well, Leo. How're you feeling?" Dr. Bollinger's face is super close to Leo's as he works to bring him around from the mild sedative. "Everything went fine. You're in the recovery room. I'll speak with your wife about how to care for the device. When you're more awake, we'll talk."

Leo mumbles something unintelligible. He takes a deep breath and his eyes pop open. "Katie?" His eyes go wide as he turns his head. "Katie? Where are you?" There's a tremble in his voice as he searches for me.

I step next to the bed. "I'm here, Leo. Right here."

"The shooting. Uh . . . explosion. You're okay?"

I look at Bollinger, who lifts a shoulder. "The meds could be causing confusion. It happens."

I touch Leo's arm. "I'm fine. We're both fine. We weren't injured. Just some bumps and bruises. You're— " I feel the sting of tears in my nose and eyes. I clear my throat. "You're getting your arm fixed up. Remember?"

"The hospital . . . "

"Yes, we're here. Dr. Bollinger finished putting the external fixator in place. You *do* look very robotic." I let out a nervous laugh.

"The hospital's intact? There isn't— " He lets out a breath and closes his eyes. "A dream?" He says something else, but the words are soft and I don't catch them.

"You're fine, honey. We're fine. Everything is okay." I look toward Bollinger, questions covering my face.

Chastity stands next to him, looking like she thinks she's the queen of the hospital. "Probably the meds. Right, Justin?"

My eyebrows shoot up at not only the use of Bollinger's first name but the soft way she says it. All kind of breathy and . . . romantic.

Either Bollinger doesn't notice or chooses not to react. He's businesslike as always. "Most likely a dream enhanced by the medication. The local will wear off soon. We'll make sure he has some proper pain relievers for the next day or two. After that, he should be fine with the herbal preparations from . . . what's her name?"

"Stella Swenson." Chastity and I say in unison.

"Right, right. Good idea for Williams to put her through the medical school. We have a few herbalist people who work at our hospital too. Don't know what we'd do without them. They work closely with the pharmacists, and . . . well, I'm sure it's the same here."

"It really is." Chastity practically gushes. "When I was a traveling doctor, I saw how each of the satellite hospitals operated compared with the main hospital. The ones where the doctors embraced herbalists, and especially wildcrafters, had a more successful program."

"There are hospitals without herbalists helping?" I ask as I use a damp cloth to wipe Leo's face. There's a sheen of sweat on his top lip. He doesn't feel hot, but I'll check his temp along with the rest of his vitals.

"Sure," Chastity continues. "When Dr. Newsome had his practice in Black Canyon, before the town burned down, he refused help from anyone without proper medical training."

I pull my lips in tight to avoid responding. This is no surprise to me. Dr. Newsome made it clear I had no place in this hospital since my training was all on the job.

"He's not the only one." Chastity bobs her head up and down. "The Canyon Lake District, they're pretty strict too."

"Canyon Lake? Really?" When she nods again, I shake my head.

My friend Opal Maher lives in the Canyon Lake District. She makes a point of always coming to our hospital, even though it takes some time to get here by horse and wagon.

That's how Merissa Weaver ended up working here—she arrived as a patient. Opal always told me it was because their hospital had so little staff and they couldn't handle anything more than a true emergency. Now I wonder if there's more to it.

I know Opal is a fan of natural medicine. She was part of the hunting party we were on when Leo fell in September. She had several different potions and treatments she suggested, and offered, in the days following Leo's injury. Opal does help at the hospital in her district. Merissa even said she was there the night of the ration center explosions, manning the radio.

"Now, Chastity," Bollinger scolds. "They're doing fine there. Dr. Lawrence runs a tight ship. He may not be as open-minded as some of the district's lead doctors." Bollinger motions his hand to indicate our hospital. "But he's a good man. Solid. Reminds me a lot of Williams."

Chastity scoffs. "In what way?"

"Well . . . he's a teacher, and he'll work himself into the ground. Same as Williams."

I don't know Dr. Lawrence, but Captain Williams, whose toe is still not fully healed, is restarting the med school tomorrow. Even with Leo out of commission for a few days and Williams in a walking boot, he's adamant we need trained doctors.

They'll only put in a few hours of schoolwork for the remainder of the week while working in the hospital and care centers. Secretly, I think part of the reason he's ramping the school back up is Bollinger. He's staying overnight at Williams's place so he can observe the school tomorrow.

"I'll agree Williams should be taking several more days off to allow his foot to heal. But with you here . . . " Chastity gives Bollinger an award-winning smile.

"Yes. Yes. I'm sure— "

Bollinger's words are interrupted by the ring of the front doorbell. Even though my husband is having surgery, I'm also the nurse on shift.

When the bell rings a second time, Chastity says, "I'll go check things out." The backdoor ringer goes off a fraction of a second later. "Uh-oh." She strides quickly to the exam room door when it pops open.

"We've got trouble." Jesse motions to the hallway.

The squelch of his handheld radio sounds. The voice comes through crackly and urgently. "Now the main hospital's hit. Lock down your buildings. Lock them down now!"

"What's this?" Bollinger practically bellows.

Leo mutters and squirms in his bed.

"Stay still, honey."

My husband's eyes pop open. "Explosions. Gunfire. Stay safe."

"Katie, stay with Leo. We'll be right back," Chastity says as they all leave the recovery room.

My upper lip starts to sweat as I glance toward my husband.

He's staring at me. "How'd the surgery go?" His voice is calm and normal.

"Um, good. Bollinger's happy." Heavy boots run down the hall past the doorway. He wrinkles his nose. "What's going on?"

"I'm not entirely sure. I think . . . we may be under attack." My voice cracks on the last word.

"Lock the doors. Get out your pistol. Where's my stuff?"

I blink several times.

"Katie. Lock. The. Door."

Coming out of my stupor, I rush to lock the door connecting this room to the surgical suite, then latch the door to the hallway. Why didn't I think of this? Because I was too focused on my husband.

I tighten my lips and slide my handgun out of the bellyband. When I turn, Leo's sitting on the edge of the gurney. "You need to stay put," I command.

More boots pound down the hallway. He lifts his chin in that direction. "Not if we're under attack. My things?"

"Your room, remember? We're still in recovery."

He lets out a sigh of disgust. "The room gun?"

He starts to lift himself from the gurney, but I lift a hand. "Stay put. I'll help you."

"Move the chair to the corner. Slide the toolbox in front of it."

The toolbox is a giant metal box on wheels that holds a variety of medical supplies. We keep one in each room, giving us everything we need to treat anything that may come up. It'll also be helpful as cover from gunfire.

I quickly have the room rearranged and help Leo from the bed to the chair.

He grimaces. "I'll take your pistol. You grab the emergency gun."

Because of the world we live in, not only does the hospital staff carry sidearms, but each room also—except the operating suite—has a hidden gun under lock and key. The truth is the gun wouldn't be much help in a true emergency. Needing to get the key before unlocking the gun takes time. But with enough warning, like now, it's good to have it.

I check the weapon, a .357 Magnum revolver, showing Leo it's loaded with five rounds. There's no additional ammo. Leo tells me he'll take that instead of my semi-auto. I place it on his right thigh. He's in the chair, and I'm sitting on the floor. The toolbox provides a barrier, but we also both want a clear view of the door.

With Leo just coming out of sedation, I'm not sure this is a good idea at all. His fresh-out-of-surgery arm is in a tight sling secured to his torso, but could the jostling be a problem?

My accelerated breathing is the only sound in the room. Even the boots crashing up and down the hallway have stopped. Leo's still in his chair, his eyes closed. Sleeping? I move my hand toward his neck to check his pulse.

My hand is partway there when he opens one eye. "I'm fine."

I pull my hand back. "What do you think is happening out there?"

"Not sure. Locking down the building."

"Why didn't they come back and tell us what to do?"

"Probably figured we'd know from the drills."

I suck in my upper lip. We've had lockdown drills before, and we were reminded of them after the explosion at the ration centers. But my mind has been elsewhere. With Leo getting hurt again, he's been my focus.

It's another ten minutes or so before there's a knock on the connecting door. "Katie?" Jesse calls out. "We're clear."

I scurry over to unlock the door.

Jesse steps in. He surveys the room before waggling his eyebrows at us. "I figured as much. Better get Leo back in bed before Bollinger sees him. They want him in his room."

"What happened?" Leo's voice is strong, with no trace of the sedative.

"They hit the hospitals."

I swallow the lump that's immediately forming in my throat. "Which ones?"

"Canyon Lake District followed by Monument."

"Canyon Lake?" I ask, thinking of Opal Maher and wondering if she was helping at the hospital today.

"Where else?" Leo asks.

Jesse's lips go into a tight line. "They were here. The sentries stopped them . . . after a scuffle."

I help Leo out of the chair. "Injuries?"

"Yeah. The assailants are DOA. Josiah was one of the sentries. He caught a knife to the bicep. Chastity has him in the exam room. It's not too bad, but she wants your help once we get Leo situated." Jesse helps Leo into a wheelchair.

"Thanks, friend." Leo puffs out his breath. "Any clues as to who's doing this?"

"I think maybe. Seemed Josiah might know something more than he's able to say at the moment."

I look at Leo, who gives a lift of his eyebrows. Glancing at Jesse, I shake my head. "Meaning what?"

He shrugs his entire body. "Not sure. They didn't bring the dead inside. Didn't even have any of us go and check them. Didn't need us to confirm the deaths."

"Okay . . . and?"

He stops all movement. "I think they knew the guys."

Chapter 24

The whispers between the husband and wife who are also in Leo's hospital room wake me. I keep my eyes closed for several minutes, hoping I can get a little more sleep. I'm on the 0600 to 1800 hours shift again today.

I take out my tiny flashlight and shine it on my windup watch—a gift from my mom and a total blessing in today's timeless world. Not even 0330. I reposition to try and get a little more sleep.

Yesterday, working while worrying about Leo wasn't easy. Add in the attempted attack on the hospital and my adrenals were overloaded. I would've loved nothing more than to go back to my little house, sit in front of the fire, and cuddle my dog with my husband by my side.

Even though I know Gerry's fine with the Harringtons, I've been wondering how fair it is to him that we've been around so little lately. For two months, Leo was there daily. Not only Leo but Gerry had his three littermates with him too.

When I went and picked up Gerry from Shaw's house, he and Tank were nestled together by the woodstove. Shaw's wife said they'd just come in from outside where they'd been rolling and tumbling in the snow.

Would Gerry be better off in a home with a second dog? Or maybe full time with the Harringtons, where Henry and his little sister can give him extra love?

My heart pinches at the thought of not having my dog. Even though he came to us under sad circumstances, he's a part of my life. *Our* lives.

The soft whispers from across the room break off. I adjust, gingerly turning over on my skinny cot, and settle back in. Soon, the noises resume. But this time, instead of whispers, it's faint crying from the wife.

The husband was injured in the explosion. She was also at the ration center and brought in for treatment, but her injuries were minor enough for her to be released. He'd fallen and injured his ribs and back—much like baby Johnny's mom—so we've kept him for observation.

Today, the doctors will decide if he should go to the long-term care facility for a few days or if they can release him to go home. The wife, like me, worked her regular crew shift before arriving at the hospital to sleep near her husband.

I've about drifted off when the crying increases. I look toward Leo's bed as the man across the room makes a shushing noise. "It's okay, honey. I'm sure someone's already making plans."

"How? It wasn't just us. All the DCs were destroyed. I think the same things were probably kept at each."

"You don't know. They might keep clothes at ours but maybe they keep, I don't know, shampoo at the others."

"Shampoo? Really? There's no shampoo now. Just that awful soap that doesn't even work right since they don't know how to make lye properly."

I almost laughed out loud. She's not wrong. Though we do have a soapmaking crew, it isn't what it should be. Some batches are more oil than soap and end up in small jars instead of bars.

The lye, a necessary component to chemically change the oils into soap, is hit or miss. There are still a few commercial bars of soap floating around, but they're getting harder and harder to find.

Lye is made from the white ash leftover after a hardwood fire. While there are a few hardwoods in the area, the bulk of wood in the Black Hills is soft, with Ponderosa Pine being the predominant species.

The hardwoods are found mainly in towns, either as furniture or planted as decorative trees. Many trees were cut down in the first winter and burned green by people who either didn't know any better or were too cold to care. Furniture was also burned, leaving us with little hardwood.

While it's true Bowski did help with the survival numbers during the first winter, there were still a staggering number of deaths. Many were from hypothermia. When the president started broadcasting again in February, that seemed to be the incentive needed to have others organize and join Bowski.

The way I hear it, up until then, even the newly appointed sheriff, Melvin Cabal, who Captain Williams referred to as a fool, pretty much sat around on his hands.

"We'll be fine, honey," the injured man, Jack, continues. "We'll find you some new clothes that fit, and we'll figure out something before the baby comes. I'm sure there were times in history when women were in the same situation."

The wife lets out a ragged breath. "That doesn't make me feel much better. And you know what, it might not even matter. You heard what they said." She starts crying harder.

I close my eyes as I remember the craziness of treating people in the hours after the explosion. I was treating someone in the waiting room. Merissa was next to me, stitching up a forehead cut by a flying piece of glass.

The lady was crying and asking when she could see her husband. Merissa told her soon. Then she said something about being pregnant and the doctor who'd first examined her said they'd need to wait and see. The woman wanted to know what that meant.

Merissa calmly told her to let someone know if she started having any cramping or bleeding. The woman cried harder. Listening to her cry now, I'm sure this is the same woman. And I do remember a bandage across her forehead when I said hello to her last night.

The memory of Elizabeth and her born-too-soon little girl floods my mind. Before the EMP, the United States had about fifteen maternal deaths per 100,000 live births. That seems like a lot for the way medicine was. In the 1800s, it was about 600 deaths per the same number of live births. In the 1600s and 1700s, double the number of deaths.

I don't think anyone is able to keep an accurate database now, but I've heard Williams and Nettie talk about the maternal death rate rivaling the seventeenth century.

Even with our knowledge of hygiene, the lack thereof thought to be a major contributor to maternal and infant fatalities, nutrition and healthcare are lacking. Although we have a functioning hospital and several people are practicing as midwives, unexplainably, many women are not seeking medical care.

Before the explosion, I'd never seen this woman in our hospital. And until the day Elizabeth was brought in bleeding uncontrollably, I'd never seen her either. Her husband said she was seeing a midwife, but I never found out who it was.

Newsome said he was going to search for the midwife and have her, along with me, prosecuted for murder. Newsome was killed later the same day as an act of revenge for the terrible things he'd done before moving to the Guard District. As far as I know, he didn't find the midwife he believed to be responsible.

As the woman's cries fade away, I drift off to sleep, making a mental note to spend a few minutes with her in the morning. I want to at least find out her work assignments and make sure she's seeing someone for her healthcare. And find out who that someone is.

When I wake again, Leo's sitting on the edge of his bed.

The woman's standing near her husband's bedside, dressed and obviously preparing to leave. "Maybe they'll let you come home today." She gives him a watery smile.

"Take care at work today. Don't be overdoing it." He grasps her hand. "I know you're tired."

"Don't worry about me, just . . . just get yourself well."

I slide off my cot, my bare feet hitting the cold tile floor. Leo wishes me good morning and gives me a loving smile.

I move to his side and plant a kiss on his cheek. "How's it feel?"

"Not bad. Clunky. *Bionic.*" He gives me a mischievous grin. "But okay."

"Give me a minute. I'll be right back." I slide into my work shoes and gather up my clothes to move to a private room to dress. The woman is still by her husband's side, seemingly delaying her exit.

As I approach their side of the room, near the door, I give her a wave. "Workday for you too?"

"Every day." She sighs.

"Seems that way, doesn't it? What do you do?"

"I'm at the water plant."

"Down Sheridan Lake Road?"

"I am now. I was at the auxiliary site, but they moved me."

I look over her attire. Heavy coat, thick boots, gloves, and a stocking cap. Well suited for outdoor work. "Do you, um . . . I heard you talking with Merissa the night of the explosion. Do you need an appointment with the doctor?"

She glances at her husband, then looks back at me and lifts a shoulder. "I'm seeing a midwife. I don't want to clog up the hospital, you know, so the truly sick people can be seen."

I crinkle my brow. "We don't ask that."

Husband and wife exchange glances. He's the one who responds. "There was a community meeting. Several, in fact. When the hospital was first set up last fall, they asked us to try and limit our visits to emergencies only."

"That's right." The woman bobs her head. "Then, when they got everything in place, they set up a clinic one day a week for issues. But by then, we were all so used to taking care of ourselves, and it seemed almost like a burden to come here. We have a woman in our neighborhood who helps with things. She knows about plants and different natural medicines. Delivers babies." The woman's hand goes to her stomach.

"Stella Swenson? She's part of our medical school now."

The woman furrows her brow. "No, not her. I don't know her. Anyway, I need to get to work."

"Please." I drop my hand on her arm. "Dr. Wolff would be happy to see you. Maybe after work today?"

"Maybe. If Jack's still here." She looks at her husband. "We're hoping he'll be able to go home today. Better rest there than here. No roommates." She waves a hand at my husband. "No offense."

"None taken," Leo says. "I'm looking forward to going home myself."

A few hours later, Leo gets his wish. Bollinger checks him over and says he's pleased with how everything looks. He wants Leo to take it easy for a few more days before returning to his teaching duties.

"Would it be possible to go over to the school and sit in on classes, as long as I don't do anything but sit?" Leo asks.

Bollinger agrees, and they walk over together so the doctor can observe.

It's Nettie, Jesse, and me on shift, with Rand Hendricks working as a janitor. Jack, the man who Leo shared a room with, is also released. Nettie asks Rand if he'll take him home and get him situated since the wife is at work.

Rand's happy to do it and says he'll make sure to get a fire going and ensure Jack has everything he'll need until the wife gets home.

"Make sure your wife comes to see us," I say to Jack. "She doesn't need to wait until clinic day. There's always a doctor on duty. If we're in the middle of an emergency, she can wait or come back later."

Jack agrees he will. After he and Rand leave, Nettie asks me what that was about. I tell her, including how the couple thought they weren't supposed to visit the hospital except for emergencies.

"That's our fault. We did put that out when we were trying to get things set up. But we made another announcement after we felt we had a handle on the hospital. We should've done more." Nettie gives a sad shake of her head.

"I know one of the things Williams is hoping for, once we get the new people trained, is a second clinic to replace our Tuesday clinic. He wants to set up a few rooms in the school like a doctor's office, operating more than one day per week. Then women like Jack's wife will come in for proper prenatal care."

"Do you think the midwife is giving proper care?"

"Oh, I'm sure she is. But . . . " Nettie bites her bottom lip. "If it's who I think it is, she's not a trained midwife."

"They said she's an herbalist."

"She isn't trained in that either. She didn't even know about herbs until after the EMP. She has some book knowledge, but she isn't like Stella, who's been honing her craft and wildcrafting for years. Williams actually interviewed the one I think it is, hoping we could put her in the school too. She . . . um . . . no." Nettie shakes her head.

"No?"

"Definitely a no. You heard she charges her patients?"

I shrug. Charging for extra things happens, even though it's considered on par with trading on the black market. There's a level of altruism during this rebuilding phase. With the ration chips, we're supposed to receive what we need to get by in exchange for the work we do.

I'll admit, like Jack's wife, I'm a little concerned about the goods lost in the explosion. While there isn't anything I desperately need, I was planning to use a few nonfood ration chips for a new blanket and a pair of mittens. But the explosion destroyed blankets, clothes, boots, shoes, and other personal and household goods.

Of course, those items pale in comparison to the loss of life—hundreds across all districts—plus another dozen killed in yesterday's hospital attacks.

Bollinger thought he'd need to go straight back but was told to stay here as planned. The attack on the main hospital was limited to the waiting room. While there were some injuries and fatalities, they were handling things.

At the chime of the back doorbell, I lean to my left to see who's entering. I lift a hand in greeting when I see Chastity.

Nettie puts her hands on her hips and huffs out a breath. "What are you doing here?"

"Wouldn't you like to know."

My gaze shifts between the housemates. Nettie straightens her shoulders. She motions to the thermos cradled under Chastity's arm. "He's not here. Besides, this hospital is no place for your pathetic attempts to woo him."

Chastity clicks her tongue. "You're the pathetic one, thinking he came here to see you. You aren't the kind of woman he wants, the kind he *needs*."

Nettie advances several feet, standing toe to toe with the much taller woman. Even with Chastity over half a foot taller, Nettie doesn't appear to be the smaller of the two.

Chastity takes a step back.

Nettie smirks. "And you think *you* are?"

"Hardly." Chastity gives a coarse laugh. "I'm in it for the fun. If you had a brain in your head, you'd realize you had fun while it lasted and now it's over. Go on to the little soldier boy making googly eyes at you if you want something long term. Bollinger is way out of your league."

Nettie takes another step toward Chastity, her hands clenched in fists.

Chapter 25

Merissa

"You're looking good, Merissa," Opal says with a knowing nod. "More color in your cheeks. How are you holding up with all the work?"

"It was a rough few days." I let out a breath. "Uh, for you too."

"It was at that. First, the distribution center explosion and now our hospital. So many dead. The hospital could've been much worse."

"How many'd you lose?" Mother Pearl asks.

Opal gives a sad shake of her head. "A nurse, support staff, and three patients."

"And the building?"

"Destroyed. We've found a new house to set up. It'll take a few days to get everythin' together."

"How often are you working at the hospital?" I lift the teakettle and motion to her cup.

She gestures for me to pour. "When they need an extra body. There's more than enough to do at the ranch, but I can't say no. With the deaths, I'll probably be there a few times a week. Everyone's excited about your med school. Especially since the captain's gonna do a nursing school too."

"I don't think that's a sure thing. I think he's going to get us through the course first before doing anything new."

Opal dunks her tea bag—a homemade muslin bag filled with dried mint from her garden—up and down in her cup. I shift my gaze toward Pearl, who's gently swirling her bag. Mine is sitting in the cup as I allow it to steep.

Opal sighs. "I sure hope it's sooner than that. I heard he's startin' the nurses in the spring."

I shake my head. "I don't know, maybe. I mean, if you think about it, it makes more sense to start with the nurses than the doctors anyway. He could've had them trained and working within six months, a year maybe. For us, it's going to take much longer."

A nursing program may be the better choice for me. I could get it done and have only one thing to focus on: going to work. Not trying to go to work and school at the same time while having a newborn. Or a toddler. Williams estimates we won't be full-fledged Doctors of the Apocalypse for about two years.

Doctors of the Apocalypse is the working name for our school. When we complete the program, we won't be actual MDs or have any designation from before the EMP. We'll be referred to as doctors and have some sort of certificate, but should the world return to normal, we'd never be offered legit positions.

Not that anyone expects our world to get back to the way it was any time soon. Probably not even in my lifetime. Definitely not in Pearl's or Opal's. Maybe some of the younger students, like Geoff Landers, should he finish the course, will have to deal with figuring out if he's a real doctor in a normal world.

"Well, I sure hope the rumors are true. We need more medical personnel. We need more farmers, ranchers, woodcutters, water collectors . . . all of it. It takes work to stay alive."

"I've been thinking I need to do more." Pearl doesn't look up from her mug as she talks. "I've been sewing, boiling water, and other duties reserved for people of my age. But I'd like to do something else."

Hiding the surprise on my face, I ask Pearl what she's thinking. As part of our rations, we're required to work. But with her age and mobility issues, Pearl is limited in what she can do. Like many of the elderly, people will drop things off for her to work on.

She's a member of the water crew, with several gallons dropped off daily. She boils them on our woodstove and returns them in the clean jugs they provide. The jugs that held the potentially dirty, contaminated water are returned empty, and the process is repeated the following day.

A few times a week, someone brings mending for her to work on. Sewing isn't Pearl's strong point, having done little of it throughout her life, but she's still able to do the simple things.

"One of the water ladies said her child goes to a daycare down the street. She said they're always needing people to help."

Opal shoots me a look—one I can't quite decipher and choose to ignore. "You think so, Mother Pearl? That might be a lot of work."

"They're babies. I could hold them, change diapers, give them bottles. Where do you think they're getting formula?"

Shrugging, Opal says, "Pretty much everyone's breastfeeding. Even the moms who are workin' keep it up as best they can. They'll stop in during the day to nurse, or they express milk. There're also some homemade formulas people are using. Not just giving them cow or goat milk but extra cream and even liver or egg yolk. I've heard about it but don't know the actual recipe. They're starting babies on egg yolk, pureed liver, and other nutrient-dense foods when they can sit up."

I'm sure I make a face.

Opal laughs. "I know. It sounds so contrary to how we used to feed babies. Stella Swenson has several books on how babies were fed in traditional societies—before the advent of baby formula and rice cereal. She convinced Captain Williams, who convinced the general and the district council. You haven't heard about this?"

"Not yet."

"Hmm. I suspect you will. I'm sure Captain Williams plans to cover nutrition in your classes."

"I suspect so. Right now, we're mainly covering trauma care. It seems the most necessary with our situation."

"I guess. But feeding our babies, plus the expectant mothers, is also important."

She doesn't say anything more, but the implication is there. I have little doubt she suspects I'm pregnant. I do appreciate her keeping it to herself until I can tell Pearl.

I've decided to wait until after the new year to tell her. By then, it'll be hard to hide, so I won't have a choice in the matter. It'll still be a couple of months before the baby can be born and possibly survive. A couple of months of handwringing worry on Pearl's part, I'm sure. Not that I'm not doing my own handwringing at times.

"So, what do you think?" Pearl asks, looking between Opal and me.

"It sounds like a good idea," Opal says. "Somethin' to keep ya busy and help the community. Do you know who to talk to?"

"Thought I'd stop by the daycare, see if they have a need. You know, after I return from the Thanksgiving weekend." Pearl looks at me. After we're done visiting, Pearl's leaving with Opal for Thanksgiving. I'm working all weekend, so I'll stay home.

I nod at my mother-in-law. "I'm sure that'll be fine. They may be doing their own Thanksgiving stuff, so waiting until you get back won't hurt a thing."

"I'll need to register with the ration office . . . once they have that sorted out. Have you heard where they're going to put it?"

"Still on Main Street, in a former restaurant," Opal says. "They should be opening up next week. They've got the staff in place, just finishing up the training. I guess all the refugees we got last summer have come in handy with findin' workers. Not that we have anywhere near enough, especially if they keep dying." Opal takes a sip of her tea.

"I do hope they find the people responsible and put a stop to this. Everyone's a nervous wreck. It is a help they found the robbers who killed Mr. Harrington. People were right on edge about those break-ins too. Poor Leo Burnett, getting his arm broken again." Opal shakes her head.

"That may have been a good thing," I say. "It didn't heal right the first time. They brought in an orthopedist, who did a less-invasive surgical procedure on it. He'll still be out several months longer, but this time, he may have full use of his arm by the time it heals."

I don't mention how I wish I could've observed the surgery. Captain Williams asked for permission for the students to watch, but Dr. Bollinger declined, saying it's not something we'd need to learn. I'm sure Williams disagreed, but he didn't argue.

I'll admit, I don't think much of Bollinger. He's pompous and argumentative. He seems to go out of his way to cause division and appears to be causing a rift between Doctors Wolff and Morrow. So much so, Dr. Morrow moved out of their shared house and into her own place. Not that I think it's a bad thing.

Chastity Morrow and Nettie Wolff aren't likely friends. While both are good doctors, their personalities are quite different. Chastity is bubbly and friendly, while Nettie is quiet and reserved. I'll admit to feeling more comfortable around Nettie.

Chastity is a lot like nurse Jacquie Haley, always going on about something and wanting me to participate in the conversation. When I don't have anything to offer, they take it as a personal affront and think I'm snubbing them.

I will say, Chastity's vivaciousness has seemed a little different lately. I can't say exactly what it is, but something's off. Maybe with the troublemaking Dr. Bollinger now back at the main hospital and her getting settled into her own place, she'll return to the way she was.

While it was sometimes exhausting to work with her, it was better than this weird way she's been acting. I wish I could put my finger on what's different about her.

"Well . . . " Opal slides her chair back from the table. "I s'pose we ought to get going. It's not terribly cold today, Pearl, but you should still bundle up."

Pearl rolls her eyes before sliding her own chair back. "Give me a few minutes, and I'll be ready."

Opal asks me about my next work shift, which I share is tonight as a medic. Then tomorrow, the day before Thanksgiving, we have classes. "In fact, I need to get going. I have classes this afternoon too."

"Do you usually only have afternoon classes?"

I shake my head. "Depends on Williams's schedule. He worked overnight last night, so he took the morning off. He's on night shift tonight also."

"This opportunity is such a blessing for you. I suspect you've wondered at times if you made the right choice. Especially with Pearl living with you and being alone so much. I think the daycare is an excellent idea. She hasn't been around babies since her own were born. It'll be good to have a refresher." Opal puckers her face and wrinkles her forehead before pulling me into an unexpected hug.

"God bless you, Merissa. You've had a time of it. But I know you're going to come out stronger. God heals the brokenhearted and binds up their wounds. That's what He's doing for you." She pulls back and gives me a smile. "Which reminds me, Shawn sent something for you."

She grabs her bag off the floor, transferring it to the chair before digging around in it. "Here it is." She passes me a thick book. "He thought you probably didn't have your own Bible."

My heartbeat quickens. "I don't. Um . . . I never have. Braedon had one, but I didn't even think to bring it." I swallow the lump in my throat. "Please thank him for me."

"I will. He put a sheet of paper inside with some verses he thought you might enjoy. Ya know, to get you started. It can be overwhelming if you don't know your way around a Bible. He also wrote out a suggested reading plan. I know you have your plate full of work and school, but I think you'll enjoy getting to know our Lord better."

"Thank you. I think you may be right." I hug the Bible close to my chest as Opal pulls me into a second embrace. I fight to keep the threatening tears at bay.

Chapter 26

Katie

"This is good." Leo pauses with the soup spoon partway to his mouth. "Nice of Crystal to make this for us."

"The Harringtons are the best neighbors." I lift my chin toward the blazing woodstove. "Starting a fire and putting soup on the stove for us to come home to. *The best.* And don't worry, the soup's made from beets, potatoes, and carrots out of their garden. Not rations."

"Yep. I know they had a great beet crop. Maybe next year we can have a garden?"

I point to the wire shelves near the big front window. It holds trays and bowls of scraggly-looking lettuce and microgreens. "You mean more than my indoor gardening attempts?"

He sets down his spoon and picks up his fork, stabbing the lettuce and microgreen salad sitting sadly next to his soup bowl. The salad is nothing special, but growing indoor greens adds a little fresh produce to our diet. One of these days, I'm going to start a mason jar of sprouts.

When we left home last June, Jake gave me a few small bags of sprouting seeds and told me to save them for winter when fresh produce is sparse. In September and October, we were given a few different seed varieties, saved from summer produce, that'll work for winter sprouting or summer planting. While nightshades, such as tomatoes, peppers, and eggplant, shouldn't be sprouted, many garden varieties of saved seeds will work fine.

In addition to the mixes Jake gave me, I have broccoli, kale, mustard greens, and . . . something else I can't remember. Because sprouting takes only a small quantity of seed and grows into a wonderful number of nutritious greens, I should have enough seeds for at least a batch of each variety and still have some for planting in the garden. There's also a rumor we'll be given planting seeds as part of our rations as soon as it's gardening time.

A sinking feeling starts low in my gut. If these new terrorists want to do serious damage, they'll target our food production facilities. The crops and farms on the outside of town, though dormant and buried in snow, are desperately needed. The ranches, like Opal's, raise our cattle, chickens, pigs, and more. There are also several greenhouses, bakeries, and commercial kitchens. Not to mention the varieties of places storing food.

Seed saving was a big deal when the crops ended last year. Specialty gardens were planted in the spring, using only heirloom seeds, and kept away from other gardens that may still be using hybrid seeds, which were common before the EMP.

During harvest time, enough fresh produce was left behind—not picked—so it could go to seed. Those plants were nurtured, and when they went to seed, they were carefully saved. Or in the case of things like tomatoes and cucumbers, with seeds on the inside, the best-looking items were harvested and carefully seeded before being used for food. Making sure our food supply can continue indefinitely into the future is important.

I look at Leo. He's back to eating his soup. "Why are they doing this?"

He finishes the bite, taking only a few seconds to chew the soft root vegetables. "The terrorists?"

"Yes. It doesn't make any sense to me. We were doing okay. Everyone was working together. Even the president has said how fabulous Rapid City and the entire Black Hills area are doing. We've been called leaders in the rebuilding."

A thoughtful look crosses Leo's face.

"What is it?"

He shakes his head. "I'm not sure. But what you said reminded me of something." He shakes his head again. "Something, but I can't remember exactly what."

"Something about what?"

"That's the thing. I'm not sure. But what you said tickled my brain."

I let out a laugh. "I hate those brain tickles. You know how it'll be. You'll be drifting off to sleep and it'll hit you. Then you'll be wide awake. Which means . . . " I narrow my eyes in a fake angry look. "Which means I'll be wide awake too."

"Never. I promise, even if I remember at two in the morning, I'll let you sleep. Last shift tomorrow before two days off?"

"Well, sort of off two days. Off a full day then the next day on the night shift. For four nights. Ugh."

"So . . . Nettie and Chastity?"

"Gads. That was something. I knew they weren't getting along too great, but I thought Nettie was going to punch her. I could see her clenching and unclenching her fist. It was something."

"And Nettie told her to move out?"

"Ordered. She ordered her to move out. But Chastity said, 'I was already planning on it. I'll be gone before you get home.' Then she flounced around and started to walk off, but not before giving Nettie an earful of what she truly thought about her. She used some words that made me blush. Nettie stared at her. I didn't know what to do after that."

I lift my shoulders. "I like both of them. I've known Nettie longer, and we've been friendly, but she's . . . you know."

"Reserved?"

"Very. She's always treated me well, but it's all surface. She'll ask me about things when we talk, but if I ask her, she changes the subject. I don't even know much about her. She never talks about her family or what things were like before she came here."

"Didn't she get a letter?"

"Yeah, but that's all I know. I shared my letter with her, but we got sidetracked and I never did find out anything about her letter. Not that she'd tell me anyway. She's private about everything. Almost secretive. I didn't even know she had a thing for Bollinger until she was fluttering her eyes at him and then with what Chastity said."

"Lieutenant Paul has the same troubles. You know, with Nettie keeping her distance. He'd like to take their relationship further and make it serious, but she isn't interested. I'm not sure it's a bad thing."

I furrow my brow. "What do you mean? I thought you liked them together. You once said we could do couple things with them."

"Sure. That'd be fine. But I don't know if they're a good match. Especially with him being Christian."

"And? I think Nettie may be also. Maybe not, um, as strong as she should be. But she's made a few comments that make me think she knows God or has at least gone to church."

"Going to church— "

"I know, I know." I flutter my hand. "But really. Has he asked her if she is?"

"I'm not sure. I think he's trying to move on. Especially after finding out about her and Bollinger."

"How does he know?"

"Shaw saw them together and told Lieutenant Paul."

"Saw them how?" I lean back in my chair and shake my head. This place is such a gossip mill. "Recently?"

"Lieutenant Paul didn't go into details, just said he realized there's no future for them. I think he knew it before but was hoping for a sign or maybe a miracle. He'll be fine. And after what Bollinger did today, if he and Nettie did have a thing, I'm going to agree with Lieutenant Paul."

My eyes go wide as my brows shoot up. "What'd Bollinger do today?"

Leo chuffs out a disgusted laugh. "He may be a great doctor, but I'm not so sure he's much of a human. I think his entire purpose of wanting to observe the med school in action was to humiliate Captain Williams."

"What? I thought they were friends."

"From the look on Williams's face, I think he thought so too. He seemed . . . surprised. Hurt, maybe. Bollinger didn't even seem to care. He just kept right on going."

"Going about what?"

"That's the funny thing. Williams was answering a question from Kerry Hendricks, something about what you do if you're overwhelmed and the injured keep coming. It was in relation to the explosion and how the hospital was too busy."

"Mm-hmm. It was too busy. And overwhelming. But Kerry seemed to be handling things fine."

"Right. Williams told her that. Said he saw how she kept doing what she knew to do. Once she gets through her training, she'll know even more and her confidence level will increase. Then he said, 'And sometimes you just have to pray. Pray God will step in and fill in the knowledge you don't have. Pray for a miracle.' That's when Bollinger started laughing. A huge, loud, fake laugh."

"Yikes. Surely Bollinger knew Williams is a believer? He's never hidden it."

"That's what Williams said. He believes in God and is a Christian. That set Bollinger off, hooting and hollering. It was almost embarrassing. After he made a show of getting himself together, he told the class they're fools if they put their trust in anyone but themselves. Williams kept his cool. Said something like, 'I've lived my life trusting in the Lord. He's never let me down. I've never been silent about it either. You've long known my beliefs.'

"Then Bollinger laughed again and said, 'I thought after all that's happened you would've wised up and realized there is no God. If there was, we wouldn't be in the mess we're in.' The class was pretty much silent, but Geoff Landers was vigorously nodding. Kerry's face was red. I think she felt bad about asking and getting Bollinger going. Williams was pretty red too."

"Angry?"

"Nah. I don't think angry as much as embarrassed and bewildered. I think he was truly shocked Bollinger went at him. As Williams said, he's never hidden his belief in God. Merissa was pretty awesome, though."

"Merissa? In what way?"

Leo lets out a laugh. "She pointed to Bollinger and said, 'So since you don't think there's a Higher Power, it's okay to mock those who do?' Bollinger's face turned all shades of crimson. Not from embarrassment or bewilderment but anger. He made a point of saying he was a respected surgeon and will not accept being spoken to in such a manner."

"Yikes. How'd Merissa take that?"

"You'll never guess."

I shake my head. "With Merissa? Anything is possible."

"True. I half expected her to give an obedient *yes, sir.* Instead, she said, 'You may be a respected surgeon and an excellent doctor, but right now you're behaving like a terrible human.' Then she motioned to Williams. 'And a rotten friend.'

"Bollinger didn't have a response. Just turned to Williams and thanked him for letting him observe the class. Said he needed to get back to Monument. They awkwardly shook hands, and Bollinger left."

"Wow. What a day. Nettie and Chastity almost go to blows. Bollinger and Williams . . . well, I guess it wasn't quite the same type of argument, but still."

"Makes me wonder if Bollinger will return to check me over like he originally said or if he'll have me go to him instead." Leo motions to his arm. "He made a special trip when I rebroke my arm, and then he returned for the surgery, but he's still scheduled to be the rotating doctor in December."

"I'm sure that won't change because of what happened today. Why would it?"

"Yeah, you're probably right. Are you . . . you're okay with going to Camp Rapid for Thanksgiving dinner?"

I dip my head and grin. My smile is a little too big, but it's still genuine. Lieutenant Paul invited us to enjoy dinner with the troops, as he put it. After all, as the lone members of the Volunteer Unit, we're under the command of the South Dakota National Guard.

Even though I'm still not entirely sure I want to be a member of the National Guard, I'm happy to be invited. Plus, it'll be good to see people we know. "I don't know how long I'll want to stay. I'm on night shift."

"We'll stay only as long as you want. Just greet and eat. Sound good?"

The look he gives me causes my heart to do the crazy little flip again. "Sounds good."

Chapter 27

"Sorry we didn't have more for today."

Leo waves me off with his free hand, the other still held tight against his body in the sling. "We didn't know the Guard would cancel their Thanksgiving plans."

"Did you hear anything more about what exactly they were called to do?"

"Nothing. Williams was tight-lipped about it when he gave me the message. If the Citizen Patrol is involved, Oscar's keeping it quiet too."

"He seems to be doing great. Walking without a limp. Is he back on regular work duty?" Oscar was shot several weeks ago. Williams and Nettie performed the surgery that saved his life. As always, infection was a concern, but he's healed nicely.

"Next week, he's back on regular patrol and sentry duty. Even so, I can't imagine he and the rest of the sheriff's department or Citizen Patrol aren't fully aware of where the Guard took off to."

I lean my head back on the sofa and pet Gerry as he snuggles close to me. "I think I'm going to take a nap. Get in a few hours before work."

"Who's on with you tonight?"

I purse my lips and think about the schedule posted in the break room. "Williams, Merissa, and Kerry Hendricks."

"That makes sense. No med school until Monday, so they all have regular work shifts."

"Mm-hmm. How's your pain? Need anything?"

"Nope. Nothing. I'm good."

I glance at the robot arm. The contraption is completely awkward and unwieldy. The pins drilled into his arm have scabs around them. Keeping it clean and infection-free is one of our main goals. "What're you going to do while I nap?"

"Thought I'd fold the laundry." He motions to the rack of drying clothes. "You did all the hard work of washing. The least I can do is put it away."

"Thanks." I grab a heavy throw we keep on the back of the couch. "I'll lie right here and watch you work."

Leo lets out a laugh. "Somehow, I think watching me fold laundry one-handed will be about as exciting as— "

"Watching paint dry? Exactly the thing to help me fall asleep."

It works like a charm. Not only do I get in a few hours of sleep but so does Gerry. He's so rested from his nap that he practically sprints to the door when Leo asks if he wants to walk me to work.

When Leo had two broken arms, Captain Williams put him under what was essentially house arrest. With both arms in casts and slings, Leo's balance was off.

Because only one arm was operated on and is now in the external fixation device, Bollinger said there's no problem with Leo walking as long as he's careful and doesn't overdo it. He even said the exercise would be good for Leo. I certainly don't mind the company on this chilly Thanksgiving.

My men see me to the door of the hospital. "You going to come in? Warm up a bit?"

"Nah. It's not that cold. Besides, Gerry gets too wound up in there. All the smells."

I nod, remembering the time we took him inside, stopping right at the front door. It wasn't so much he was wound up; it was more like he was frightened. The hospital was just too much for him.

I squat down and give him a goodbye rub. "Take care of your daddy while I'm gone."

Gerry lets out a whine and whips out his tongue, catching me on the chin.

After finishing my doggie goodbye, I stand and stretch up on my toes to kiss Leo. "See you in the morning."

Dr. Nettie Wolff and the rest of the day shift are wrapping things up. The hospital is quiet again, with all but two of the explosion survivors released to home or one of the long-term care facilities. The two still here need more monitoring than the doctors thought wise at the care facility.

That's one thing the med school will help with when the training is done: staffing the care centers. Even though the med school seems to be off to a rocky start, I've heard Williams is going to start a nursing school too. I'm glad. We certainly need nurses.

"Is Captain Williams here yet?" I ask Nettie as she finishes up her charting.

With paper and pens as a finite resource, we were fortunate someone was organized enough in the early days to secure many boxes of copy paper for our use. The former dentist's office, owned by a relative of the captain, was well stocked with office and medical supplies.

Paper is being made now, but it's not the smooth commercially processed paper of the past. Instead, it's made from recycled paper and sawdust, resulting in bumpy, obviously handmade material.

There's even someone making parchment, but I've heard it's even rougher than the homemade paper. I'm sure, given enough practice, the parchment made from animal skins will become a decent product.

"In his office." She gives a wave of her hand. "Said he wanted to work on next week's school schedule. You hear anything more about why the Guard went out?"

"I didn't. You?"

"Nothing. It's been mysteriously hush-hush. Josiah Talbot isn't even talking." She flares her eyes at me, causing me to laugh.

"Well, if Josiah is quiet, it must be serious. Looks like Shaw's people from the Citizen Patrol are covering sentry duty today. I guess the threat of attack is still there."

She's instantly solemn. "My guess is the threat of attack will be around until they're sure they have the perpetrators. That's another thing Josiah is being quiet about. I asked him about the guys who tried to attack us. He hemmed and hawed and said pretty much nothing."

"Have you talked to David Paul? Does he know anything?"

She drops her gaze back to her papers. "Um, no. David and I— " She lets out a sigh. "He wanted more than I could offer."

I slide into the chair next to her. "You want to talk about it? I'm a good listener."

Nettie snorts out a laugh. "I know you are. And I also know you aren't a gossip. But . . . no. There's nothing to talk about."

She writes a few more words before picking up the paper and sliding it into the manilla folder, also salvaged from the well-stocked office supplies. "That's it. I'm done. Hope you guys have a quiet night. The last few hours have been calm, but the morning started off pretty busy. Did Jacquie give you the lowdown on our new patient?"

"She did. You think it's bacterial and not a virus?"

"Seems so. But we're treating it like a virus anyway. Don't want to spread a respiratory virus through the community." She hands me one of the manilla folders.

I read the name and age on the outside. The sixty-three-year-old woman is pretty sick. I even heard her coughing when I came inside the building. Merissa, who arrived before me for our night shift, was in the room with her, as well as Jesse. Jacquie was checking on the two explosion patients.

As the time clicks past 1800 hours, I say goodbye to Nettie and the others before getting my things together to visit the patient rooms. Nettie gives a quick knock on Williams's office door and then pokes her head in.

I hear her faint goodbye and reminder that she has the radio if he needs her before she moves to the back hallway where her coat and snow boots are stashed.

I've already checked on all my patients and recorded their vitals when Williams comes limping down the hall. "Katie, did you and Leo do okay on Thanksgiving with the feast being canceled?"

"Feast? I didn't realize we were missing out on a big feed."

He lets out a laugh. "Well . . . I may be using the term liberally. Alice and I enjoyed our quiet meal. How about you?"

"Very much so. We made pumpkin soup and baked potatoes. It was . . . nice." I point to his booted foot. "How's the toe?"

He wipes the back of his hand across his forehead. "Troubling me some. Wondering if I could bother you to take a look. I was going to unwrap it myself, but you know what they say about acting as your own doctor and having a fool for a patient." He wipes his forehead again.

Is he sweating? I narrow my eyes and realize his color is also a little off. "Let's go into exam room one. I'll grab Merissa and meet you there."

When Merissa and I go into the room, he's sitting on the guest chair. He's already removed the walking boot and is staring at his foot. Even with the bandage still on, the stench of infection is unmistakable.

Merissa sucks in her top lip and shakes her head. "When was the last time you had the bandage off?"

"This morning. Alice helped me with it. It was . . . well, a little angry but not terrible. We did a good soak and cleaning. I thought . . . " He lets out a sigh. "I think I have a fever too."

Merissa takes his vitals. He has an elevated temperature of 102°. His heart rate and respirations are both slightly fast, and his blood pressure is a little low. As soon as she's done with his vitals and is recording them, I take care of unwrapping his foot.

Williams makes a slight gagging noise as we see what we're dealing with. "It didn't look like that this morning. I would've . . . I'd have come right in if it did. I'm not *that* much of a fool. Alice is going to kill me."

I resist the urge to tell him only if the infection doesn't get him first. "I'll call Dr. Wolff. This is— " I shake my head. "We need her."

"It's going to have to come off."

I breathe through my mouth to try and avoid the smell. "I'll use the base to call her. Then I'll, uh . . . I'll get the operating room ready, just in case."

"Can you get Alice too? She'll have my hide if I don't include her in this decision." He shakes his head. "Not that there's much discussion to be had about it."

He leans forward slightly and looks at his foot again. "I don't see any other way. Not with the way the infection's tracking up my leg."

Merissa steps forward. "I'll go to your house. Kerry can help Katie get the OR ready. We'll get you taken care of properly, sir."

Within the hour, Alice Williams, Nettie, and Chastity are all at the hospital. Nettie and Chastity have put their differences aside and are 100 percent professional as they discuss the plan with Williams.

"What if we take off the big toe and second toe, along with this section of the foot?" She motions toward the middle of his swollen and purplish foot. "Make sure we have good bone. We might be able to save part of it. You'd have a limp but could still get around."

"Maybe." Williams looks sick. "My guess is you'll know when you get in there. Use a local so you can tell me everything you see, and we'll decide as we go."

They've already given him a loading dose of antibiotics with plans for another dose as soon as the procedure is over. Like everything, antibiotics are in short supply and reserved for use only in the most serious cases.

Well, not exactly the most serious cases, but the cases where a reasonable amount of the drugs will save a life.

The surgery goes better than any of us hope. There's good bone right about where Chastity had suggested there might be. While the big toe, second toe, and upper middle portion of his foot are gone, the rest is saved.

We're all hopeful we stopped the infection in time and, along with the help of the coveted antibiotics, Captain Williams will make a full recovery. He's even saying he'll be ready to teach on Monday. They've had enough interruptions, and the school must go on.

Chapter 28

"Burnett? May I see you?"

There's a snip to Geoff Landers's tone, which raises my eyebrows.

It's been two weeks since Captain Williams's partial amputation. True to his word, med school was back in session on Monday, with Williams getting around in a wheelchair and his assistant teacher Leo with his arm in a tight sling. The irony of the two primary medical school teachers being in such bad shape wasn't lost on anyone.

Even with their injuries, the decision to teach was probably the right choice. Everyone realizes how easily things can go wrong in our current world and how desperately we need additional medical personnel.

At least it's been somewhat quiet lately—no new terrorist attacks or mass deaths. The hospital is still under extra protection from the National Guard, the Citizen Patrol, and the regular Pennington County Sheriff's Department.

We never did get details about the Guard's Thanksgiving Day mission. We have, however, been invited to join them in a few weeks for their Christmas celebration.

I understand the necessity of extra security at the hospital, but it's starting to get old. Especially when people who need medical attention are being delayed.

So far, the delays haven't resulted in any catastrophes, but it was close yesterday when a woodcutter showed up with a massive bleed injury. Someone new on the Citizen Patrol was a little too ambitious with his security and was quizzing the injured man as he nearly bled out.

I smile at the woodcutter who nearly lost his life as I finish refreshing his bandage. "Feeling good?" Though it was a close call, the man is recovering well. Captain Williams reeducated the sentry directly and has called a training session for all potential sentries to ensure this doesn't happen again.

"Now, Burnett." Landers taps his foot at me.

I tilt my head at my patient. "Give me a few minutes. Lunch just got dropped off, so I'll be back with it shortly. We may even be able to send you home later today."

"Sure. That's fine." The woodcutter's voice drops to a whisper. "Better go see what his issue is. The way he struts around like he owns the place . . . " The man shakes his head. "Near as I can tell, all he's good for is dumping my bedpan."

I pull my lips in tight to avoid the snicker I feel bubbling up. Geoff Landers does strut around like he's God's gift to medicine. But out of all the students, he's the one who seems to struggle the most.

The funny thing is, I'm not even sure he knows he's struggling. He's convinced he's right and everyone else—even Captain Williams—is wrong. The way Leo tells it, Landers is teetering on the edge of being booted from the program.

Landers is standing outside the door. "About time, Burnett. Do you keep the other doctors waiting?" He jabs a finger at my chest, actually making contact.

I take a step back and narrow my eyes as a surge of anger bubbles up in my belly. "You— "

"What's the problem?" Doc Nettie steps out of the exam room across the hall where she's been reorganizing and inventorying the supplies.

Landers waves a hand. "Nothing to concern yourself with, Nettie. This is between me and Katie."

Doc Nettie adjusts her stance and seems to add several inches to her diminutive frame. She gives him a cold smile. "Dr. Wolff." She points at her chest, then motions toward me. "Sergeant Burnett—as *Captain* Williams has stressed to you several times. Now, Mr. Landers, what seems to be the problem?"

Although her use of mister when addressing him sounds less than complimentary, it's the term Captain Williams has asked us to use. The men in the medical school are all referred to as mister and the women are either missus, if married, or miss if not.

It shouldn't even be a big deal how we're addressed, but Geoff Landers made the distinctions necessary in his continual bid to degrade people.

Okay . . . not people so much as women. Nettie, Kerry, Merissa, me . . . he seems to go out of his way to try and show his superiority.

He's especially demeaning toward nurse Jacquie Haley and herbalist turned med student Stella Swenson. The two women, both in their forties, are often the target of age-related wisecracks.

Dr. Chastity Morrow is the only one who seems to escape his denigration. *With reason.*

Leo and I were walking by her house the other day when we saw Landers on her porch. The two were hugging and kissing. I'd seen them chatting at work but hadn't realized the extent of their friendliness.

I asked Leo if Williams knew about the pair. Leo doesn't think so and is considering if it's something that needs to be known.

Geoff Landers huffs out a disgusted sigh. "Someone— " he jabs his finger toward my chest again, making sure not to connect this time " —used the last of the elderberry tincture and didn't say anything."

A laugh bubbles up from deep inside me. I do my best to control my facial expressions. I fail.

He shoots me a dirty look. "Sergeant Burnett thinks she's the only one around here who matters. She's continually using the last of something and not replacing it."

"Continually?" I croak out the word. "Seriously?"

"It's completely unacceptable! She thinks she's special and doesn't need— "

"Enough!" Nettie raises her hand. "I'm not exactly sure where you're getting your information— "

"I saw her using it! And now it's gone."

"It's not gone." Nettie steps closer to Landers. "It's been moved. You were at the meeting yesterday when we discussed supplies going missing, right? The tinctures are some of our missing items. I've moved them all to a secure location. If you need a tincture to treat a patient, you need to get the key from the doctor on duty." She jiggles the key ring in the pocket of her scrub top. "Now . . . who are you treating?"

With the medical students now several weeks into their studies, they've been given medic, nursing, or janitor shifts to work on their own. Whether we think he's ready or not, Geoff Landers is the medic on duty with Nettie and me today. He furrows his brow. "Um . . . well . . . it's, uh, for me. I have a tickle at the back of my throat and want to get ahead of it."

Nettie gives him a tight smile. "All right. Let's give you a quick exam."

She turns to me. "Sergeant?" When we're alone, she still calls me Katie, but in front of others, she makes a point to use the titles specified by Captain Williams. "Can you start a chart for Mr. Landers? I'll meet you in exam room two in ten minutes."

Landers waves a hand. "That's not necessary. I'll be fine."

"It most certainly is necessary. If you're coming down with something, we need to take precautionary measures. You can't be here, working in a hospital, with a virus that could spread to our patients. Now, go in and put a gown on. We'll see you in a few minutes."

He lets out a few huffs and then slinks off to the exam room.

Nettie shakes her head. "Well . . . that could explain some of our missing meds."

"Meaning?"

"Meaning, I think he may be choosing to self-medicate."

I chew on my bottom lip. "I've never seen him lurking around the supplies. Have you?"

She shakes her head. "Nope. But there's no doubt someone's taking things. We'll check him over and see if he's coming down with something. I've noticed he's seemed a little tired lately and even more surly than usual."

Nettie pulls a watch from her pocket. While the timepiece still works, the band broke, and she hasn't found a replacement. "What time did Dr. Bollinger call?"

I glance at my wristwatch. "It's been almost three hours now. He should arrive within the hour. Both Leo and Captain Williams said they'd be here by 1300."

Bollinger is on his all-district rotation. He's been covering one of the other districts and is scheduled for us next. He'll arrive today and check Leo and Williams, then he'll start his hospital and care facility shifts tomorrow.

Nettie tightens her mouth. "It's good he's going to check Williams too. I'm fairly happy with the job Chastity and I did, but a second opinion is always a good idea. Even if it is Bollinger's opinion."

After the last time Bollinger was here, and she and Chastity almost went to blows, I've learned a few bits and pieces of the situation.

Although Nettie is tight-lipped about her private life, Chastity isn't nearly as quiet.

She was more than happy to tell me about how Nettie and Bollinger were an item in the early days of the attacks when Nettie was doing an internship. She was especially happy to point out Bollinger is the reason Nettie was transferred here instead of staying at the main hospital. He got tired of her.

Chastity had way too big of a smirk when she shared this gossip. She took even more delight in pointing out how she and Bollinger started dating a few months ago, while she was a rotating doctor, before she was also transferred to the Guard District.

I don't think she even realizes the parallel between the two women and their stories. In her mind, she wasn't transferred because he got tired of her but because this was where she was most needed, and he had gone out of his way to make sure she knew she was doing a good thing helping here after Dr. Newsome's death.

Maybe she doesn't care, considering she was playing kissy-face with Landers. The whole thing is almost funny—in a soap opera sort of way. Why Chastity would date Geoff Landers is beyond me. He's several years younger than her, and . . . well, he's the way he is. Pompous and annoying.

When I think about Bollinger, he's kind of the same. Definitely pompous but in a different sort of way. The man is a good doctor—a good surgeon—and he knows it. He likes to make sure other people know it too.

When Leo and I first met him, I didn't think much of him at all. He was too condescending. After the attack on the festival when he saw us helping, he was a little less jerkish. Plus, he seems to have done well with the recent surgery on Leo's wrist. At least, I'm hopeful we'll get a good report about it today.

Nettie does a surprisingly thorough exam on Geoff Landers. He does seem to have some sinus drainage and a slightly red throat and eyes, but there's no fever or severe congestion. She asks him to wear a mask when tending to patients, and if he does spike a fever, he's to go home until it passes.

She also gives him a dose of elderberry tincture and sends a small bottle home with him, telling him how and when to take it. "Be sure you bring the bottle back. Stella had these in her personal inventory and only gave us a few for home use. We're keeping close track of them."

He makes a face at the mention of fellow med student Stella Swenson. He seems to want to say something before seeming to think better of it.

"No more self-treating." Nettie gives him a stern look. "It's important all of us approach our health in the same way as regular patients. Not only to keep sickness from spreading but to best use our resources. What we have . . . " She shrugs. "It's what we have. Even though we're able to make things like the elderberry tincture, we have only what we have until next season."

"I know that." He rolls his eyes.

"Good. I'm glad we understand each other." She gives him a cold smile. "Get dressed, and we'll get back to work."

In the hall, she shakes her head and says in a low voice, "I don't know why Williams accepted him into the program. The way he is . . . " She lifts her hands. "Everyone else brought some serious knowledge with them—Merissa, Kerry, Stella. But Landers, he's as useless as . . . as . . . I don't know what. He thinks of himself and himself only. Then goes out of his way to badmouth everyone else. The way he talks about Stella, I can't stand it."

I like Stella Swenson. She was an important part of this hospital and community before the medical school even started. The medications and knowledge she's provided have been amazing.

A few days ago, I asked her about the midwife I heard about, the one the pregnant woman mentioned who Nettie seemed to know also. Stella took a deep breath and pursed her lips. "Um, yes. I know her. She's . . . have you asked Captain Williams about her?"

I told her I had only learned about her recently, and with Leo's surgery and then Captain Williams's surgery, I hadn't asked him. I did tell her I'd heard the midwife was interviewed for the med school but was not accepted.

All Stella said was, "You should talk to Williams about her. It's not my place to say anything."

I still haven't had a chance to ask the captain. Maybe today after Bollinger sees him.

Chapter 29

"Hey, babe." Leo leans in and delivers a light kiss to my lips, causing my heart to give a little flutter. Even though things still aren't perfect between us—what marriage is always perfect?—we're doing better. "Is Bollinger here?"

"Yup. About twenty minutes ago. He's in the break room. Williams hasn't arrived yet, so I guess you can go first."

"Dandy." His good hand moves to the arm in the sling. Other than taking the arm out to clean the pins and check for infection twice per day, he lives in the tight sling, which functions more as a splint. We're hoping that'll change today. If Bollinger likes the looks of Leo's arm and is happy with the healing, he'll possibly let Leo move to a more loose-style sling.

I get my husband set up in the exam room and then let Nettie and Bollinger—who are both in the break room in some kind of heated discussion—know he's ready.

Nettie gives me a barely noticeable bob of her head as she purposely avoids looking at Dr. Bollinger. "Will you need my assistance, Doctor?"

"Nah. I'm sure the sergeant will be able to help." He gives me a smarmy smile. "Should be just a quick look-see. I'm sure the surgery was a success. Williams, though, I'll want your accounting of what you did when we check him over." Bollinger hefts himself out of the recliner. "I'll make a quick bathroom trip and then be right there."

"Yes, Doctor." Nettie gives a roll of her eyes as Bollinger leaves the room. "I'll check on our other patients. Let me know how things look with Leo."

"Are you . . . " I motion to the room. "Is everything okay?"

"It's fine. I needed to clear the air and make sure he knew . . . " She clears her throat. "I wanted him to know exactly where I stand." She winks. "It truly is okay."

As I step out of the break room, Captain Williams slides in the back door with his wife pushing his wheelchair. Or I should say, his *outdoor* wheelchair.

Jesse enlisted the help of a few other men to rework an older wheelchair we had in storage to replace the front wheels with tiny skis. The skis on the front allow the wheelchair to glide over the snow and ice as opposed to sinking in. Alice Williams reports, while not perfect, it does make pushing her husband around in the snow much easier.

Williams raises his hand in greeting, while Alice Williams gives me a smileless nod and helps her husband from the outdoor wheelchair to the normal one he uses inside the hospital.

"Captain Williams." I return the greeting as I walk toward them. "Dr. Bollinger is here. He's in the bathroom. I have Leo in exam room one. But, uh, he can wait if you're ready."

Williams lifts a hand and shakes his head. "I'd like to sit in on Leo's exam and see how he's healing. I'll wash up in my office. Give me a few minutes."

I meet his wife's gaze. "Mrs. Williams, it's nice to see you."

"You too, Katie." She gives me a half smile. "Hope it's a good report for both of our husbands."

"Now, Alice." Williams makes a clicking noise with his lips. "I'm coming along fine."

"You said the same thing the morning of the amputation. Remember, Chris?"

He touches her hand. "It'll be fine."

The door to the bathroom opens with a clunk, causing all of us to look in that direction.

"Well, there you are, old friend." Dr. Bollinger strides toward us. "What're we going to do with you?" He shakes Captain Williams's hand, as Williams mutters something about not believing the trouble he's caused.

Bollinger greets Mrs. Williams with a kiss on the cheek. "You keeping him out of trouble?"

"As if I could. Did you hear he's still teaching each day? Took only three days to recover from major surgery before he was back at it. I hope you'll talk some sense into him today."

Bollinger throws back his head and gives a big, fake laugh. "As if I could. I was going to check Burnett's arm."

Captain Williams dips his chin. "Thought I'd join you and see how my co-instructor is healing. Give me a few minutes to wash my hands and change?"

"Yup. That's fine. I'll get another cup of tea while I'm waiting. The wagon ride over here was freezing. Think we've got a storm coming in."

"Seems so," Williams agrees. "It's dark to the west and much colder than it was. Might be a doozy. You sure you're okay staying in the call room? You're welcome to stay with Alice and me."

"Nah. Might as well stay here in case we get snowed in."

"All right. See you in a few minutes." Captain and Mrs. Williams step into the office, softly closing the door behind them.

I go to Leo's exam room to tell him it'll be a few minutes and we might as well visit while we wait.

The wait's only about ten minutes before Bollinger pushes Williams's wheelchair into the room. Both doctors greet Leo and break into a discussion about the impending storm. I stand by, acting as a nurse and wife. It's a strange combination in times like this.

I'm about ready to politely suggest we get on with the exam when Bollinger says, "Let me wash up and we'll take a look. Nurse, can you get him out of his sling?"

I hide my response to his addressing me as *nurse*. Leo gives me a wink and says, "If you can hold this here, Katie, that's all I need."

I help Leo clean his fixation device and pins twice per day, which means we're pretty good at getting him in and out of the tight sling, so it takes us only seconds.

I look over everything as his arm and the device come into view. There's still quite a bit of bruising and some light swelling around the incision sites. His skin is pale from months of being in a cast prior to this new robotic-looking one. The skin's wrinkly and there's been some noticeable atrophy of the muscles.

Both Chastity and Nettie have looked at his arm a few times since the surgery, and both said they thought it looked like it should.

Bollinger doesn't bother with gloves, just washes his hands and uses sanitizer. He's holding his hands in the air, allowing the sanitizer to dry, as he steps to the exam table. "Hmm. Okay. The incisions look good. You getting much pus out?"

"Very little. We've been cleaning it like you said, pushing on the incisions slightly to encourage any fluid to exit."

"Good, good." He pauses as he touches a spot near one of the pins. "There's a little more bruising and swelling than I'd hoped to see." He looks over his shoulder at Captain Williams. "Chris, have you looked at this?"

"Nope. I haven't been working in the hospital since— " He motions to his foot. "Both Dr. Wolff and Dr. Morrow have checked him. They've reported to me about the progress."

"Mm-hmm. I'm not sure either of them has ever seen an external fixation before."

"Neither have I, friend." Williams wheels himself closer to the exam table. "The skin looks a little . . . waxy?"

"Times like this I wish we had our x-ray machines. How's the pain level, Leo?"

"Uh . . . not terrible. Better than it was maybe, before the new break."

"Yeah. A malunion can be painful. You sleeping well?"

Leo looks at me. I'm doing my best to stay calm. The conversation sounds like Dr. Bollinger isn't overly happy with Leo's progress. "He sleeps okay. We leave the splint on, like you said."

"It's been, what?" Bollinger scrunches up his nose. "Almost three weeks?"

Leo and I both nod in response.

"I'll be here for three days. I want to have you come in each day. I'll check it and clean it." Bollinger looks at me. "Not that there's a problem with how you're cleaning it. It looks fine. But I want to see if something jumps out at me. So, you'll still do the twice-a-day cleaning as you have been. I'll do a third. Hopefully, the weather will cooperate so we can do this. Today's Saturday. Your school's closed until Monday?"

"That's right," Williams answers.

"Alrighty. Don't worry, Leo, Mrs. Burnett. We're still fine. Me being here these few days will make all the difference in this arm healing."

I swear the room seems to shrink as his head swells. "Thank you, Doctor."

"Get the sling back in place. We'll take a look at Captain Williams. Or . . . would you prefer I have Nettie assist me so you can visit with your husband?" He raises his eyebrows at me.

"I'm happy to help, sir. I'm on shift today."

"I'll get myself set up in exam room two, if that's okay, Sergeant Burnett?" Captain Williams gives me a slight smile.

I appreciate him using my rank and name to remind Dr. Bollinger of my status here. "Yes, sir. I'll be five minutes."

When the doctors leave, Leo lets out a sigh. "That Bollinger . . . his bedside manner is awful."

"Really? I think he's great with you."

"Yeah, well, maybe my judgment is clouded by him referring to you as *nurse.*"

I sigh. "That's better than how Newsome used to refer to me. What do you think of what he said? Is there . . . is something not right?"

With his unbroken arm, Leo motions me to step closer. He pulls me into a single-arm hug. His breath tickles my ear. "Let's not worry about it right now. I think he maybe feels the need to show his importance."

I snort out a laugh. "Probably true. Let's get you put back together so I can help with Captain Williams."

Dr. Bollinger gives Captain Williams a glowing report on his recovery. "Those girls did a good job. Not sure I could've done much better myself."

"Yes." Williams nods. "Doctors Wolff and Morrow were stellar. They're a huge asset to our hospital."

"They've come a long way for sure. Both of them were like frightened little rabbits when they first started working at the main hospital." Bollinger raises his eyebrows at Williams. "Anyway, I'd like to think I had a hand in molding them into the doctors they're becoming. Of course, under your expert tutelage, they've blossomed."

"Thank you, I appreciate you saying so."

"Looking forward to seeing how your medical school turns out. You happy with how things are going?"

"For the most part. We have a few wrinkles to iron out, but most of the students are performing even better than expected."

"Got some deadweight?"

"Well . . . you know how it is."

"Cut 'em lose. We can't afford slackers in today's world."

Williams huffs. "If only it were that easy."

I keep my head down and my eyes averted, wondering if they'll continue the conversation with me in the room. They don't. Instead,

Captain Williams says, "So whadda ya say, Doctor? Think I'll be dancing with Alice soon?"

"Did you dance with Alice before?"

"Never. But she always wanted me too."

"I think if you stay off it another week, and keep using the chair, you can graduate to crutches. Save the dancing until Valentine's Day. And then only slow dances. Did you hear I'm going to be a regular on the rotation circuit? Once a quarter at least, so I'll be back in March at the latest."

"Oh? You happy about this?"

"Surprisingly, yes. Going to the different satellite hospitals has shown me how much my expertise is needed. You run a tight ship here, Chris. But some of them . . . "

Bollinger shakes his head. "Did you hear they set up shop at Canyon Lake Hospital in a new building? 'Course, they lost a good portion of their staff in the explosion and are short-staffed like everyone. We all hope your med school experiment is a success. We need more doctors. Like I said, cut the deadweight." His eyes pierce Williams. "And when are you starting the nursing school? We need nurses too."

"I guess it'll open on February 15 if you think I'll be up to dancing on Valentine's Day."

Bollinger gives a hearty, not quite so fake laugh. "Good on ya. Good on ya."

Chapter 30

"Um, so that's about it. I don't really do anything special. Just try and think about how I'd feel if I was on the gurney or in the bed." I shrug and glance around the room.

I'm teaching at the med school today. *Teaching.* Not exactly the word I'd use for what this class is. While learning the nursing aspect of the job is part of the lessons, and I do help with those classes on the days I'm not on shift at the hospital, Williams calls this class *learning empathy.* I'm supposed to help the future doctors develop a good bedside manner.

I'd much rather be teaching how to help transfer a patient or change their bedding while they're still in the bed. Even sponge bath training would be better! At least there's a specific way to do those things.

How in the world does one *teach* empathy? Especially to adults. Adults who are already set in their ways. My gaze catches Geoff Landers. He has the usual smirk on his face, which he curls up into more of a sneer.

I quickly look away from him to find Kerry Hendricks smiling at me and raising her hand.

"Um, yes?"

"How much do you think our personal feelings about things come into play when we're caring for others?"

I shrug. "Keep in mind, I don't have any specialized training on mental health or anything."

Geoff scoffs and mutters, "No kidding."

"Something to add, Mr. Landers?"

"Nope. Nothing at this time, Captain. I'm ready to move on to the next class. What're we doing? Phlebotomy?"

Williams straightens in his wheelchair. "We'll move on to the next class when Sergeant Burnett's time is up. You may think this is a throwaway—a waste of your time. It's not. Having a good bedside manner can determine how successful you are as a doctor. If your patients don't like you, you may not get honest answers to your questions. Questions that can make a difference to their life."

Williams motions to me with a hand and then nods at Leo. "Both of the Sergeant Burnetts are naturals. Each of them knows how to communicate. How to ask the questions and gauge the responses. And not just the verbal responses. They watch for nonverbal clues in body language and facial expressions." He turns to me. "Tell us about how you take a history."

"When the patient first comes in?"

"Yes, the initial history, before the doctor comes in."

"I ask the basic questions about why they're there."

"Do you have them sit on the exam table?"

"Oh, uh . . . no, not usually. Sometimes they want to, but if they're looking around the room, I ask them to sit in a chair. Then I sit down next to them."

"Like you're friends?" Landers scoffs, earning a glare from Williams.

"Sort of, I guess. I want them to be comfortable."

Kerry, Merissa, and most of the others are scribbling in their notebooks. Landers is sitting back in his chair with his arms crossed and his legs stretched out.

Captain Williams asks a few more questions about my method for taking a patient history, before returning to Kerry's question about personal feelings affecting how we care for others.

"Burnett's life experiences are probably a big reason she's the way she is with patients. She didn't have any real medical training before the attacks started, just a few first aid courses. She told you she was an artist. Possibly, that's one reason she's able to communicate so effectively—she didn't go into medicine on purpose. Any other questions for Sergeant Burnett?"

After the class wraps up, and the students get a break before moving on to phlebotomy, Leo motions for me to join him. We sit at the back of the now-empty classroom.

"You did great today."

I let out a sigh. "I know Williams thinks this is something important for them to learn, but I'm not so sure I should be teaching it."

"Rather teach phlebotomy?"

I roll my eyes. "I'm sure Landers will have plenty to say at my class later this afternoon when we're discussing the excitement of inventory."

Leo lets out a soft laugh. "Pretty sure he got a crash course when Nettie found him nipping at the tinctures."

"True. Not only from her but also from Williams when he read the daily report. I thought that was going to be it for Geoff Landers and his medical training."

"Same." We sit quietly for a few minutes. In a barely audible voice, Leo asks, "Do you think it's odd it wasn't?"

"Wasn't the end of Landers?" I shrug. "I think it's odd he was accepted in the first place. I know there was a reason—you know, with someone who knew him and asked for him to be let in. But I'm not sure who thought it was a good idea."

"My guess is it's someone who doesn't know what's needed to be a good doctor." He sighs. "You've got a break for the next couple of hours, then you teach your inventory class?"

"I do. I thought I'd go to the new ration house. I'd like a pair of mittens."

"Mittens?"

"To go over my gloves. The last cold snap we had . . . remember how much I complained about my fingers?"

"Have you heard if they were able to replenish much of what was lost in the explosion?"

"Some. I think one of the main reasons was, even though it was the main ration centers that were destroyed, not all of them kept the same goods. Some of the DCs didn't even keep supplies there. It was strictly a spot to get ration chips."

He answers with a knowing nod. "Right. That did help."

"And the main supply buildings, where they keep all the supplies collected since the collapse— "

"You mean hoarded?" He wiggles his brows at me.

"Exactly." I let out a small laugh.

What they did here in the Black Hills is much like what we did in Bakerville. Vacant houses—places where the occupants were gone on vacation—were emptied of usable goods. With so many businesses and industries available around here, the same thing was done. Sadly, in some cases, it was too little too late.

The grocery shelves were stripped bare long before the EMP hit as the smaller attacks weakened and scared everyone. By the time of the pulse, supplies were already depleted, with zero hope of restocking.

Then, the military—Camp Rapid National Guard and Ellsworth Air Force bases—stepped in at the request of the governor to commandeer whatever could be used to help people survive.

That was before the governor decided using the national military didn't fit with the best interest of the state of South Dakota. Now Ellsworth is back to being a nonpolice entity since the immediate disaster is over.

I guess they still have plenty to do; we often see or hear different aircraft. Jacquie Haley said there are a lot more types of aircraft flying around than the bombers they used to have.

She also had a lot to say about what she perceived as a lack of response to the initial attacks and EMP. She's vocally opposed to the governor not allowing Ellsworth to give us more aid. Others are just as vocal about agreeing with the governor and thinking it was the right decision to limit the powers of the federal military in the state.

At least South Dakota has made a huge effort to beef up the numbers of their Army and Air National Guard Units, more than tripling the number of soldiers and airmen they had before the EMP, and with a plan to add even more.

Soon, I'll be one of those. Even though it isn't looking good for Leo to be able to take his oath after the new year as planned, and they're reviewing his waiver to extend his oath for another three months, I'm not asking for a waiver.

I'm still on the fence about the eight-year commitment to the Guard because of being so far away from my family, but I'm beginning to accept it. My life will change little. I'll still be working at the hospital, and we'll live in our little house. I'll be under Captain Williams's command, same as now.

A few weeks ago, Williams mentioned he should add me to his school, make me a med student. He hasn't said anything more about it. Maybe I misunderstood? I've replayed the conversation in my head many times, trying to determine how I misinterpreted it. Or maybe he changed his mind.

He has detailed how I'll move from the United Volunteers to the National Guard and what will be expected of me training-wise. We'll have an abbreviated basic training course for only two weeks. I'll be required to train with Camp Rapid two days a month, working around our hospital schedule.

With the push to increase the Guard numbers, I'm not the only one who'll be joining. There're several others from the community enlisting after the new year.

"Can you see if they have mittens for me too? Or at least one mitten." He lifts his good arm and wiggles his fingers.

Bollinger checked Leo's arm each day he was working in our hospital. While he agreed there was no sign of infection, he mentioned several times how he wished he could x-ray the arm to make sure the pin placement is right. He still thinks the skin looks a little off, but maybe it's from being in a cast for so long before the external fixation device was put on.

Bollinger wants us to go to him after the new year for a checkup. In the meantime, we keep cleaning it, and Leo needs to keep the tight sling in place. If there are any obvious changes, we're to call him on the radio immediately.

With Bollinger happy about Williams's recovery, too, the captain is back to taking hospital shifts in addition to teaching. But with his mobility limitation, he needs an assistant. Mrs. Williams or Leo take turns in this capacity.

I was surprised to learn Alice Williams was the captain's original nurse. When he first opened his small doctor's office, it was just the two of them. She worked as his nurse and receptionist. She even handled the billing for the first couple of years until the practice merged with another set of doctors.

After that, she continued as his nurse for a few more years, "retiring" about five years prior to the EMP to pursue her own interests. Why she hasn't been working at the Guard Hospital before now is a question I haven't asked.

As soon as the break is over and Williams announces for everyone to meet in the lab, I give Leo a goodbye kiss. "I'll be back soon."

"Be careful." He moves his hand to my back. "I know they've upped the security everywhere, but keep your eyes open. I think there's something weird going on."

"Weird?" I snort out a laugh. "This whole thing is weird."

"New weird. The general's aide was here first thing this morning. He brought a note to Williams. I'm not exactly sure what it was about, but Williams seemed concerned. He scribbled a note back, and not half an hour later, Lieutenant Paul was here. Williams had me take over the class while they went off to the office, so . . . " Leo lifts his shoulders.

"Military secrets. Always fun. I'll be careful. But like you said, there's security everywhere. Between the Guard, Citizen Patrol, and Shaw's deputies, I'm pretty sure the new ration house is fine. Speaking of, did you hear anything new about their quest to find the perpetrators?"

"Perpetrators?" He gives me a wink.

I playfully narrow my eyes. "Are you making fun of me?"

"I'd never." He drops a kiss on my nose. "But no. To answer your question, if they know who did it, they aren't saying. I think even Captain Williams is in the dark about it. You know that sheriff friend of his— "

"Friend? I'm not sure about that."

"True. Anyway, he was here a couple of days ago."

I shake my head. "I hadn't heard."

"Sorry. I didn't even think about it. They had a meeting, and the guy stormed out."

"The county sheriff? Melvin . . . something?"

"Melvin Cabal. He came strutting in, waving and smiling at people, but went out red-faced and stomping. Williams didn't say anything about why he was here or what happened." Leo shrugs. "Even Josiah Talbot is still tight-lipped. I don't think he's even told Jesse what he knows."

Leo gives me another kiss as he heads toward the lab.

I go to the back door and slip out of my tennis shoes and into my boots. I've finished tucking my shoes into my backpack and am reaching for the back door when it opens. I jump when I see Jesse Talbot on the other side. "You scared the daylights out of me." I let out a small laugh.

"Sorry, Katie. Heading out?"

"Just for a bit. Going to see if I can find a pair of mittens." I splay my gloved fingers at him. "What're you up to?"

"Got a call on the radio. You know Kittleson, Young, and the others arrested for the theft ring? There's been a jailbreak."

"What! How?"

"They were finally moving them from the National Guard holding cells to the main jail and . . . something went wrong. There're injuries. Deaths too. We're expecting casualties."

Chapter 31

Chastity and Jacquie are at the hospital, along with Jesse as our medic and Rand Hendricks taking care of all the custodial duties. Chastity gives me a pinched look. "Nettie's on her way. The med students?"

"I met Jesse at the back door on my way out. I assume they'll be here shortly. Do you know what to expect?"

Her pinched look increases. "Shaw said there was an incident when moving the prisoners. They have casualties. Jesse asked if they needed transport, and he said they were already on their way."

"I'd better change." I grab my hospital clothes out of my locker and slip into the small closet we use for changing. I'm halfway finished when there's a soft knock at the door. "Just a minute."

Dressed enough to be decent, I step out and Merissa slips inside the room.

Stella is getting her things out of her locker. "We should move some of the lockers to a separate room. Give the men and women their own spaces. If we had separate changing rooms, we could simply lock the door." She motions to the break room door as it opens.

Geoff Landers and another man from the class walk in.

"See?" Stella says. "I'm going to go change in the firewood room."

It takes me only a couple of minutes to get my tennis shoes on and move to a mirror to try and contain my hair. Chastity gave me a few more hair bands, ones she'd had in her personal supplies.

She cut her hair short a few months before she transferred here and no longer needs them. I've been thinking about doing the same thing. My too-thick, too-curly hair isn't practical in today's world. Cutting it short would make things easier.

Back in the hallway, Leo is waiting in the lobby. He's still in the street clothes he was wearing for teaching, along with his heavy jacket and boots. "They're a couple minutes out. I thought I'd see what a one-armed man can do to be of help."

"Your sling's tight?" I move to his side and fiddle with the fabric.

"Seems to be fine."

"Okay. Just . . . just be careful. We don't need— " I take a deep breath. A wave of unreasonable anger builds in my gut.

There have been plenty of emergencies since Leo broke his arms the first time. He's done what he can to help with each while trying to prevent further injury to his arms. After the explosions at the festival and our ration distribution center, he jumped right in and did what was needed.

We already knew about the malunion before those events, so they weren't at all responsible for it. But with this new surgery and the bionic-looking arm, I'm concerned. Perhaps unreasonably, but I'd like him to take a seat and stay out of the way.

"Hey." His gaze meets mine, his green eyes looking deep into mine. "I won't do anything dumb. I promise."

I drop my shoulders from my ears and let out a breath. "I just worry. You've had such a hard time— "

"So have you." He tilts his head. "Thanks to me going out of my way to be a jerk."

"They're here," Jesse calls from the window. He and Rand Hendricks are in their boots and coats, ready to get the injured inside.

"We're good?" Leo asks as he takes a step back.

"We're good. Just be careful."

Ritchie Kasubowski is holding one end of a stretcher; Jesse has the other end. I do a quick evaluation of the injured man and send him to exam room one where Chasity and Jacquie are already waiting.

Once all the injured—seven altogether, some of Shaw's men and some from the theft ring—are inside and triaged, I take a quick minute to write up an incident report. Bowski, now sitting in the waiting room, helps me with a few details.

I move next to him. "Were there any deaths?"

He rubs his hands over his face. "One of ours and one of theirs."

I bite my lip to prevent asking what exactly he means. Although everyone else seems to support Bowski and his integrity, saying there's no way he was part of the robbery ring, I'm still not convinced. He seems to be too intertwined with some of the shady things that happen around here.

"Three men escaped. That's why Shaw isn't here. He took Josiah, Reeves, and a few others, plus called in the National Guard. They'll find them."

I shake my head. "How'd this happen?" I don't need the information for the incident report but ask out of my own curiosity.

"Ambushed. Someone knew we were moving them today. They were waiting for us. Kittleson didn't even seem surprised when it started."

I suck in a breath. RJ Kittleson. The man with the bad onion breath who'd surprised us the night we saw the two men sneaking around. The man who faked being tied to a tree to look like a victim. The man who had a hand in my husband rebreaking his arm. One of the men responsible for the death of Mr. Harrington.

I narrow my eyes. "Where is he?"

"He's one of the ones who got away. Along with Bryson Young and the one they call Mouse."

"Bryson Young? Your friend? The one who disguised himself in the dyed-red Santa beard?"

He gives me a hard look. "My friend? What are you implying?"

I clear my throat. "Nothing. Just . . . the first time I met him—*met you*—was at the hunting camp. Remember? You introduced me to him."

Bowski sits back in his chair and seems to relax. "Sure, yeah. I forgot about that. I've known Bryson for a few years. We're friendly, sure. I knew he was— " He tilts his head to one side. "He'd been doing what he could to help his family. His brother."

"By stealing?"

"I didn't know about that. Until the arrests, I didn't know he was involved in the burglaries." He points to my clipboard. "What else do you need for your report?"

Staring at my paper, I confirm seven injured were brought to the hospital and two were dead at the scene. I ask if Hugo, the man who acts as coroner and undertaker for us, was called.

Bowski says he was, and the dead will be taken care of.

I fill in a few more details we may need before thanking Bowski for helping me with my paperwork.

As I shift forward in my chair, Bowski puts a hand on my arm. "Look, Katie. I know you don't trust me. I understand. Some of the things I do may seem— " he purses his lips " —unsavory. Illegal, even. With the way things are these days, we do what we must. I know you've heard about me being part of the . . . "

He leans forward and lowers his voice. "About me being able to get things other people can't. I'm not against the new setup, with the ration chips and everything. But I don't think it's enough. We're going to need a proper trade system set up soon. That's the way we'll get back on our feet. I do what I can to help my community. The more people we can save, the better."

"Because of your daughter?" I blurt out the question without thinking.

"Yeah." He nods slowly. "She and my wife. My *former* wife. I'd like to think they were able to get someplace safe and they're getting the help they need. Maybe— " He lets out a noisy breath. "Maybe if I do what I can, God will notice my efforts and make sure my family's taken care of."

I lean back in my chair. I don't know Bowski well. Not at all, really. But I feel the need to say something about this, about his statement of God noticing his efforts and taking care of his missing family. What to say is hanging me up, though.

I've gone to church most of my life. At one time, while I was in college before I met Leo, I'd thought I might devote my life to Christ by becoming a missionary. The college church I attended had a mission trip planned for the summer. I'd done a little fundraising for the trip then Leo came along. I experienced a crisis of faith and put my plans to serve God on hold.

Bowski's statement sounds a whole lot like thinking his good works will get him into Heaven. Many Bible verses remind us we're saved by grace not by our works. But at the same time, he isn't asking for his own salvation. He's hoping if he can make a difference here, in the Black Hills of South Dakota, God will make sure his family is okay wherever they are.

He lifts a hand. "I know what that sounds like. Believe me, I've had more than one person remind me how it works. I've spent enough time in church to know what they're talking about. I'm not getting into Heaven because of the things I do, that is through Christ alone. *I get that.* I do. I also know there are verses about doing good and sharing what you have, that those sacrifices will please the Lord."

I dip my chin. "Hebrews. Leo and I were reading it the other night."

"Besides, I'd probably go nuts thinking about things if I didn't stay busy. One thing is for sure, there's never a lack of work in the apocalypse." He lets out a wry laugh. "Sometimes, I forget how easy we had it before."

His words remind me of something. I can't quite remember what, but something. Or someone.

"What's wrong? Did I say something to upset you?"

"Oh, no." I wave my hand and relax my face. "What you said, it reminded me of something. I just can't remember what exactly."

"Maybe some other Bible verse you've read?"

I tilt my head. "Yeah, maybe. That's probably it. Thanks for helping me with my report. And for talking with me."

I pass off the incident report to Captain Williams, who's in his office with his foot elevated, and ask if he needs me to stay.

"No, no. Obviously, school is done for today. This— " He motions toward the main part of the hospital. "This is why they're here. You take the rest of the day off. I know, with the regular nursing shifts and helping at the school, you must be tired. Plus, with Leo still not at full capacity, you've got extra work at home too."

"Home isn't so bad. People have been so kind to us—giving us food, making sure we have water, firewood . . . everything. I'm going to go home and get my dog. I want to find a pair of mittens. Um, if you're sure you won't need me?"

"Nope. You're fine. Did you want Leo to go? I think he's overseeing our med students right now."

"I'm fine. Gerry and I can use the walk. I'll let Leo know I'm leaving."

Twenty minutes later, I'm out of my hospital clothes and back into street clothes and my snow boots. Leo walks me to the door and gives me a goodbye kiss. "See you soon."

"What time do you think? 1800?"

"Probably around there."

"I'll have dinner waiting." I stretch onto my toes to give him another kiss.

Outside, I consider jogging to our house, but there are too many patches of snow and ice to make jogging safe. Instead, I speed walk in the clear spots and pick my way through the slippery areas.

This winter is milder than last, but I'm already done with it. And it's only the seventeenth of December—not even winter yet on the calendar!

Christmas is a week from tomorrow. My sister Sarah is getting married a week from today, a Christmas Eve wedding. I sent her a letter a few weeks ago and slipped in a small gift. Nothing elaborate since those days are over and I'm not even certain it'll reach her.

But I did find the perfect little wedding gift. A lady stopped by the hospital a few weeks ago. She'd been feeling dizzy. She apologized up and down for bothering us, saying she knew we needed to be available for emergencies.

I tried to allay her concerns, but she continued to apologize throughout the history I took of her and the exam Nettie did. Her blood pressure was too low.

When we told her why we wanted to keep her, because of extremely low blood pressure, she shook her head. "Nope. I have high blood pressure. I'm taking medication for it."

"Really?" Nettie asked as she eased into the chair next to the exam table. "What're you taking?"

The woman slammed her lips shut and stared at her hospital-gown-covered knees. She muttered something neither Nettie nor I could make out.

"What was that?"

"Nothing. It's, uh, something I thought might help. Before, my blood pressure was a little high—you know, when I weighed more." She motioned to her thin frame. "Never enough to need medicine, but I had to monitor it. I thought the dizzy spells were from it being too high. It never occurred to me it could be too low. The doctor always told me, if I took off a few pounds, it would do me a world of good." She let out a coarse laugh.

Nettie gave me a look. We ended up keeping her for a couple of days to rehydrate her and make sure she was eating properly. Plus, to try and get whatever she'd been taking—she never shared what it was or who told her about it—out of her system.

A few days after she was released, with her blood pressure normal and looking much better than when she was admitted, she and her son showed up bearing gifts. I ended up with a couple of beautiful and dainty tatted lace bookmarks. One, a series of hearts, is what I sent to Sarah for her wedding gift. The second is a cross, which I kept to use in my Bible.

When I open the door to my house, I'm met with a burst of cold air. Much colder than usual. The woodstove must have gone out.

As I shut the door, I notice a chilling breeze, like the backdoor was left open. Gerry, who was shut in the laundry room when we left this morning, lets out a bark from the bedroom. I reach for my sidearm. "I wouldn't do that if I were you."

Chapter 32

"Did you hear me, lady? Keep your hand away from your gun," the gruff voice of the unseen intruder commands.

"Katie. Her name's Katie Burnett." Bryson Young, the man Bowski introduced me to at hunting camp, the one who was wearing the dyed-red Santa beard as a disguise, steps into view.

Gerry lets out a howl from my bedroom.

I swallow and blink away tears, willing my turned-to-spaghetti legs to keep me upright as I lift my hands away from my body. "Why are you here?" My voice comes out in a squeak.

"You're a nurse, right?" Young lifts the muzzle of his gun in my direction. "Royal was injured. You need to fix him up."

I move my gaze from Bryson Young to my sofa, where RJ Kittleson is lying, his gun in his left hand pointed haphazardly in my direction, his right hand pushing on his stomach.

I blink a few times as I take in what I'm seeing. Stomach wound. Memories of my own gutshot early in the days of the trouble, even before the EMP, wash over me. At that time, we still had a good supply of antibiotics and doctors who knew what they were doing.

In today's world, even with our good doctors, we lose over 50 percent of our gutshot victims to secondary issues. And those are the ones who make it to the hospital. Most die before.

A shiver runs through me. "Why's it so cold in my house?"

Young points at Kittleson. "Back door was locked. He thought knocking out the window with his gun was a good idea. That's when the dog freaked out and broke through his door. I grabbed him and put him in the bedroom."

"Be glad I like dogs, little missy, or else . . . " RJ lifts his gun slightly to punctuate his point. The extra movement results in a grimace.

I straighten my shoulders. "The first thing you need to do is put the gun down and stop moving around." My voice isn't as strong as I'd like.

I clear my throat and point to Bryson. "And you—get something over the window and then start a fire. It's too cold in here for RJ." I make a point of using his first name, hoping it'll make me seem like I care about his condition. I take a step toward the sofa.

Kittleson tracks me with the pistol.

I lift my hands out from my side, the classic display of showing they're empty. "Put it down. Every time you move, you could be doing more damage."

Young goes to Kittleson's side and whispers, "Let her fix you up. That's why we're here." He takes Kittleson's pistol and tucks it in the back of his pants.

Bryson points to me. "Your gun?"

I move slowly and take it out of the holster. I step backward into the entryway, my eyes never leaving the men. Shifting slightly, I put my pistol on a shelf.

I wish I was wearing my backup. Even though I should, I never wear it to work, reserving it for the times we're away from home for other reasons, like when we went to the hospital in Monument.

I lift my hands again to show him they're empty.

"You need to help Royal. I'll fix the window, get it warmed up in here."

I grab a blanket off a nearby chair and cover Kittleson's legs. "There are a couple of cardboard boxes over there." I point to the well-used box holding leaves and debris collected in the fall for starting fires.

"You could use them to patch the window. Blankets are in the linen closet by the bathroom." I pinch my face. "I think there're nails and a hammer in the laundry room."

Bryson sets off to warm up the house, going first to the laundry room. I can see the hollow-core door to the small room from here. It's splintered, with a Gerry-sized hole in it. How my little dog managed that is beyond me. I squat next to Kittleson.

He narrows his eyes. "I suppose you'd be happy to let me die."

I slide my backpack off and unzip it.

"Hey!" Bryson suddenly appears, waving his gun. "What are you doing?"

I swallow hard, fighting down both fear and anger. "You want me to help him? I need my supplies." I motion to the backpack. "I have a small med kit."

He motions with the pistol. "Dump it. Let me see it all."

With shaking hands, I empty the contents of my daypack on the floor.

"Spread it out."

I oblige his order. "See? Happy?"

The man narrows his eyes. "Yeah." He looks to Kittleson. "You okay?"

Kittleson gives a slight nod. "You heard she's good, right? Knows what she's doing?"

"That's what I heard. I guess we could've gone to one of the women docs' houses instead, but . . . " He lifts a shoulder. "We're here now."

"Look," I squeak. "All I want is to fix you up and get you on your way."

Gerry must hear my voice; he lets out a soft whine.

"Humph. You and your husband . . . you two messed up everything. This— " Kittleson motions to his stomach. "This is on you."

"Where's the other guy?"

"What *other* guy?"

"The reports said three of you escaped."

"Dead. At least probably by now. His death—also on you."

I let out a slow breath. I don't like the sound of this.

"Get him fixed up," Young says. "Then we'll get out of here." He turns and heads toward the back door.

I quickly organize my supplies. "Let me check your vitals."

A loud racket from the laundry room causes me to look over the back of the couch.

Bryson sees me. "Figured I'd use one side of the door to cover the window. Found the nails and hammer. Just a few minutes and I'll get the fire going."

Gerry whines again. I want to go to him. Tell him everything is okay. Snuggle him.

I let out a sigh before turning back to my patient. I check Kittleson's pulse.

He opens one eye and wrinkles his forehead. "You gonna fix me up or what?"

"I'm going to do my best."

After checking his blood pressure with my manual blood pressure cuff and stethoscope, I begin to work on cleaning out the wound. The bowel smell is pungent, almost overwhelming. He needs a surgeon and massive antibiotics, none of which are happening here.

It takes me only a few minutes to know, even at our small hospital, he'd be in the 50 percent. Not the 50 percent that survives, but the ones that don't. The damage is so extensive, we'd do little but keep him comfortable.

Even though there's little chance of survival, I'll do what I can to at least make him comfortable. I dread letting Kittleson or Young know what I truly think. What I'd like more than anything is to get Kittleson to a place where he can leave, where he can go somewhere else to live out the remaining time of his life.

Leo expects to be finished at the hospital around 1800. That's less than five hours from now. I need these men gone before Leo gets home.

Kittleson's eyes are closed, and his breathing is shallow. He may not have five hours.

The cold wind is no longer blowing through the house.

Young stops his hammering and goes back into the laundry room. He returns with several pieces of scrap from the former door. "Looks like there's still embers. Shouldn't take much to get the fire going."

Within a couple of minutes, he's standing near the couch, the soft roar of the fire filling the silence of the room. He makes a gagging noise. "Bad, huh?"

"It's not good. If we take him to the hospital— "

"Not happening." Kittleson's voice is weak, much softer and shakier than when I got here and he was ordering me around.

I tighten my jaw. "Look around. You're lying on my living room couch. There's smoke from the woodstove and who knows what all blew in when you broke my window. Not to mention, I have a dog. Does this seem like the kind of environment you should be in for treating an open wound? I don't have everything we need. I can't even stop the bleeding, not with the damage. You've lost so much blood you need fluids. Intravenous fluids at the least, more likely a transfusion. If we get you to the hospital now, you may have a chance."

"You think he would?" Young motions to Kittleson's gaping wound. "He'd have a chance at the hospital?"

I pause while I consider how to answer. They broke into my house, knowing I'm a nurse. If I tell them I can't help them, where does that leave me? Unneeded. *Possibly dead.* I decide on the truth.

I lean back on my heels and meet Bryson Young's eyes. "I can't save him. Not with my supplies in this environment. His bowel is perforated. The bullet is still inside. Getting it out— " I shake my head.

"Even if I could get it out and sew him up properly, infection is likely—very likely. I don't have antibiotics." I scrunch up my face. "Do you? I know they found some of the things you, um, had. But do you have medical supplies stashed somewhere?"

Bryson kneels next to the couch. His voice is a whisper. "No. There's nothing left." He takes Kittleson's hand. "What do you want to do, brother?"

Brother? I look from one to the other but don't see a resemblance. Maybe it's a term of endearment and not indicative of being related.

Kittleson's eyes flutter. "No. Hospital." His words are slow and labored, stretching out hospital so it sounds like three separate words with a pause between each.

I take his wrist to check his pulse. It's slow. I watch as he struggles to breathe. He shivers.

"Pull the blanket up. Let's keep him comfortable."

I slide back from the side of the couch and let him move near Kittleson's head. He's holding his hand as he speaks softly to him, telling him it's okay.

I move toward the woodstove to add another log to the fire. My eyes are stinging, and my nose is burning. Both from tears and fear.

After putting the wood in, I dip my hands in one of the pots of water we have on top of the stove to add moisture to the air and to have instant hot water. It's warm but not boiling. I take my time cleaning the blood from my hands.

I stay facing the stove as I wave my hands in the air to dry them. When I finally turn around, Kittleson's entire body and face are covered with the blanket.

Chapter 33

Bryson Young sits on the floor, leaning against the couch and staring in my direction. "Thanks for doing what you could."

"What now?"

He shakes his head, causing his now unzipped jacket to move.

I narrow my eyes as I look at his bloodstained jacket and shirt. Wrapped around his stomach, in almost the same area as Kittleson's wound, is blood-soaked sheeting of the same material as the bandage Kittleson had. I point to the bandage. "You were shot too?"

"Royal was my half brother. We had the same mom. He was eight when I was born. He lived with his dad and stepmom but had weekend visits with our mom. He was a great big brother, especially because he wasn't there all the time, so I didn't annoy him too much." He gives a small, tear-filled smile.

"He was a lawyer, you know. Before all this." He motions around the house, but I know he means the apocalypse. "Successful. Always looking out for me when I did stupid things."

"Shaw said he knew RJ . . . um, Royal. Is that from before? When he was a lawyer?"

"Yeah. I s'pose it was." He leans his head against his brother. The movement causes him to grimace.

"Can I check your injury?"

"No need. Royal and me—we're about the same. He got hit first. Then me. When we got away, he even joked about how I was still copying him. Nothing was ever his own. I'll just sit here. Rest a few minutes."

"Can I get you a blanket?"

"Nah. The fire's warming things up. It's fine. Sorry about your house."

I step out from in front of the fire to allow the heat to better fill the room. I slowly make my way to one of our easy chairs. We're quiet for several minutes, listening to the crackling of the wood.

Young lifts his head. "No one was ever supposed to get hurt. No one was supposed to die. Mr. Harrington—he and Oscar were supposed to be at work that night. We figured the women would stay upstairs."

"Why the Harringtons?"

He gives a slight tilt of his head. "Kirstie. She traded on the black market a few times. Had some good stuff, so . . . " He lifts a hand.

"Is that how you picked the houses? By traders on the black market?"

"Mostly. After Mr. Harrington, though, we took a break. Figured it'd be too dangerous. Then they found one of our stash houses. Killed a couple of our guys, and Oscar Harrington was injured. The rest of us figured it was over. We only started up again after the explosions, thinking Shaw and his men would have their hands full looking for those guys."

"How'd you escape?"

He smirks and shakes his head. "If I tell you, I'd have to kill you."

My eyes go wide, and my mouth dries out.

"What I will tell you, though, is I think I know who's behind the explosions."

"The ration centers?" I lean forward in my chair. "You do?"

"Yeah, maybe. Royal thinks he did anyway. There's a guy, he's a preacher of some sort now. Always going on about how God brought on the original attacks and the nukes to teach us to turn back to the old ways. He talks a lot about how rebuilding will put us back where we were and that isn't God's plan for us. He's pretty much a nutball."

"Wait." I lift my hand. "I think I heard him. Before the first explosion at the festival—the church by Monument Hospital."

He scrunches his face. "You were there?"

"With my husband. We were at the festival when it happened. But anyway, outside, beforehand, a guy was preaching, saying how we should embrace our new life. Grow our food and not try to get back what we once had. He had a bunch of people around him."

I lift my shoulders. "Honestly, I never thought— " As I say the words, I remember my conversation with Bowski earlier today. He said sometimes he forgets how easy we had it before. The preaching man, that's who I was reminded of when Bowski said that.

"What is it?"

"Nothing." I shake my head. "Just thinking about a conversation. Why do you think it's this guy? The preacher?"

"Royal knew him. He was his lawyer before, helped him with some contracts for something he was doing. He wasn't a preacher back then. Owned an IT business. Royal ran into him over the summer and ended up talking to the guy.

"Told me later he's nuttier than a fruitcake. Started his own church that Royal said sounded more like a cult than a church. When the attacks first started, Royal didn't connect the two, but he heard something from someone, and— " He wrinkles his nose. "I don't know for sure. It's only a theory. Royal's theory."

"Did you tell anyone?"

"I didn't. We got arrested, and that was that. Doubt Royal said anything either. Probably would've if he thought it could get us a get-out-of-jail-free card."

"I guess you didn't really need a card, though, did you?" I stare at him to see his reaction.

He grimaces. "Good point. But things didn't quite work out as well as expected. You'll make sure my brother is taken care of?" He leans forward and hoists himself off the floor. He wobbles a bit before getting his feet under him.

"I will. Please, let me check your wound. It might not be as bad as . . . as you think."

He snorts and sways back and forth before putting a hand to his head. He takes a few steps and then slips into our other easy chair. "It's as bad as I think. Guess I'm not going anywhere yet." He slides back.

We're silent for a few minutes until Gerry whines, likely asking if anyone is still here. I'm sure he smells us and knows we are.

"Go ahead." Young lifts his hand in the direction of the bedroom. "Take him out."

I raise my eyebrows in a question.

He shakes his head. "I'm not going to hurt him. Or you. Never planned on it. Royal needed help. That's the only reason we're here. I know you and your husband both work at the hospital. We hoped you'd come alone. You did. You've been good about all this. Go ahead and get your dog. Take off. I'll . . . I'll just sit here." He gives me something resembling a smile.

I bite my upper lip. "You're sure you don't want me to look at your wound?"

"Go on." He motions toward the bedroom again. "When they get here—Shaw and his men—make sure they know I won't put up a fight. No need for them to come in guns a'blazing and messing up your house even more."

I don't wait for another invitation to leave. I practically run to the bedroom and scoop up my growing dog under my arm. He plants several kisses on my chin and anywhere else his tongue can reach.

I glance back toward the living room where I can catch a glimpse of Young in the chair, his chin on his chest. I scoot toward my nightstand where my backup gun is tucked away, still in the ankle holster. I don't take the time to put it in place and instead put the whole thing in my pocket.

"You're okay, Gerry. We're okay. Let's go find Leo."

Young is still in the chair in the same position when I step out of the bedroom. "Thanks for doing what you could for my brother."

"I'm sorry for your loss," I mutter as I scurry to the front door, grabbing Gerry's leash from one of the hooks. I clip the hook to his collar and open the door, my wiggling dog still tucked under my arm.

Still wearing my coat and boots, I grab a stocking cap from a basket by the door and slip it on my head. I take a few steps so I can see Young. "We'll bring the handcart and get you to the hospital."

"Yeah. Sure." He motions around my living room. "Sorry again about your house. The window and everything."

I want to say something more, something profound and hopeful, but nothing comes to me. I silently leave the house.

Once we're off the front porch and on our small walkway, I set Gerry on the ground as my tears start flowing. I can barely see as I quickly move to the sidewalk. I sniff at my runny nose and rub the back of my hand against my eyes. "Let's go, Gerry. Let's hurry and get to the hospital."

A shiver runs through me. Without stopping, I zip my coat to my neck and then fumble to get my gloves on. "All right. That's better." I rub my gloved hands against my cold, tear-dampened cheeks. "Let's get Young some help."

Walking as quickly and safely as I can, I replay the events of the past little while. How long has it been since I walked into my house? An hour? Less? One man is already dead on my couch, and the other didn't look good. What a stubborn man to not even let me check his wound. When we reach a clear section of pavement, I urge Gerry on to a slow jog.

There's a band of sweat underneath my stocking cap when I arrive at the hospital guard shack.

"I need help. The escaped prisoners broke into my house. Um, two of them anyway." I motion to his radio. "Can you call Shaw?"

"Ma'am?" the young sentry asks; he's part of the new recruits working with the Citizen Patrol.

I take a deep breath, purposely slow my words, and repeat what I said before. This time, he springs into action, using his radio to locate whoever it is he reports to. Not Shaw but someone between this new sentry and Shaw.

"Tell them one man, RJ Kittleson, is dead on my couch. The other, Bryson Young, is wounded. He won't put up a fight. He'll need transport to the hospital." I give my address, then move toward the hospital. They'll radio the hospital with the official details and tell them where to wait while they secure the house before bringing in medical.

Leo and Geoff Landers are at the desk nearest the door when I go in. The ringing of the bell causes them both to look up. Leo's eyes go wide.

Landers points to Gerry. "Don't bring him in here."

"I'm not. Just to here." I motion around the waiting room.

Leo moves toward me, asking what happened.

I get it all out in a rush without even taking a breath. The tears are threatening again. My knees are shaking, and I feel sick to my stomach. I'm cold all over and having trouble catching my breath.

Leo's by my side, ushering me to a chair. I hear the squawk of the radio but can't make out the words. Everything feels fuzzy. Leo sounds far away when he says my name.

Chapter 34

Merissa

Captain Williams looks around the break room, taking a moment to make eye contact with each person. He called an all-staff meeting, including the med school students.

He lets out a sigh and sinks back into his wheelchair. "We've had quite the time here, with the explosions and now the escapees taking one of our own hostage." His gaze rests on Leo Burnett.

Leo straightens in his chair and dips his chin. "Thankfully, with a little time, she'll be fine. I suspect she'll be back to work in a few days."

The captain gives him a brief smile. "I'd like to tell you things are going to get better, but that's not a promise I can make. While it's believed the robbery ring has been eliminated, there are still some questions about how they managed to escape. Deputy Shaw, in conjunction with the Military Police, will continue to investigate exactly what happened. They're also still looking for the perpetrators of the explosions thanks to a recent lead."

Leaning forward in my chair, I wonder what the lead is. I've yet to hear anything about this. Based on the murmur of surprise going around the room, I'm not the only one who hasn't heard about this.

Williams lifts his hand. "I can't say anything more, just that we need to be ready to receive wounded. We also may be needed in the field. Jesse, Ryan, and Merissa—make sure the radios are always charged and ready. Once we know more about the operation, we'll determine who, if any, of our personnel are needed.

"In the meantime, we continue as we have been. The med school will take a brief break over Christmas. The last day of class is December 23. We'll resume after the new year."

Geoff Landers pumps his fist in the air, and Chastity Morrow lets out a giggle at his shenanigans.

Williams sends them both a stern look. "Don't think you'll have a vacation. I made it clear this school is a full-time endeavor. There're no real holiday breaks. While we won't have classes, you'll have a list of reading material to complete, and you'll continue working regular shifts at the hospital.

"We're going to have at least one med student on every shift, either shadowing a hospital employee or handling things on their own. You might shadow a medic one day, a nurse the next, or a doctor."

Williams looks directly at Landers. "You may even take a shift as one of the janitors, and you'll be grateful for the opportunity to learn how this hospital truly functions."

Landers makes a face but wisely keeps his trap shut.

"On another note, Deputy Shaw brought a new issue to my attention. Well, not entirely new but of increasing concern. It seems trying to survive in this new world isn't enough for some people. We've long known about the prohibition announcement from the president and how that's not stopping a few enterprising people from constructing stills."

Several people talk at once, but Williams raises a hand.

"I'm not talking about the legit operations providing hand sanitizer and alcohol for cleaning and disinfecting. Really, this isn't even about the booze being made. It's about booze not being enough for some.

"There're several versions of a synthetic drug going around. This was a problem before the EMP and something we'd hoped would not return—at least not anytime soon. One of the drugs, something being referred to as Ploy, is suspected in the deaths of four people in the past week."

Chastity Morrow, eyes wide, quickly raises a hand. "How do you know the drug killed them?" There's a noticeable catch in her voice.

"We don't know for sure. I heard about this a few days ago when Shaw told me they'd found someone dead with this drug on them. A couple of others were found the week before. Another person yesterday. To my knowledge, we haven't had anyone come into the hospital with signs of a drug overdose."

Dr. Morrow and Dr. Wolff both agree they don't think they've seen anyone like that.

Williams goes over the symptoms: slurred speech, hallucinations, changes in mood, anger, paranoia, poor coordination, memory impairment, and more. Pretty much the symptoms that could go along with a bunch of other issues too.

"The trouble with this drug and others being made are the ingredients. There's no way to know exactly what's in each batch. One dose and it could be fatal. In the past, some drugs had things like rat poison in them. Now, with our limited supplies— " He lifts his hands out.

"We just don't know. Finding the people making these drugs is going to be a challenge too. From our end of things, if we suspect a drug overdose or even usage, we'll let Shaw and his people know."

Stella Swenson raises her hand. "Do they have any leads on who's making these drugs?"

"Nothing concrete. There's a thought it's coming out of Deadwood, but we don't know for sure. Any other questions?"

"Is it the black market?" Rand Hendricks asks. "You know, running the drugs? Maybe the robbery ring was part of it?"

Williams shrugs. "Could be, though Shaw is fairly confident they aren't being sold via the recognized black market."

I scrunch my forehead and try to comprehend his words. The black market is an open secret. While it's officially prohibited, everyone knows it's happening and does nothing to stop it. Not law enforcement, the National Guard, no one.

I even heard from Jacquie Haley that the governor knows the black market is operating and turns a blind eye. Not only here in Rapid City and the Black Hills but throughout the state. Officially, ration chips are the way of the state. Unofficially, survival is the ultimate goal, and the black market helps with that.

Jacquie also said Ritchie Kasubowski is one of the main organizers. It started last year, before the ration chips were put into place. But the underground deals still continue.

"If there's nothing else, regular staff are dismissed." Williams motions toward the door. "Sergeant Burnett and med school students, stick around."

As the other hospital workers slip out of the break room, Jacquie Haley is gesturing and chattering loudly about the drug problem. I'm sure I'll get an earful next time I'm working with her.

Once the room has cleared, Williams gives us a smile. "I know this first month has been a challenge for everyone. With the explosions and my foot troubles, things haven't gone as planned." Williams shakes his head.

"At the same time, this has been a real-life education. You don't have the luxury of learning the way I did, in a safe and structured environment. The frequent chaos has been a challenge. For the most part, you've conquered this challenge. Before I dismiss you today, Sergeant Burnett and I will meet with each of you privately. While we've been providing feedback as we go, today is your first official evaluation. Merissa, you're first."

Geoff Landers smirks at me before muttering, "You're out of here."

Ignoring him, I follow Leo and the captain from the room. I consider asking the captain if he'd like me to push his wheelchair, but he seems to be doing fine.

Leo holds the door as we leave the break room and enter the captain's office. Instead of going to his desk, the captain motions me to the sitting area as he wheels himself into position.

I perch on the edge of the loveseat while Leo takes a straight-back chair. He looks like a wreck. I don't blame him, considering what his wife went through earlier today.

When Katie showed up at the hospital a few hours ago with their little dog, I only caught a little of what was happening. The next thing I knew, she was going down—fainting.

Katie kept it together long enough to tell the guardhouse sentry what was happening. Jesse's radio went off, requesting a medic to help with a field operation. Because of the jailbreak, the other medic, Ryan, was also on duty, so he and Jesse went out.

"Comfortable?" Williams asks, interrupting my thoughts.

"I'm fine, sir."

"I know this has been quite the day. I'll keep this brief. You're off tonight?"

"Correct, sir. Well, I have studying."

He chuckles. "The life of a med student. That's one thing that hasn't changed in this world. You're doing fine, Merissa. You aren't just keeping up, you're excelling. I know it's a lot for you with still taking the medic shifts too. I have a lead on another person who we may bring on to help."

"Another medic?"

"Yes. Hopefully, after the new year. Think you can handle the workload until then?"

"I'm fine, sir." My conscience is pricked, knowing now is the time to tell him about the baby.

He must see it in my face. "Something you wish to add?"

I swallow hard and straighten my spine. "Yes, uh . . . yes, sir, there is. I'm pregnant."

Leo's eyes open wide in surprise. The captain tilts his head. "That's truly a blessing. I know you lost your husband recently . . . "

"I was able to tell him about the baby before he was killed."

Williams gives me a broad smile. "Congratulations. Have you been examined?"

"Yes, by Dr. Wolff, before you added me to the hospital staff and the med school. I realize I should've told you, but I wasn't sure if I'd be able to sustain the pregnancy. It's been a difficult time."

"Indeed. No need to apologize for keeping your private business private. Although, I am concerned about your workload. I'll see if there's something we can do about that sooner rather than later. Are you eating as you should?"

"I believe so. The rations have been fairly generous."

"Do I have your permission to share this news with my wife? She'll mother hen you and help make sure you get what you need."

"Um . . . " I let out a sigh. "I haven't told my mother-in-law yet. It's been difficult for her, with losing her son . . . both her sons. This child will be her only blood."

"Understood. We'll be discreet."

"Thank you, sir."

He asks if I have anything else I wish to share or any questions about the program. When I tell him I don't, he dismisses me and asks me to send in Stella Swenson.

I'm glad he knows about the pregnancy and seems fine with it. A few more weeks and I'll tell Pearl. Part of me wishes I'd simply tell her and get it over with. But the rest of me . . . I can't. Not yet.

Not only do I not want to get her hopes up when there's still a chance I could lose the baby, but I need this for me. Just for me and Braedon. Once Pearl knows, everything will change. I'm not ready for that. Not yet.

Chapter 35

Katie

"Katie?"

"Mm-hmm?"

"I brought you some tea and a piece of bread. Can you eat?"

I open my eyes and look around the dimly lit room. The curtains are opened, and soft, barely-there light is streaming through the window. I narrow my eyes. "Where are we?"

Leo furrows his brow. "Shaw's house. Remember?"

I close my eyes and let out a breath as the events of yesterday sweep over me.

I'm not going to cry. I'm not going to cry.

Repeating this to myself does zero good, and more tears come. You'd think, after eighteen months of death and destruction, I'd stop being such a baby.

Leo awkwardly wraps his good arm around me.

After what feels like forever, I give a loud sniff. "Gerry?"

"With Tank, of course. He's completely fine."

When I reached the hospital, I got woozy and almost passed out. Maybe I did a little bit. There were a few minutes where everything was sort of "out there" and I couldn't really make out what was going on.

When things came back into focus, my head was between my knees and Leo was reminding me to take slow breaths.

Jesse and Ryan took the handcart to the staging area to await Shaw and his team to clear the house. It turned out the handcart wasn't needed. Bryson Young was dead, by his own hand, when Shaw arrived.

I'm feeling a lot of guilt over that. If I'd stayed, insisted he let me check his wound, would he still be alive? Maybe it wasn't as bad as his brother's wound, and he could've survived.

Maybe, maybe, maybe. The maybes are driving me crazy.

With two dead bodies and a broken window in the backdoor of our house, Shaw offered to put us up for a few days. We'll need a new sofa and chair, plus a better repair job on the door—or a completely new door. Maybe one without a window. I close my eyes and take a deep breath. Definitely one without a window.

I quickly open my eyes and sit up straight in the bed. "Was it him? Did they find him?"

Leo gives me a confused look. "The preacher? The one Bryson told you is behind the explosions?"

Nodding vigorously, I ask again if they found him.

"Not sure. Shaw passed the info along to the deputies in the various districts, and the National Guard is involved too. I heard— " He drops his gaze and clears his throat. "Sheriff Cabal is treating it like any other unsubstantiated tip . . . which I guess that's what it is."

"He doesn't think the preacher is the one behind the attacks?" I furrow my brow.

"The way Shaw put it, they're proceeding with the investigation but not going in with guns blazing. Which— " he lifts his hands " — if you think about it, that's the way it should be."

I nibble on my lip as I glance at the mug on the nightstand. The piece of bread next to it is topped with a generous smear of butter.

Leo turns his head to follow my gaze. "Tea first?"

After a few sips of mint brew, I nestle the mug between my hands and ask Leo what time it is.

"A little after 0700."

"We'd better get going. School— "

"We have the day off. Captain Williams is having the students work in the hospital this morning. He'll take care of the classes this afternoon. They did well yesterday with the onslaught of injured from the jailbreak." He gives me a wobbly smile. "Most of them anyway."

"Let me guess. Geoff Landers was the weak link."

"As always. I did learn a little more about why he was a last-minute admission."

"Really? Why?" I lean toward the nightstand to exchange the tea for the bread.

"He's Melvin Cabal's nephew."

"The county sheriff is his uncle? Okay? So? How does that get him into the new med school when he isn't qualified?"

"That's a good question, isn't it? Shaw's wife is the one who told me about the relationship with Landers and Cabal. Captain Williams said he's known Melvin Cabal for years, right?"

"They went to school together. Williams doesn't like him much, though. So why give his nephew a spot in the school?"

"Shaw's wife didn't know. Said it seems suspicious for sure. I'm thinking about asking the captain."

I shake my head. "Don't, Leo. It's his school. We can speculate all we want, but . . . " I lift my chin. "Besides, he's your superior officer." I bite into my bread. The homemade butter is creamy and delicious but not as salty as I prefer.

Leo gives a noisy sigh. "You're right."

We're quiet for many minutes while I eat my bread. When it's gone, I go back to the tea. "So . . . I guess we should find some new furniture today and get a new door."

"We should. The Shaws said we're welcome to stay here until we get things put back together. I'm hoping, if we can find the door today, I can get that installed."

I point to his arm. "Really? How?"

"Well, I didn't mean *me* exactly. I'll find someone. I have a few leads on who can do it. We can move back home without the new furniture. We'll need to do a little cleaning, though." He grimaces.

When I left the house, there were blood smears in various places from Kittleson—probably Young too. The couch was obviously ruined by Kittleson bleeding out on it. I'm sure it's even worse now, though I didn't ask for details on the way Bryson Young ended his life.

The guilt goes through me again, wishing I would've done something different.

After I finish breakfast and get dressed, Leo and I leave Gerry with Carol Shaw and Tank while we go in search of a new door.

Yesterday, after the all-clear was given, Leo went to the house while I stayed at the hospital to rest and rehydrate. They were worried the stress of everything might cause me to go into shock.

Leo packed a bag of night clothes and a change of underwear. He also put in some extra winter gear, which was good thinking. It's about twenty degrees colder today than yesterday and has been snowing for several hours. At least there isn't too much wind, so it's not terrible outside.

One of the ration stations is set up for building materials, so we start there. Building materials are a specialty ration and not included in our regular ration chips. We need to apply for it at the front desk, and if we're approved, we'll be allowed to shop.

Deputy Shaw gave us a special wooden token to indicate his involvement in our situation. In some ways, it reminds me of our life before the apocalypse and needing to get an insurance company involved to replace things after a fire, burglary, or accident.

We find a steel door, and the woman running this station says she'll hold it for us until the next day. Captain Williams gave us permission to use one of the handcarts to get our stuff back to the house. Jesse and Josiah Talbot are going to help us load and operate the cart. I know Leo feels bad about needing so much assistance, but with his arm, there's no choice.

Furniture is part of our regular ration packet under the household goods category. A former furniture store houses all the couches, chairs, beds, and tables you could imagine. While there are new items, there are also a lot of used things salvaged out of houses.

The couch we had was a long, minimalist style. It wasn't super comfortable for sitting but great for lying on. I'd like something similar but maybe a little less minimal and fluffier. A couch I can sink into after a long day at the hospital.

As we're moving around the warehouse, someone calls Leo's name. We both turn and see a man near the door who's well bundled in winter gear and waving. I tilt my head in the man's direction. "Who's that?"

"Lieutenant Paul, I think." As the words leave Leo's mouth, the man slides the gaiter down from his face. "Yep. Paul." Leo lifts a hand.

We move toward him as he scurries in our direction. "Mrs. Shaw said you may be here." The men shake hands. "How are you doing, Katie?"

"Better, thanks."

"I wanted to make sure you knew I heard about Young giving you the information about the preacher. We'll check it out."

I stiffen my back. "I thought the sheriff was treating it as fake?"

He constricts his mouth. "The National Guard does not need his approval to pursue leads."

"Uh . . . I didn't . . . " I feel my face flush from embarrassment.

Lieutenant Paul shakes his head. "Sorry, that came out wrong. Let me try again. We're moving forward with or without the aid of the sheriff. We believe the information provided is valuable. And . . . unofficially, I suspect there will be others who can help us pursue this lead."

"Shaw?" Leo asks.

"I'm sure you know Deputy Shaw would never blatantly go against the wishes of his superior."

"Of course not."

"Right. Anyway, I'm taking this personally. If the preacher, or cult leader, thinks he's acting on behalf of God with the massacres . . . well, I'd say he needs to read his Bible. It's proof to me how badly we— " Lieutenant Paul motions to the three of us " —and other believers need to be sharing the true word of God with people."

I look from the lieutenant to my husband, who's aggressively nodding. "Just like we talked about," Leo says. "People are looking for something. *Anything.* If we don't share the Gospel, someone else will distort it to their own use. It's happened before. It'll happen again."

My heart fills with pride as I listen to the men talk for a few minutes about their men's group and how they want to expand and bring more people to God.

After a few minutes, Lieutenant Paul puts his cap back on. "I've got to go. I wanted to make sure you were okay and tell you we appreciated the information. Oh, and another thing we're pursuing, whether the sheriff chooses to or not, is exactly how Kittleson and the others managed to escape."

"An inside job," Leo mutters.

"Mm-hmm," Lieutenant Paul agrees. "That's something we're looking into. You two are still planning to join us on base for Christmas dinner, right? You'll come as our guests this year. Next year, you'll be official."

A smile breaks across my face. "Thank you, sir."

Though I've gone back and forth about committing to the National Guard, hearing him say we'll be official sends a thrill of excitement through me. I don't know exactly when things changed, when I stopped dreading staying in the Black Hills and committing to the National Guard.

Maybe it's because I've come to love this area, both the town and the people. Maybe it's a belief God is nudging me to stay here, to make this my mission field. Hearing Leo and Lieutenant Paul talk about the need to share the Gospel and how hungry people are for the true word of God helps solidify this feeling.

God knew what He was doing when He sent us to South Dakota. We're needed here. Needed not only at the hospital and to help rebuild the beautiful Black Hills but to share the Gospel. Together, Leo and I can make a difference in this new world. *Together.* I grasp Leo's hand as he asks Lieutenant Paul to keep us posted.

Once the lieutenant leaves, Leo turns to face me. "You've made your decision?"

"I think I have. Even with everything . . . all the troubles . . . this is where we're supposed to be. Where *I'm* supposed to be. Working at the hospital, training the new doctors, and even joining the National Guard—it feels right."

"When did you decide?"

"I'm not sure. Not exactly. I've been praying about it, pondering it. I guess today. When Lieutenant Paul invited us to Christmas dinner, I just knew." My eyes search his face. "It's still what you want?"

He puts his hand on my cheek. "What I want is to be with you. To continue to build a life together."

As we stare at each other, someone shopping nearby clears their throat. I let out a laugh. We're going to be okay. Even with the troubles of this world, Leo and I are stronger together than apart.

Together. As God intended.

The adventure continues in Inflicting Mayhem: Dakota Destruction Book 3.

Inflicting Mayhem: Dakota Destruction Book 3

They thought the Black Hills would be safe . . . they were wrong.

The promise of safety led Merissa to the beautiful Black Hills of South Dakota. But safety is only an illusion when a mysterious force emerges, inflicting chaos and destruction.

Katie and Leo Burnett strive to rebuild their lives after a world-changing event and personal struggles rocked their existence. But with so many changes in such a short time, rebuilding may prove impossible.

In a world teetering on the brink of despair, Katie, Leo, and Merissa navigate treacherous terrain, where danger lurks at every turn.

Can they survive this chaotic new world? Or will their time in South Dakota—and possibly their lives—come to an end?

Thank you for spending your time on our new South Dakota
adventure.

If you have five minutes, you'd make this writer very happy if you
could write a short review on Amazon, Goodreads, Bookbub, or
your favorite review site.

I appreciate you!

Join my reader's club!
As part of my reader's club, you'll be the first to know about new
releases and specials. I also share info on books I'm reading,
preparedness tips, and more.

Please sign up on my website:
MillieCopper.com

Also by Millie Copper

The Havoc in Wyoming Series

When a series of coordinated attacks devastate the United States, the people of Bakerville, Wyoming, must come together to survive. Unfortunately, not everyone has the town's best interest at heart. Some are striving for personal gain during the apocalypse.

The Montana Mayhem Series

A group from Bakerville, Wyoming strikes out on their own while searching for the desires of their heart. Unfortunately, the road will not be easy, and sometimes the heart is hardened and deceitful. When things don't work out as they hoped, will they become stranded in the wilderness? Or will each be able to find their way home?

The Dakota Destruction Series

After a series of coordinated attacks devastate the United States, Katie and Leo sacrifice everything to help their country. But some things aren't as they seem. Is it time to go home and start fresh, or can something good come out of this terrible situation?

Nonfiction Books

Millie has penned seven nonfiction, traditional food focused books, sharing how, with a little creativity, anyone can transition to a real foods diet without overwhelming their food budget. Many of her books also include preparedness and food storage tips.

Find these titles at:
MillieCopper.com

Acknowledgments

Thanks to:

Ameryn Tucker, my editor, beta reader, and daughter wrapped in one. I had a story I wanted to tell, and Ameryn encouraged me and helped me bring it to life.

Dee from Dauntless Cover Design.

My husband, who gave me the time and space I needed to complete this dream and was very patient as I'd tell him the same plot ideas over and over and over.

Three more adult daughters and a young son, who willingly listen to me drone on and on about storylines and ideas while encouraging me to "keep going."

My amazing Beta Readers! Thanks to Barbara, Becky, Glen, Ilona, Judy, Linda, Tammy, and Tracy for your help in creating the final story. Your insights and abilities to see the things I miss are very much appreciated!

A special thank you to Kristy who gave me a peek inside the world of the Coast Guard and Forest Service. And also a special thank you to Tim, a specialist in all things that go boom, for always answering my questions and pointing out things I wouldn't even think about.

And to you, my readers, for spending your time on our new South Dakota adventure. If you have five minutes, you'd make this writer very happy if you could leave a review. I appreciate you!

About the Author

Millie Copper, writer of Cozy Apocalyptic Fiction and preparedness mentor, was born in Nebraska but never lived there. Her parents fully embraced wanderlust and moved regularly, giving her an advantage of being from nowhere and everywhere.

Millie Copper lives in the wilds of Wyoming with her husband and young son, tending chickens and attempting a food forest on their small homestead. After living off the grid for several years, they've recently gone back on the grid. Four adult daughters, three sons-in-law, and five grandchildren round out the family.

Since 2009, Millie has authored articles on traditional foods, alternative health, homesteading, and preparedness-many times all within the same piece. Millie has penned seven nonfiction, traditional food focused books, sharing how, with a little creativity, anyone can transition to a real foods diet without overwhelming their food budget.

The twelve-installment *Havoc in Wyoming* and six-installment *Montana Mayhem* Christian Post-Apocalyptic fiction series use her homesteading, off-the-grid, and preparedness lifestyle as a guide. The adventures continue with the *Dakota Destruction* series.

Find Millie at www.MillieCopper.com
Facebook: www.facebook.com/MillieCopperAuthor/
Amazon: www.amazon.com/author/milliecopper
BookBub: https://www.bookbub.com/authors/millie-copper